"Loren, I'd like you to meet my daughter, Daphne."

For Loren, the scene took on a surreal quality. How could Adam have a daughter named Daphne? That was supposed to have been *their* daughter's name. She thought about her own son, Josh. Daphne and Josh! Just as they'd planned. Except for one small detail. She and Adam had both married other people.

Daphne walked forward and held out her hand. "Glad to meet you."

"Same here." Loren wrenched her perspiring hand out of her pocket and put it into Daphne's cool, manicured fingers. She looked up at Adam. He'd purposely hidden his identity, probably waiting for this dramatic little moment. Well, she wouldn't give him another ounce of satisfaction.

"I wish you'd told me you were the client I'd be dealing with," she said. "I'd have given you a discount." That should get him, with his fancy red plane.

He looked unfazed by her patronizing gesture. "Maybe I was afraid you'd raise the price."

"I wouldn't dream of gouging you. After all, we go way back."

"How far back?" Daphne glanced from her father to Loren.

"I was a cheerleader when your dad played football for Flagstaff High." There was no need to tell the young woman more.

After all, it was ancient history...wasn't it?

Dear Reader,

Most of us fell in love for the first time in high school, and it's a love we'll never forget, even—and perhaps especially—if we ended up marrying someone else. I thought it would be fun to explore the fantasy of reuniting two high school lovers. To complicate the reunion, Adam has a sophisticated eighteen-year-old daughter, and Loren has a naive eighteen-year-old son. Because I'm the parent of a son and daughter aged twenty-four and twenty-two, I thoroughly enjoyed writing about Adam and Loren's almost-adult children.

This book is also special to me because my father, still a pilot at seventy-four, helped with the research by flying me into Sedona Airport, a decidedly tricky maneuver. He also served as my consultant on matters of piloting. In additon, I'm grateful for the help of Glenn Lewis, aerial photographer. If I've made any mistakes on matters of flying or aerial photography, they're my goofs and not the fault of my excellent advisors.

Sincerely,

Vicki Lewis Thompson

Vicki Lewis Thompson

Adam Then and Now

Harlequin Books

TORONTO • NEW YORK • LONDON
AMSTERDAM • PARIS • SYDNEY • HAMBURG
STOCKHOLM • ATHENS • TOKYO • MILAN
MADRID • WARSAW • BUDAPEST • AUCKLAND

For my father, Darold Shutt, and Echo Romeo.
Neither of you looks your age.

ISBN 0-373-70637-5

ADAM THEN AND NOW

Copyright © 1995 by Vicki Lewis Thompson.

Adam
Then and Now

PROLOGUE

May 25, 1972

LOREN MONTGOMERY was about to surrender her virginity. Stretched on a picnic blanket deep within the cool recesses of Oak Creek Canyon, she lay beside Adam Riordan. His touch played a melody far sweeter than the song of the water rushing beside them over the smooth stones of Oak Creek. The erotic scent of greening moss and sprouting ferns, the sound of crickets chirping, made chastity seem the most unrewarding of virtues.

She closed her eyes against the soft moonlight and turned into Adam's embrace, the chiffon of her dress rustling against the blanket. Eventually, slowly, the dress would be removed, for even at nineteen Adam knew how to stage a seduction. As his mouth covered hers, his kiss tasted of the champagne her parents had allowed them to sip at the graduation party.

"You're really sure?" His teeth caught her earlobe and she shivered.

"Yes."

"I have to tell you something first."

She opened her eyes. This wasn't the way she'd scripted this moment in her head. "Now? You have to tell me something now?"

"I should have told you before, but when I looked at you lying there in the moonlight, I . . ."

"Adam, for heaven's sake, tell me!"

"I got my draft notice."

She sat straight up and the breeze felt like ice on her heated back. The draft lottery. "No."

"I report June fifteenth."

"No," she said again, fighting nausea. The sweetness of Adam's kisses had turned to the bitterness of fear. A year ago, she'd had a few weeks of panic when all student deferments had been canceled, but then, when nothing had happened . . .

"I'm sorry, Lor." He sat up, too, and ran his fingers through his hair. "I couldn't bring myself to tell you before. You were so happy tonight, and we had this plan to come down here to the creek, and damn, I want you so much."

A minute ago the crickets had sounded romantic. Now they screeched like violins in a horror movie.

"But the more I thought about it, the more I realized it wasn't fair to make love without first telling you about the notice."

She struggled for breath. "Adam, you're not going."

The wind sighed down the canyon, and shadows of leaves caressed his face. "Sorry, but Uncle Sam says different."

"You don't mean you're *considering* it?"

He shrugged.

She scrambled to her knees and gripped him by the shoulders. "You most certainly are not going! I won't let you sacrifice yourself in this horrible war!"

Sliding his arms around her waist, he pulled her between his knees and buried his face in her breasts. "You can march and carry signs all you want, but the draft still exists, Lor," he murmured, biting her nipple through the material of her dress.

She pushed him away. "How dare you be so offhanded about it! Don't you realize you could be killed?"

"We all have to die sometime."

"Don't give me that nonsense! We have to stop this. We'll get married."

He grew still. Slowly he gazed up into her face. "No, we won't."

"Why not? We'll tell everyone I'm pregnant, and then I really *will* get pregnant with little Josh or little Daphne, just like we planned. The draft board will let you off for that. Don't you remember when Eddie and Sue—"

"Loren." He cupped her face and drew her down until she could look directly into his eyes. "Don't go off the deep end."

"I'm not!"

His voice was tender. "Yes, you are." She wasn't convincing him. She fought panic as she gazed into his eyes—pale gray in the moonlight, a fierce, irresistible blue in the warmth of the sun. Those eyes had been her undoing from the day she and Adam had started going steady a year ago. That summer, he'd kept the pavement humming up and down the Oak Creek Canyon road that connected Flagstaff, where he lived, and Sedona, where she lived. Everyone had predicted they'd break up during Adam's freshman year at Arizona State University in Phoenix, but here they were, more in love than ever.

Her throat constricted with grief and she blinked back tears. "We have to do *something*," she said.

"Getting married now isn't a good idea. Think it through. You're just barely eighteen."

"And you're only nineteen! Pretty young to die, wouldn't you say?" Hysteria threatened to overwhelm her. She couldn't lose him. Not to this hateful war.

"Your parents won't pay for college if you're married. And if you had a baby...well, it's just out of the question. I can't do that to you."

Desperation made her reckless. She reached between his legs and caressed him. "I think you're very capable of doing that to me."

He caught her hand firmly in his. "We're not getting married and having babies. Not now."

She had to keep touching him, trying to convince him. She moved both hands to his face and stroked the dark sideburns that made him look like a movie star. "Then we'll go to Canada. We'll work ourselves through school up there."

"And be outcasts for the rest of our lives? I couldn't hurt my parents like that, and neither could you."

Loren's desperation grew. "You think they'd prefer you dead or maimed?"

He smiled the confident smile that could beguile or infuriate her, depending on the context. Tonight the smile filled her with terror. "You know nothing's going to happen to me. In a couple of years I'll be back, and you'll be halfway to your degree, and we'll finish up together.''

"Oh, yeah?" She had to break through this rational approach of his. Her Adam in combat was too grotesque a possibility to be entertained with such cool logic. "If you're so sure you'll be back, why did you have to tell me about the draft notice before we made love?''

"Because . . ." Uncertainty flickered in his gaze for a moment. "I guess because making love is like a commitment. If we make love, I'd expect you to wait for me, and I'm not sure that's fair. You might meet someone else.''

How like him. Her noble, fair Adam. But tonight fairness was the last thing on Loren's mind. For a few moments, she thought of other ways to influence the draft board somehow, but gave up those ideas as unworkable. Only one thing might hold him. One thing might keep him alive. "I don't want to wait for you.''

He looked as if he'd been slapped.

"Not without a wedding ring on my finger.''

"Are you crazy? For one thing, I'm too young to get a license.''

"You've got ID showing a fake birth date, don't you? We could drive to Vegas tomorrow night. I'll tell my folks I'm spending the night with Sherry. No one has to know but you and me. We can make love all night, Adam." She captured his gaze. "All night," she murmured, and became giddy with relief as his eyes darkened. "You can't guarantee you'll be back. Give me this, please. Give us both this.''

He stared at her, his desire a palpable thing. She gathered him close, tears seeping from the corners of her eyes as she squeezed them shut and prayed. "Please," she whispered.

The moment of decision lasted so long she almost screamed out in fear and frustration, but she forced herself to keep holding him as tears dripped down her cheeks.

At last he nodded, his breath easing out in a long sigh.

She choked back a sob of relief and hugged him hard. Thank God. She had a chance now.

They drove home in silence, the car radio switched off, as if music was too frivolous for a time like this.

"I'll meet you at Sherry's at seven tomorrow night," Loren murmured at her front door.

"All right."

"It's what we need to do," she said, kissing him with all the passion she possessed. Then she went into the darkened house where green, white and brown streamers still hung from the ceiling, along with the peace symbols she'd insisted on. Through the window, she watched his red Capri pull away into the night. Trembling with emotion, she leaned against the cool glass. She must not doubt her power over him. Once they were married, once they'd spent a long night together making love, he wouldn't want to go to Vietnam. She was gambling everything on that.

May 26, 1972

LOREN MADE SURE she said hello to Sherry's parents, who were sitting in the den watching the latest war news. Loren averted her gaze from the obscene pictures flashing across the screen as she answered questions about how her folks were and what she was majoring in next fall. She wanted Sherry's mother and father to record the fact that she was definitely here and was spending the night. She carried her favorite Fleetwood Mac album under one arm as an added prop. Finally, she excused herself and went to join a breathless Sherry in the bedroom.

"This is *so* romantic, Loren," Sherry whispered, although there was no need to whisper with the door closed. "I almost wish Greg would get drafted, so we could run away, too."

"Don't say that." Loren peered out Sherry's window as the setting sun glowed tangerine on the rocky buttes that circled Sedona like ruined medieval castles. Ten more minutes. "Nobody should be drafted. Why do you think we went to all those rallies?"

"Well, of course, but if Adam hadn't gotten his notice, he'd be working some highway construction job this summer, as usual, and you'd be developing other people's vacation pictures at the photo lab, and your most exciting adventure would be going down Slide Rock on Sunday afternoons." She caught Loren's glance. "Well, your second most exciting adventure, then. I forgot you two were planning to become lovers this summer. But besides that, your lives would be pretty boring." She sighed. "Like mine."

Loren's stomach felt like a hardening chunk of cement. "I'd take boring right now."

"What's in the overnight case?"

"My graduation dress, and I used some of my graduation money for a negligee."

"Ooh! Can I see?"

"I guess." Loren's attention remained on the street. Any minute Adam's red Capri would appear, and then maybe the petrification of her insides would reverse itself.

"Oh, Loren, this is *sexy*."

Loren glanced over her shoulder. Sherry held up the skimpy black nightie in admiration. Loren had debated white or black, and decided on black. She'd heard men went crazy over the naughty-girl look, and she wanted Adam to go crazy tonight. And every night thereafter, until he got over this temporary patriotic phase of his. Until he was safe from harm. "Better put it back. Your parents could come in."

"Right." Sherry reverently folded the negligee and tucked it back in the overnight case. "Good thing you went to Planned Parenthood for those pills last month, huh?"

"I've stopped taking them."

"What?" Sherry slapped her hand over her mouth and glanced nervously at the door, but the television set was on loud enough to distract her parents. "Does Adam know that?" she whispered.

"No, and if you tell him, you're in deep trouble."

"You want to get pregnant?"

"Sherry, I'll do anything to keep him from going to Vietnam."

"Wow."

The sound of a car engine brought Loren's attention back to the window, although she knew it wasn't the Capri. Like a mother who can pick her own baby's cry out of a nursery full of children, Loren could recognize the Capri's individual growl from among all the other cars on the streets of Sedona.

She knew whose car had pulled up in front of Sherry's house, though. The turquoise Mustang belonged to Jimmy Denton, the tight end on the football team and Adam's best friend. Jimmy got out and glanced anxiously at the house. The chunk of cement in Loren's stomach twisted, and she whimpered softly in distress.

"What's wrong?" Sherry came to the window. "Uh-oh." She squeezed Loren's arm. "Stay here. I'll see what he wants. Maybe it's nothing."

Loren stayed. She didn't want to talk to Jimmy. Nothing Jimmy had to say could be good news tonight.

She stood at the window and watched as Jimmy walked back to the car, his head down. Sherry came quietly into the room a few moments later. Loren didn't turn around.

Sherry came up behind her. "Loren..."

Loren shook her head.

"Adam's enlisting. He's staying with a friend in Phoenix until his papers are processed."

Loren put her hands over her ears.

Sherry's voice rose a notch and she tried to turn a resistant Loren to face her. "Look, I'm supposed to tell you why. Jimmy said I had to. It's important."

Loren took her hands down and balled them into fists. She didn't look at Sherry. "I don't care why."

"But, Loren—"

"If he'd rather go to some stinking jungle—" Loren's voice rose to a wail and the red buttes seemed washed with blood "—if he'd rather *die* than stay with me, then who gives a damn why?"

CHAPTER ONE

July 15, 1995

AS LOREN STOOD in front of Sedona Airport's terminal waiting for the red twin-engine Cessna 414 circling the field, she hoped the pilot knew what he was doing. The airfield's only runway bisected a plateau with steep drops on all sides. Loren's father compared it to touching down on an aircraft carrier, minus the water. Loren would hate to lose Scorpio Steel as a client because the pilot misjudged the runway.

The plane sailed in low and slow, wings steady. Loren let out her breath and admired the black scorpion logo on the fuselage as the pilot taxied in. Scorpio Steel was the perfect sort of client, meaning they had lots of money. And Loren needed money. She'd even agreed to overlook an Icarus Enterprises policy and let a representative from Scorpio ride along on today's photographic survey trip.

Having a client come along had already become a nuisance. She'd considered modifying her outfit of comfortable shorts and tank top to appear more businesslike, but anything else on a July morning would be too hot and restrict her movement. Restricted movement meant bad pictures, and she'd decided good pictures were more important than propriety.

A small pickup with a Follow Me sign guided the red plane to an open-air tie-down near a row of hangars, and Loren walked over to meet the plane's occupants. As she approached, a young woman in a denim miniskirt that displayed spectacular legs climbed down from the pilot's seat. A *very* young woman, Loren noted with surprise. Couldn't be much more than eighteen, with tousled blond hair cut in a wash-and-shake style. Apparently, Scorpio trusted her to fly some senior exec around, although Loren had pegged the company as too conservative for that.

The movements of the man who swung down from the passenger seat were oddly familiar. When he turned to face her, she smiled automatically, as she would at any client, but something about the shape of his face and his carriage sent a rush of adrenaline through her that pushed the smile away.

He wore dark aviator glasses, an open-necked sport shirt and faded jeans. His mahogany hair was gray at the temples and smile lines bracketed his mouth, although he wasn't smiling now.

Slowly he took off his glasses, and she stared into the cobalt blue eyes of Adam Riordan.

"Hello, Loren." He smiled slowly, gently, as if she were a wild animal that might bolt at any minute.

Her ears buzzed; her head swam. She put out a hand to steady herself, but there was nothing there to hold on to, so she thrust both shaking hands into the pockets of her shorts to maintain her balance. Swallowing, she opened her mouth to say something, but nothing came out. *Hello, Loren.* The words, spoken in that achingly familiar voice, reverberated like the ending bass notes of a beloved song.

"Daddy, the plane's tied down. Am I cleared to pick up the rental car so I can unload the luggage?"

Loren's shocked gaze veered to the pilot, who had a designer tote bag slung over her shoulder.

"Yes, you are." Adam's attention remained focused on Loren. "But before you go, I'd like you to meet an old friend of mine, Loren Mont—I mean, Stanfield. Loren, this is my daughter, Daphne."

The scene took on a surreal quality. How could Adam be introducing her to a daughter named Daphne? That was supposed to have been *their* daughter's name. Then she remembered her son, Josh. Daphne and Josh, just as they'd planned, except for one small detail. They'd both married other people.

Daphne walked forward and stuck out her free hand. "Glad to meet you."

"Same here." Loren wrenched her perspiring hand free of her pocket and put it into Daphne's cool, manicured fingers. This was one sophisticated young woman. Years ago, Loren had heard about Adam's wedding to a Phoenix socialite named Anita McFarland. And here was the result, Loren thought, forcing a smile and releasing Daphne's hand.

Damn him. Shock was slowly giving way to anger. How dare he do this to her? What sadistic impulse had possessed him to hire her, of all people, to photograph a construction site? There were aerial photographers in Phoenix. Had his former passion faded to casual curiosity? She didn't think she could stand that. He'd known all along who he was dealing with, and he'd hidden his identity, probably waiting to enjoy this dramatic little moment. Well, she wouldn't give him another ounce of satisfaction.

"I wish you'd told me you were with Scorpio," she said earnestly as she glanced at Adam. "I would have given you a discount." That should get him, with his fancy red plane and macho-looking scorpion logo.

He looked unfazed by her patronizing gesture. "Maybe I was afraid you'd raise the price."

Or refuse the job, Loren thought. But no, she'd take anybody's money these days if it meant keeping Josh in school. Out-of-state tuition wasn't cheap. "I wouldn't dream of gouging you on the price. After all, we go way back." Her jolly tone cracked a little around the edges, but she thought she was pulling the nonchalance off.

Daphne glanced from Loren to her father. "How far back?"

"I was a cheerleader when your dad played football for Flagstaff High." That was all this self-possessed young woman needed to know.

"Oh." Daphne didn't seem completely satisfied, but the tote bag must have been getting tiresome to hold, because she shifted it to the other hand and tipped her head toward the terminal. "I'll see about the car. I hope you got a convertible."

"I didn't."

She made a face and started off. "Maybe I can work out an upgrade," she said over her shoulder.

Loren gazed after her; it was safer than looking at Adam. Luggage and a rental car? "I didn't know you planned to stay in Sedona," she said.

"Daphne asked to come along, so when I've finished with business, she and I will have a long-overdue father-daughter vacation."

"I see." She gathered her courage and faced him again. "That sounds like a nice idea. We should be through with the photo run sometime this afternoon, and then you can do. . .whatever you had in mind."

What *did* he have in mind?

He continued to stare at her. "I don't know why, but I thought your hair would still be long."

Loren touched her brown chin-length bob and could think of no response.

"It's good to see you again, Loren."

He hadn't replaced his dark glasses, and she gazed into his eyes for a second too long. Her heart gave a painful jerk and she turned away lest he see through her veneer of nonchalance. "Well. We'd better get started. The clouds are already building up. Can Daphne find us if we head over toward the hangar?"

"I don't doubt it. In case you hadn't noticed, she's not the shy retiring type."

"I noticed." But shy and retiring exactly described her son Josh, Loren thought as they headed for the hangar. Suddenly, she had a desperate need to make contact with Josh and her father, as if they might safeguard her against the emotions threatening to engulf her. Josh—sweet, quiet Josh, who probably loved working on airplane engines because they didn't require conversation.

"I haven't spent as much time with Daphne as I should," Adam admitted. "Besides, at eighteen, kids think they know everything."

"Mmm." Loren didn't want to discuss the behavior of eighteen-year-old girls. His sudden appearance had thrown her back to a time when she'd thought she knew everything about Adam Riordan. And she'd been humiliatingly wrong.

She walked beside him, aware of the scent of an unfamiliar cologne, no doubt chosen by his wife. Loren wished she could freeze-frame Adam for a moment, back off and study him at her leisure. She was too disconcerted by the rolling film of their interaction to form an objective impression.

She sneaked a glance at him from the corner of her eye, then another glance. Each stolen picture made her heart beat a little faster. Some other woman loved him now. Some other woman kissed those lips, gazed into those eyes now crinkled at the corners from years of squinting into the Arizona sun.

Her photographer's eye picked out telling details—the jut of his chin was a little firmer, the width of his shoulders a little broader, but he was still Adam, still the first man she'd ever loved. All at once, she could hear the rush of water over the rocks of Oak Creek Canyon and taste champagne and desire as if she and Adam had held each other only yesterday.

"Does the aerial photography company belong to you?" he asked, interrupting her thoughts.

She dropped a curtain over the memory. "To me and Dad. We've combined his engine-maintenance business with the aerial photography, so the corporation that covers both is Icarus Enterprises."

"Then I could get your Dad to tune my plane while I'm here?"

No! "I doubt it." What was he trying to do with all this togetherness stuff? Tear her into little pieces? The suspicion that this was all a lark for him chilled her. "He's scheduled the time today to fly us over to the construction site, but the rest of the week he and Josh are booked up with repair jobs."

"Josh?" He glanced at her, but he'd replaced the sunglasses and she couldn't read his expression.

"My son." She delivered the line with a flourish and reveled in the flush that tinged his cheeks. Maybe he wasn't as blasé about this reunion as he seemed. Maybe he could still be pricked with the pain of what-might-have-been. Good. "I always liked the name," she said oh-so-casually.

His mouth tightened and he gave no response. She felt the scales tilt just a little; he no longer held the advantage. But she wanted him to go away. He was making her heart ache in a way it hadn't for a very long time.

They approached the hangar labeled Icarus Enterprises, where her father and Josh were poised on stepladders on either side of a Mooney MSE, their heads stuck under the open cowling.

They both had grease on their hands and shirts and protective goggles over their eyes. Her father's baseball cap, lettered with the name Icarus, covered the generous bald spot he'd developed over the years. Josh's identical cap sat backward on blond hair so short it was almost a military cut. Loren felt a rush of love and pride.

"Hey, guys," she called out. "Our client's here." She wondered what her father would say when he

learned who his extra passenger would be today. She'd
never been sure what her parents had thought of
Adam's going to war. They'd comforted her and
agreed he should have said a proper goodbye, but they
hadn't joined her in damning Adam to the farthest
reaches of hell.

She, on the other hand, had been judgmental and
uncompromising. And eighteen. But even making an
excuse of her age, she winced a little at the memory of
those unbending beliefs. She'd called Adam a traitor
to humanity, but years later she'd been concealing
wounded pride and paralyzing fear. She'd shoved him
out of her life because she was afraid his death would
destroy her. And she was sure he would die in that war.

Her father moved out from under the cowling and
glanced down at her. "I can be ready in five minutes.
I just want to—"

"Don't worry, Gramps," Josh said, his voice muffled under the cowling. "I've got it under control."

"The boy's right." Loren's father pulled off the
goggles and left them hanging around his neck as he
backed down the stepladder. When he reached the
bottom, he straightened with a grimace. "Besides, his
back's younger than mine." He wiped his hands on a
rag and stepped forward to shake Adam's hand. "I'm
Walt Montgomery, Loren's father and the pilot."

Adam had once again removed his sunglasses, and
Loren wondered how her father could fail to recognize him, but then, her father hadn't memorized
Adam's every feature as she once had. "Dad, remember Adam Riordan?"

"Well, of course I..." He paused and squinted at Adam. "Well, I'll be damned. It is you." He shook Adam's hand again. "It's been a long time."

"A long time," Adam repeated. "I asked Loren if you might be able to tune up my 414 Cessna while I was here, but she seemed to think you were too booked to squeeze me in."

"Well, now..." Walt scratched his chin and glanced at Loren, who tried to relay with a frown that she didn't want him tuning up Adam's plane. They weren't that hard up for money.

A slight smile crossed Walt's face and he turned back to Adam. "Might fit it in tomorrow. Josh and I have an overhaul, but with both of us working, we probably could tune that Cessna for you. Going to be around Sedona for a while, are you?"

"A few days."

"Well, we're glad for the business," Walt said with another casual glance at Loren. "Have you met my grandson?"

Loren felt betrayed. Didn't her father understand what having Adam around was doing to her equilibrium?

"Josh, why don't you stop a minute and meet Adam Riordan?" Walt said. "He went to high school with your mother."

Loren wanted to hide somewhere, but she was a grown-up now, supposedly equipped to handle situations like this. She prayed her father wouldn't embarrass them all with some story about a time she and Adam had broken curfew or been caught parking by the Flagstaff police. Thank God her parents had never found out about the aborted elopement plan.

Josh came down the ladder, dutiful kid that he was, although Loren knew he hated to leave the engine tune-up. He wiped off the oil and shook hands with Adam. Loren watched the two of them sizing each other up. Josh was about the same height, but Josh would never have Adam's solid muscularity. Josh's father was wiry, or at least he was the last time Loren had seen him fourteen years ago. Josh took after him in looks, fortunately not in temperament.

She wondered if Adam was looking at Josh and searching for evidence of the man she'd married, just as she'd tried to find clues about Anita from meeting Daphne.

"Are you in college?" Adam asked.

"I'll be a sophomore at MIT this fall."

Loren loved the sound of that statement. *Eat your heart out, Riordan.*

"That's great," Adam said. "It's a tough program."

"Yeah." Josh's sigh was heartfelt. "To tell the truth, paying out all that money seems crazy when I'd just as soon join the military and get training there in aircraft mechanics, but—"

"But his mean old mother won't let him," Loren said. "People can get killed in the military, although Josh refuses to admit that." Her chest tightened. That last had slipped out, escaped from a dusty storehouse of memories and resentments. It wouldn't happen again. "The clouds are building in the west, Dad. I think we'd better saddle up."

"Right." Walt glanced at his grandson. "Caldwell wants that Mooney by five-thirty. See any problem with finishing by then?"

"No problem, Gramps."

Pride shone in Walt's eyes and he clamped a hand on Josh's shoulder. "Good. Then I guess we'll—"

A horn beeped from the tarmac outside the hangar and a bell-like voice called out, "Hey, Dad, what do you think of this baby?"

All four of them turned. Daphne waved from the driver's seat of a black Geo Storm convertible. The top was down and luggage was piled high in the back seat.

Josh blinked. "Who's that?"

"My daughter," Adam said, resignation in his voice. "Looks like she wrangled a convertible, after all."

Daphne flung open the car door and stepped out. Loren wanted to cover Josh's eyes before he glimpsed that long stretch of tanned leg, but Josh was way past the stage when she could order him not to look. And look he did. Daphne had a model's languorous walk and she twirled the car keys in one slender hand as she approached the hangar.

Loren knew the exact moment Daphne sighted Josh. Her chin went up, like a predator scenting game. She paused imperceptibly before continuing toward them. Loren could see the girl's focus narrow from the general to the specific. Loren tried to be amused, but something about Daphne scared the hell out of her.

When Daphne reached them, she pushed her sunglasses to the top of her head and Loren saw for the first time she had Adam's eyes, but with a subtle difference. In the time Loren had known him, his gaze had never been calculating.

Adam introduced Daphne to Walt and Josh.

Daphne glanced from Josh to the Mooney. "You been working on that?"

"Yes."

"How d'you like the Lycoming engine?"

Josh stared.

She gave him back an exaggerated stare. "Girls can know about airplane engines, too, you know."

"Maybe," Josh said, "but I've never met one who did."

"You have now."

Loren felt as if a trapdoor had opened beneath her. Or more precisely Josh. Her son would be a sitting duck for someone who looked like Daphne and understood airplanes, besides. She didn't want Josh to know Daphne was a licensed pilot, too, and a good one, judging from her landing this morning.

"I flew my dad up here today," Daphne said. "In Scorpio's twin-engine."

"No kidding?"

"Don't look so surprised. I got my single-engine rating when I was sixteen, my twin-engine last year."

"Me, too," Josh said, his gaze never leaving Daphne's face.

Loren glared at her father, hoping he was satisfied with the mess his welcoming attitude toward Adam had helped create. Walt shrugged as if to say there was nothing much they could do; the forces of nature had taken over.

But Loren wasn't ready to surrender the field. "That Mooney has to be done by five-thirty, Josh," she reminded him gently.

"Uh, right." He returned to the ladder, and for the first time in Loren's memory, he seemed reluctant to return to an airplane engine. "Nice meeting you, Daphne."

"Same, here." Daphne showed no signs of leaving as her gaze followed Josh up the ladder.

Adam cleared his throat. "I'd like you to drive down to the Los Arboles resort as soon as possible, Daphne. I'm not convinced Greta got the reservations right."

Daphne looked up at her father with a sunny smile. "Sure, Dad. What time do you want me back here to pick you up?"

Adam glanced questioningly at Loren.

"About four, I'd say," Loren told him.

"I'll be here." Daphne walked to the convertible, and Loren forced herself not to check out whether Josh was watching. A confirmation of her suspicions would be far too unsettling.

TWENTY MINUTES LATER, the single engine of Icarus Enterprises' Cessna 206 roared as Walt took the plane down the runway. Loren usually felt a sense of elation and release from worldly concerns as the plane took off on an assignment. But there would be no contentment for her this trip, she knew.

Adam sat in the passenger seat next to Walt, Loren behind them on the floor. The other four seats had been taken out to make room for the Wild RC-10 camera mounted over a manhole-size opening cut in the fuselage.

Adam relaxed against the seat, his broad shoulders settling into the cushion as if he'd ridden there hundreds of times. Loren studied the back of his head and his nape, which she'd never really seen because hairstyles had been longer when they'd dated. The slight wave she remembered combing her fingers through was still there in abbreviated form, and it made the back of his hair swirl gently, defying the barber's attempt to make a neat vee cut at his nape.

A small white scar just beneath the hairline caught her attention. Had it been there before? Or did it mark the path of a Vietcong bullet? Her stomach clenched with the nostalgic pain of an old fury. After all this time, why did she even give a damn? And why, in the deep recesses of her heart, was she shouting with joy because he was whole?

She turned her gaze to the window as Walt took off like the seasoned professional he was, banking the plane to allow Loren a view of the red-rocked buttes. Streams the color of melted pistachio ice cream laced the rusty ground. Loren couldn't imagine a more beautiful, or more treacherous, place to fly. Updrafts could flip a landing plane in a second, which made Daphne's feat this morning all the more amazing.

Daphne. Loren glanced back at Adam and wondered if he suspected the same thing she did—that Daphne would check in at Los Arboles and return to the airport and Josh.

As if in response to her thoughts, Adam turned in his seat and spoke over the drone of the engine. "Josh seems like a nice kid."

"He is." *And keep your daughter away from him.* Loren was supposed to return the compliment, she knew, but Daphne didn't fit the description of a nice kid. "Daphne's very beautiful."

"Unfortunately she knows it."

"Josh isn't very..." She searched for the right word that wouldn't make Josh seem immature. He wasn't, but he was reticent and had recently been dumped by the only girlfriend he'd ever had. "I think he feels more comfortable with airplane engines than with girls," she said at last.

"And he's damned good with airplane engines," Walt chipped in. "Mark my words, that boy will be a master mechanic one day."

Loren smiled as Walt launched into his favorite subject. Maybe she'd deliberately given him his cue because she wanted Adam to hear Walt rave on. From the day Josh was born, he's been his grandfather's sun and moon, earth and stars. Which was another reason Loren couldn't let him enlist in the military. If Josh ended up injured—or worse—it would tear her apart, but it might kill Walt.

Loren glanced at Adam's profile as he listened to Walt cataloguing Josh's virtues. The contours of his face were essentially the same as she remembered, except the skin seemed stretched tighter over the bone, and there was a tense set to his mouth that hadn't been there before. She wondered if he was happy.

"Josh has a bright future in avionics," Walt said. "Plus he's a decent kid. Although I'm sure he had a few beers his first year away at college. All kids have fake ID cards by that age, don't they?"

Loren held her breath. Did Adam remember that she'd suggested using his to get a marriage license?

"I certainly had one," Adam said easily.

Of course, he'd probably forgotten all that, she thought. She was the fool who'd allowed stupid details to stick in her mind all these years.

"But Josh hasn't been in any serious trouble," Walt continued. "He's a credit to his mother."

Adam turned to her, his eyes gentle. "I can see that."

"Thank you," she managed. *He could have been your son.* She was amazed the past still inspired such anguish in her. A long time ago, she'd fantasized about tracking Adam down and pointing out to him how his heroics had destroyed their lives. But time had shifted her perspective, allowed her to accept some of the responsibility. If she'd read at least one of his letters, instead of ripping them to shreds, if she hadn't married an antiwar protester, which she now could admit had been an act of revenge, things might have been different.

Then again, maybe not. Adam had run out on her, left without a word. Something else had been more important than her love. Had they reconciled, she might have lived in fear that he'd abandon her again if another noble cause came along. She looked away from the heartbreaking kindness in Adam's eyes. Perhaps everything had happened for the best.

CHAPTER TWO

ADAM'S GAZE caressed Loren's face, relearning its curves and hollows. She turned away before he got his fill of her fawn-brown eyes. *Come back to me,* he pleaded silently, but she refused to meet his glance again.

"By the way, I brought turkey sandwiches and bottled water to drink," she said, moving toward the back of the plane, away from him.

"That's fine. I didn't even think about food." A gigantic understatement.

"You're the client. You're not supposed to." Her comment emphasized the line she'd drawn between them. "If you'll excuse me, I'd better recheck a few things on the maps." She pulled out two rolled topography maps from a compartment in the back and made a great pretense of studying them. At least he figured it was a pretense. She'd surveyed this area for him before and knew the routine.

She sat cross-legged and unrolled the maps on her bare knees. He remembered she used to be so limber she could sit like that for hours, involved in a debate about social issues with Sherry and some of her other friends. He'd loved standing in the background watching her spirited conversation, her animated expression.

He'd imagined this meeting for so long that he could hardly believe she was here, little more than an arm's length away. "Everything checking out?" he asked, wanting to maintain conversational contact.

She didn't look up as her supple fingers smoothed back the corners of the map. "Just familiarizing myself again."

And so was he. When he'd stepped off the plane, the sight of her had weakened his knees. He wondered how long he'd stood there staring like an idiot, his heart hammering and his palms sweaty. Seeing Loren had stripped away the years, the experiences that had jaded him, the stagnation that surrounded his heart. She stole his breath with the picture she'd made walking toward him, her skin sheened with moisture in the summer heat, her smile welcoming. For a wild moment, he'd imagined the smile was one of pleased recognition. Then he'd taken off his sunglasses, and the smile had faded.

"Your daughter must be a good pilot if you trusted her to land at Sedona," Walt said.

He turned to Walt. Pride tightened his chest. "She's so good it astonishes me."

"Does she plan on a career in flying?"

"I wish I knew. Right now she seems to be... drifting."

"Mmm." Walt's nonanswer didn't disguise the note of disapproval in it.

"She's still young. Eighteen's a tough age," Adam said defensively. Secretly he believed Daphne was too talented to waste her time like this. She'd learned to read before she'd started school and he'd recognized an intelligence in her that matched, sometimes surpassed, his own. But from the time Daphne was born, Anita had appropriated her, accusing Adam, with his ideas for stimulating her mind, of "trying to turn her into a son."

Consequently, Daphne had become somewhat of a mystery to him. She'd hired a stranger to teach her to fly, rather than take lessons from him, which had hurt like the devil. But he'd been afraid to ask her why she'd done that, afraid to discover she hadn't wanted his guidance. Anita had hinted that was the case, that Daphne didn't think he was on her wavelength.

After the divorce, he realized he'd lose her completely if he didn't try to establish some sort of common ground, whether or not Daphne welcomed it. They'd had a few dinners together, and he had to admit he didn't speak her language, especially when it came to designer clothes and musical groups. He'd learned that she favored short skirts and fast cars, attended college because she liked sorority life, had no clue as to what career she wanted and went through boyfriends with the speed of an F-14.

On the plane ride up here today, he'd seen the first glimmer of hope as they found something they both loved to discuss—airplanes. Maybe this was how they'd finally connect, even though she apparently hadn't trusted him enough to teach her to fly them.

He sensed some movement behind him and turned to see Loren putting away the maps. Then she began cleaning the lens on the camera. Every brisk, professional movement she made filled him with ridiculous, unfounded pride. He'd had nothing to do with the woman she'd become. Although, if he'd given in to her demands and presented her with a baby twenty-three years ago, her life might have been far different. Maybe he could take some satisfaction in his refusal to saddle her with that sort of responsibility before she'd been ready for it.

When she'd mailed Scorpio Steel the results of her first assignment for the company a few months ago, he'd cherished those mundane shots, because she'd taken them. He'd traced her left-handed, back-slanting signature on the accompanying invoices. If his own signature hadn't become so illegible over the years, she might have deciphered his name at the bottom of the checks she'd cashed. Never in his life had he paid out money with such excitement.

"Seems like things have gone well with you," Walt said, obviously wanting more information.

Adam broke off his reverie. "Financially things are fine," he said. Adam understood Walt's curiosity, but he didn't want to get too specific about his personal situation until he could look into Loren's eyes while he explained it. "I was sorry to hear about your wife," he said, shifting topics.

"It was pretty bad. Cancer's gotta be the worst way to go." Walt lowered his voice and tilted his head back slightly. "It was real tough on her."

Adam's heart twisted. "I'll bet."

"Who told you about Fran?"

"I keep in touch with Jim Denton."

"That's right," Walt said. "You and Jimmy Denton were friends in high school. I'd forgotten that. Guess you know he's getting a divorce. Hell of a thing."

"Yes, I know. There's a lot of that going around."

"Your folks still in Flag?" Walt asked.

"No, they bought a retirement place in Sun City."

Walt made a noncommittal sound deep in his throat. "Don't suppose I'll ever retire. I'm having too much fun."

"That's great." Adam realized he envied Walt a little. Flying and working on airplane engines sounded like a pretty good life compared to the pressures of running a multimillion-dollar company. "It's beautiful up here."

"Wouldn't trade it for the world."

Adam watched the plane's shadow skim over the nubby desert. Walt had taken them northwest over Prescott National Forest to pick up Interstate 40, a dark gray ribbon stitched between Williams and Kingman. The highway would lead them most of the way across to the bridge construction site on the Colorado River, just south of Laughlin, Nevada. To their left marched gray-blue mountains, backdropped by another range, then another, each jagged silhouette tinged a lighter blue than the one before, like the shades of a color wheel.

"Remember you once offered to teach me to fly?" Adam asked Walt.

"Yep."

"I should have taken you up on it." Except flying lessons would have interrupted his time with Loren, and all he'd wanted in those days was to be with her, to hold her, kiss her...

"Well, you learned how to fly, I take it."

"Yes, I learned." More than how to fly, he thought. But flying had been the saving grace in a life where other satisfactions danced perpetually out of reach. A plane was the first major toy he'd bought when Scorpio Steel began turning a sizable profit.

Walt pulled the nose of the plane up a little. "Is the bridge construction going along on schedule?"

"No, it's not, which is the reason for all these pictures." Part of the reason, he amended to himself. Ever since Jim Denton had mentioned that Loren was an aerial photographer, he'd been looking for a reason to hire her.

"Figured as much." Walt called back to Loren. "Bridge isn't on schedule, just like I told you."

"Have you figured out what's wrong?" Loren's voice held the same husky, rich tone he remembered. Back in high school, they'd talked on the phone for hours, and he'd never tired of that sultry sound. Sometimes he still heard it in his dreams.

He turned in his seat. "The contractor claims he's getting shorted on the steel shipments."

"But you're shipping the right amount?"

"I've spent several hours going over the invoices, and everything checks out. I think he's getting the steel and off-loading to another site."

"Really?" Her brown eyes grew alert with interest. He remembered how she'd always hated injustice. "Embezzling the steel?"

He nodded.

"Do you know the contractor?"

"I know him. His name is Barnaby Haskett." Considering Loren was obviously still hostile toward the military, he decided not to add that he'd served in the same unit with Haskett in Vietnam.

"I've never worked with anybody by that name," Loren said. "How long have you known him?"

"Quite a while. I helped him get his contractor's license."

"And this is how he shows his gratitude?"

Adam shrugged. "That was a long time ago. He's probably forgotten." While they'd shared the choking humidity of the jungle, Adam had convinced Haskett that Arizona was the place to live. But after he'd helped him settle in and get his license, they'd lost touch. When Adam noticed Haskett was the contractor for the bridge project, he'd invited him over to the house for dinner, for old times' sake. Then, only days afterward, Adam had come home unexpectedly and found Haskett in bed with Anita. So much for esprit de corps.

"If you helped him get his license, why do you now think he's the type to be embezzling the steel?" Loren asked.

Adam didn't want to go into Anita's indiscretions at this point. "I know him a little better than I did back then," he temporized. Haskett and Anita were engaged now. His anger over her adultery was tinged with guilt at not having given her enough love and attention during their marriage. Maybe he could make partial amends by keeping her from marrying someone who would ultimately end up in prison. Daphne didn't need that kind of embarrassment, either, so he hoped to wrap this up before the wedding.

As a by-product, he had an excuse to see Loren. Hiring her to work for him while he found out what Haskett was up to seemed like a logical, low-pressure way to find out if he and Loren still had anything between them. Jim had failed to tell him that Loren had a son about Daphne's age. Josh. So Daphne and Josh had become a reality. Anita hadn't wanted the name Daphne, but that was a battle he'd won.

"What exactly are you looking for in the pictures?" Loren asked.

"I'm hoping to get lucky, see Haskett's crew actually transferring steel somewhere else."

Walt nodded toward the burgeoning gray thunderheads on the horizon. "Those clouds may screw up our chances this morning."

"Aw, Dad, we can make it," Loren said.

"Easy for you to say. You're not flying this baby to the exacting specifications of a lady photographer I know."

"I'm not that critical."

Walt snorted and glanced at Adam. "Not that critical, she says. When Loren's taking pictures, she wants the plane steady enough to balance a martini on each wing without agitating the olives."

"That's a gross exaggeration!"

Walt winked at Adam. "Just watch. And listen." He handed Adam a headset and put on his own.

Adam needed no invitation to study Loren as she worked at the job she obviously loved. The film canisters looked heavy, but she used leverage and economy of movement to load the film with the same grace he'd admired when she'd turned cartwheels in front of the grandstand of Flagstaff High. They'd met when she turned a cartwheel right into his arms. He'd never believed it was an accident. She wasn't that clumsy.

"Five minutes," Walt said. "How low do you want us to get, Adam? Population's sparse enough here to go in at five hundred feet if you want."

"No, that might create undue suspicion. Twelve hundred feet is fine. This should look like a typical survey run, unless I spot a truck going in the wrong direction with a load of steel."

"So we'll do a normal grid pattern," Loren said.

Her voice, so intimately close, stirred memories of holding her, and he felt as if someone had just drop-kicked his heart. "Yes."

"If we can," Walt muttered as wisps of cloud shrouded the plane momentarily and moved on. The bulk of the storm lay directly in front of them, ragged tails of rain unraveling from the underside of the cloud bank.

Adam peered down at the bridge construction on the Arizona side of the river, where steel supports sprouted in a row across the turquoise water of the Colorado. The trucks and cranes on the bank beside the river looked like the scattered toys of a five-year-old who'd been called in to lunch.

"Rolling," Loren murmured in his ear just as the clouds moved overhead and blocked the sun, turning the river water gray.

Walt guided the plane as if stringing a loom, with each pass parallel to the last. Then the plane hit an air pocket and lurched.

"Steady, Dad," Loren said, her tone breathless with concentration. "Steady." Another pocket. "Dammit!"

"Can't hold it. Storm's moving in," Walt said as a few drops hit the windshield.

"You can do it," she barked. "Left wing down! Come on, Dad, hold that course."

Adam saw an eighteen-wheeler pull away from the site. Which way was it going? A layer of clouds moved under them, obscuring the view.

"Shi—shucks," Loren said.

In spite of his own disappointment at missing the direction of the truck, Adam smiled.

"Keep going, Dad."

Walt turned the plane and started back.

"Hold that line . . . hold it. . . . Now back across."

Adam had lost sight of the truck. He didn't think Loren was getting much with the cloud interference.

"Easy does it," she said. "That's it. You've . . . No!"

The jolt of the plane threw Adam against his seat belt as Loren groaned in frustration.

"Give it up, sweetheart," Walt said, banking the plane. "I'm heading home before we get socked in."

"Damn. We almost had it."

Adam spoke into the small microphone attached to his headset. "We'll adjust, Loren. Maybe the weather will be better tomorrow. We could start early in the morning." He thought about Daphne and figured he wouldn't be taking time from her. She'd already announced she wanted to sleep in on this trip.

"We could try another run in the morning," Walt said, "but you'll have to choose between that and a tune-up. I can't be two places at once."

Adam knew an opening when he saw one. That instinct had made him the best running back in Flagstaff High's history. "What if I flew the plane for Loren?"

Loren's reply was like a shot. "Our insurance wouldn't cover it."

He wasn't giving up his advantage. That time alone would be the perfect opportunity to explain about his divorce. They could talk, maybe clear the air about what had happened all those years ago. "My lawyer could fax a release."

"I still wouldn't want to do it."

He knew what she didn't want to do—be in a plane alone with him. Disappointment dampened his mood.

"Seems like a reasonable solution to me, Adam," Walt said, "assuming you can put up with the drill sergeant in the back."

"I can." He mentally crossed his fingers.

"But, Dad," Loren said, "I don't think—"

"Now, Loren, I'm sure Adam can manage this plane. I'll let him fly us the rest of the way home so he's checked out on everything. I don't think the insurance is a real problem, do you?"

Adam waited through another period of silence.

"I guess not," she said at last.

"Then it's a deal," Adam said, closing his eyes with relief. Tomorrow he'd be alone with Loren for a few

precious hours. It was the most he could hope for at
this stage.

DAPHNE RIORDAN DROVE fast over the winding roads
to Los Arboles, trying to wipe out the memory of how
her father had looked at Loren Stanfield. Daphne
certainly recognized sexual tension; despite her youth,
she'd stirred up enough of it. And she'd solved the
mystery of why her dad had hired an aerial photographer from Sedona when he certainly could have
found a more convenient service in Phoenix.

What a bitch of a situation, to be hanging around
while her father tried to light up an old flame. Not that
Daphne had really expected him to spend all that much
time with her. Years ago her mother had warned her
that her father cared about business first and family
second. Since the divorce, he'd seemed a little more
interested in her activities, though.

Besides, she tried to remember that his success with
the steel company allowed her and her mother to live
in Fountain Hills, wear boutique clothing and drive
sexy cars. His preoccupation with business seemed
normal; she could take it. But Loren Stanfield wasn't
business. And if he found another love, what would
happen to what little attention she'd been getting from
him in the past few months? She knew the answer to
that. Most of her friends' parents were divorced, and
a new lover usually meant the kids could go hang.

She pulled into the valet-parking area, tossed the
keys to a uniformed guy who was semicute and allowed a bellman to deal with the luggage while she

whisked in the door. The place was nice, Spanish tile and all that, but Daphne was used to nice.

When she reached the room that was to be hers, she gave it a cursory glance and walked back out the door. Orienting herself to all the amenities—pool, spa, tennis courts, golf course and health club—took less than twenty minutes. She had the rest of the day until four o'clock to fill. She'd planned to spend it shopping at Tlaquepaque, a cluster of shops that had some cool stuff, but now she had a better idea.

In minutes, she'd retrieved the black convertible and headed up the airport road. She loved airplanes. She'd taken flight lessons in the first place to impress her father. She'd even followed her mother's advice and hired someone else to teach her so as not to disturb her father's busy schedule. She'd looked forward to surprising him with her expertise.

He hadn't seemed all that surprised or impressed, although he'd let her fly his plane once she was rated for a twin-engine. But it turned out she didn't care so much now whether he was impressed, because flying was the neatest feeling she'd ever had. If she couldn't be flying, she'd rather hang out with mechanics than with her regular friends.

Except she'd never met a mechanic as cute as Josh. What made him extra tempting was that Loren obviously didn't want her within a thousand miles of him. Daphne intended to get a whole lot closer than that.

LOREN COULDN'T believe it. Her father was a turncoat. He'd practically pushed her into this survey trip with Adam, and now the two men were swapping flying stories like long-lost buddies. If her father even *dared* to move from flying stories to accounts of his days on board an aircraft carrier, which would naturally bring up Adam's war experiences, she'd strangle them both.

She dimly remembered that her father had taken a shine to Adam back when she'd been dating him, but she hadn't ascribed much significance to it at the time. Later, she was sorry her father hadn't shown the same affection for Jack Stanfield. But then when she and Jack had parted ways, she'd thought it for the best that her father hadn't been attached to him.

Adam taxied past the terminal and parked the plane just outside the open Icarus hangar. From the way Walt praised his flying ability, Adam could have been a reincarnated Charles Lindbergh returning from his flight across the Atlantic. So the guy was passable at the controls. So what?

Both men got out of the plane still talking. Loren handed her father the partially used canister of film, and he headed off to find out how Josh was coming along on the tune-up.

As Loren started to climb out, she realized Adam had his hand extended to help her down. She had a split second to decide whether to be ungracious and safe from harm, or cordial and in danger of making a fool of herself. Her mother's training in manners won out and she placed her hand in Adam's.

The result was as disastrous as she'd feared. The familiar warmth of his hand clasped around hers unsettled her so much that she stumbled on the way down, which meant he had to catch her around the waist to keep her from falling to the tarmac and skinning both knees.

For one sizzling moment, their bodies touched before she jumped back in what must have looked like a ridiculous overreaction. "I—I'm sorry," she muttered, hot with embarrassment. "I'm usually not so clumsy."

She heard a little sigh. Startled, she glanced into his eyes.

"I know," he said with too much feeling for the remark to be empty conversation. "Loren, I—"

"I'm gonna tar and feather that boy!" shouted her father from inside the hangar.

Loren spun toward the building in alarm. "What's wrong?" she called, hurrying to her father, who stood next to the workbench, his feet braced and his hands on his hips.

He gestured toward a note held down by a large wrench. "Seems he's left for *ice cream*. Seems he'll be back at four. Look at this place!"

Loren surveyed the tools left out, the rags lying around, the goggles tossed in a corner. Her stomach churned when she saw the uncharacteristic mess. "Did he finish the tune-up?"

"The note says he and *Daphne* finished it together."

"Daphne?" Adam asked, coming up behind Loren. "Daphne was here?"

Loren whirled to face him. "Look, Adam, this is a business. You'll have to explain to your daughter that she can't—"

"We can't blame it all on Daphne," Walt said, and Loren knew how much the admission cost him. He liked to think his golden grandchild could do no wrong. "Josh knows better than this."

"But he's never left the shop a mess before," Loren persisted. "He's never left the shop, period, without checking with us first. But now that Daphne—"

"I'll speak to her," Adam said.

"Well, you'd better, because I can't have—"

"I said I'd speak to her." Adam's blue eyes flashed a warning.

Loren was shaking, but she had to assure herself that Josh would be protected from Daphne. "It may take more than one conversation, Adam. I saw the way she looked at my son. She has her moves all figured out. He's no match for her, and you know it."

He didn't respond right away. Then he smiled ruefully. "That's right, he probably isn't. No more than I was a match for you at that age."

Loren felt the blood drain from her face.

"But don't worry, Loren." An intensity in his eyes contradicted his easy smile. "I'm more than a match for you now."

CHAPTER THREE

THE IRONY of the situation, Loren protecting her son from his daughter, didn't escape Adam.

"I don't think this is the least bit funny," Loren snapped, her dark gaze indignant. Just then, the black convertible wheeled across the tarmac toward them, Daphne at the wheel, blond hair flying.

Loren stiffened. "Well, they're back."

Adam welcomed the reprieve. Loren couldn't see the humorous side of the incident, and he really didn't want to fight about their kids. "Then I guess we'll take off. I'll meet you here in the morning, say six?"

"Six is fine." She kept her attention on the black car as it braked to a stop a few yards away.

Adam noticed how good Daphne and Josh looked together as they got out of the car—blond, heartachingly handsome examples of the next generation. How could he blame them for wanting to taste everything life had to offer? He'd wanted to at their age. So they'd taken off for ice cream. Big deal.

Nevertheless, he adopted a stern expression as he approached the car. "Let's go, Daphne," he said.

She smiled. "Okay. I'll drive."

"No, I'll drive."

She glanced at him, shrugged and walked around to the passenger side of the car. "Whatever." Then she turned and waved at Josh. "See you."

"Yeah," he called, sticking his hands in his pockets and slouching in seeming nonchalance. "Thanks for the ice cream."

"Anytime."

Adam shoehorned himself into the Geo and adjusted the seat several notches to accommodate his long legs. He wadded up a chocolate-stained paper napkin and brushed aside sugar-cone bits on the console before he turned on the ignition and shifted into first gear.

"Josh is sweet," Daphne said as they drove out the airport gate and started toward town.

"That may be, but you've caused him some problems today."

"*I've* caused him problems?" She didn't look very innocent behind her aviator Ray-bans, but her voice was filled with ingenuous amazement.

"His mother and grandfather have entrusted him with quite a bit of responsibility for an eighteen-year-old," he said. "They don't expect him to run off for ice cream and leave the place a mess. His grandfather was really upset when he saw everything still lying around."

"But he said he'd clean it up later, Dad," she said, her tone martyred. "How was I supposed to know his gramps would wig out about it? Like, we went for *ice cream*. It's not like I invited him to the resort to do drugs, or something."

"*Where* you went wasn't the problem." Although Adam figured Loren would have found something wrong with any plan involving Daphne and Josh. It was as if they'd come full circle. How well he remembered his parents lecturing him about the dangers of becoming too involved with Loren. "Leaving without cleaning up was the problem."

"Well, it's not my fault if he was hot to ride around in my car. I did what I was supposed to. I was there when I said I'd be there to pick you up."

"Yes, you were." He didn't contradict her about whose car this was. "I appreciate that." He turned into the wide driveway leading to Los Arboles. Not three miles down the road was a rambling house on the creek side of the canyon, where Loren's parents had lived. He wondered if Walt still did.

Los Arboles hadn't existed then, and Adam could imagine Walt complaining about the increased traffic its presence brought. The resort was elegant to look at, though, nestled against the cliffs, the massive Spanish architecture softened with juniper, spruce and countless beds of flowers.

"I am always very punctual," Daphne announced with pride, crossing her arms over her chest.

Adam braked the car at valet parking. "Yes, you are. It's a good trait to have." One of the few successful moves he'd made as a father was giving her an alarm clock when she'd turned five. She'd been responsible for getting herself up every morning after that. It was one area in which she differed greatly from her mother, who was always late.

Adam glanced in disapproval as the valet opened Daphne's door and ogled her legs as she got out. Short of asking her to wear less revealing clothes, which he was smart enough not to do, he had no choice but to put up with the reaction of most males.

After handing the keys to the valet, he followed Daphne into the lobby.

"This way, Dad." She led him out a side door and down a path between fragrant junipers and beds of petunias. "I have this place all figured out."

Smiling to himself, he allowed her to direct him to their adjoining rooms. Daphne had always prided herself on her navigational skills. It was another thing that helped make her a top-notch pilot. He'd like to see her turn her skill into a profession, but he hated to push, was wary of making even the suggestion for fear she would think he was trying to plan her life and would stubbornly resist.

She handed him his key, and they unlocked both doors, then the one between the two rooms. Each room had a flower-bedecked patio and a view of vermilion cliffs jutting up behind the resort. "Let the vacation begin," she said, standing in the doorway between the two rooms, her glasses shoved to the top of her head.

"That's right. Except for one small thing I still have to do. But it shouldn't affect you."

Her expression became guarded. "What do you mean?"

"The weather was uncooperative today, so we didn't get the photographs. We have to go back to Laughlin in the morning. I should be through before you get up, though."

"Why do you have to go? Can't she do it alone?"

He noticed the bitter emphasis on the word *she*. "Actually, Loren needs someone to fly the plane, so I volunteered. Walt and Josh are tied up with repair work."

Daphne's mouth tightened and her blue eyes grew cold. "I think you just want an excuse to be with her."

The truth of her statement jolted him. He regarded his daughter with caution. "What do you mean by that?"

She let out an exasperated breath and looked up at the ceiling. "Dad, I'm not *stupid*." She glared at him and began ticking off items on her fingers. "First you hire an aerial photographer from Sedona, when there must be companies in Phoenix. Then you decide you have to go with the aerial photographer while they're taking pictures. And after we get up here, I find out you knew her back in high school. I saw the way you looked at her. And she looked pretty freaked out, herself. She was your girlfriend in high school, wasn't she?"

Adam met her gaze. "Yes, she was."

"Dad, is the ink even dry on the divorce papers?"

His jaw tightened. "Daphne, don't pass judgment on something that isn't your—"

"It *is* my business. You said you had to get some aerial photographs. You didn't say anything about looking up an old flame. Do you think I'd have asked to come along if I'd known that?"

He felt trapped. "I didn't know what would happen when I saw her again."

"Well, I guess *that* question's settled. You're both hot to trot."

"That's enough, young lady!"

She shrank back a little, but the fire never left her eyes. "So tell me I'm wrong."

He gritted his teeth. A shouting match wouldn't be helpful, but boy, she could be mouthy. Anita had taught her that. "You're wrong," he said quietly. "I don't know what will happen between us. She may be involved with someone. But she was important to me once, and I wanted to see her. Maybe I should have told you, but—"

"You should have."

"You're being pretty hard on me, Daph. It's not the sort of thing a father usually discusses with his daughter."

"How would you know?"

He caught his breath at the pain that knifed through him. "Dammit, Daphne, I—"

"Forget it." Eyes bright, she turned and stormed into her room.

Just before the lock clicked, he grabbed the knob and pushed.

She stepped away from the door, obviously amazed he'd barge in on her and spoil her dramatic exit. But he'd lived with Anita for twenty years, and so knew pretty much what to expect from Daphne, who'd trained at her mother's knee.

"No, I won't forget it," he said. He took a deep breath and spoke more gently. "Whether you believe it or not, I care about you."

Her throat moved convulsively as she seemed to be struggling not to cry.

"I was glad you wanted to come along on this trip, even if I had misgivings about bringing you. I decided to chance it. We can still have a great time—if you'll try not to judge me so harshly."

She hugged herself and stared at the floor. Finally, she lifted her head. Her lashes were wet, and she looked very young. "Okay," she whispered.

When she was little, he would have gathered her into his arms to comfort her, and he longed to do so now. But they'd lost that closeness along the way. "Dinner?"

She nodded.

"Great." He started back to his room.

"You know what, Dad?"

He turned. "What?"

She sniffed and wiped her nose. Then she gestured around the room. "This is nice. I'm not complaining. But you know what I always wanted to do for a vacation?"

"No, I don't," he said. "I don't know a lot of things about you, Daphne," he added softly.

"You'll laugh."

"Try me."

"Camping."

He was too astonished to laugh. "Daphne, are you sure you mean that? Camping, as in no washrooms and no electricity for hair driers, and sleeping in tents that sometimes leak, and trying to keep the creepy-crawlies out of your sleeping bag? That kind of camping?"

"Yeah." Her smile trembled. "I've *always* wanted to do that. Remember Jenny?"

He nodded, vaguely picturing one of her friends from school. He hadn't known any of her friends very well, another unfortunate fact he regretted.

"Jenny and her family went camping every summer. Sometimes they came up here to Oak Creek Canyon. It sounded so neat, Dad. They asked me to go with them once, but..."

"What happened?" He prayed he hadn't been the one who'd refused to let her.

"Mom had planned this big shopping trip for that weekend to San Diego. She'd bought plane tickets, and everything." Daphne shrugged. "I couldn't tell her I'd rather go camping. I mean, I wanted to go shopping. We bought lots of cool stuff, but I still wish..."

Adam walked over and gave her the hug he'd been afraid to try earlier, and she hugged back. "We'll go camping," he said.

"Really? You know how?"

Adam thought of pitching a tent in a steamy jungle clearing, of trying to start a fire in the midst of a drizzle, of eating reconstituted food and trying to sleep while gunfire echoed in the distance. "Yeah, I know how," he said. He gave her another squeeze. "So, are you ready to eat, or did all that ice cream spoil your appetite?"

Daphne beamed at him. "I'm starved."

"IT'S JUST NOT like you, Josh," Loren said as she sat on the edge of his bed after dinner. Outside his open window birds twittered as they settled down for the night, and the creek gurgled over jumbled rocks. They'd had many talks sitting on this bed. As always, she gathered her thoughts by smoothing the blue corded spread beneath her fingers. "I think Gramps reacted like that because he was just so surprised. So was I."

Josh plucked at a loose stitch on his running shoe and wouldn't look at her. "I didn't think it'd be such a big deal cleaning up after we came back. Daphne had to pick up her dad at four, so we had just enough time to go into town." His chin jutted forward. "And you guys were early."

Loren ignored his belligerence. "What if someone had come by the shop?"

"Nobody was scheduled to come by. I checked."

"But still, someone unexpected could have shown up."

Josh thumped both feet to the floor. "Will you get off my case? You act like I'm some sort of criminal." He glanced at her, a sneer on his face. "Busted for ice cream. Big whoop."

She stood, her stomach clenching. She hated to see that expression on his face, hated fights with him. They hadn't had one since his high school graduation, when he'd wanted to enlist. "I don't like that girl, Josh. I don't think she's good for you."

He gave a bark of laughter. "Like it matters! In two or three days she'll be history. A girl like her would never be interested in somebody like me, anyway, so cool your jets, Mom.''

"That's exactly my point. She's the kind who could lead you on and drop you. I think you should stay away from her."

"And what about your divorced friend?" His gaze skewered her. "What type is he?"

Loren stared at him.

"I take it the steel man didn't tell you he's wife-less."

"No. There... wasn't much time." It was a stupid excuse and she was sure Josh saw right through it. She averted her gaze and focused on an Arizona Cardinals poster hanging over Josh's bed. The predominant color in the poster was red. Adam's favorite color.

"Five months ago," Josh announced. "Split city. Daphne thinks he's up here for more than one reason. So maybe you'd better take some of your own advice, Mom."

AT FIVE FORTY-FIVE the next morning, the red twin-engine with the scorpion logo, its cowling up, crouched inside the Icarus hangar. Walt and Josh worked without conversation, but that wasn't unusual, Loren told herself as she prowled the tarmac in front of the hangar. Besides, in her present coiled state, she was no judge of tension. She'd spent the night tossing around, sleeping little. So Adam was divorced!

A muted roar coaxed her gaze upward, where a commercial jet opened a white seam in the denim sky. There were no clouds this morning, at least not over Sedona. But the weather report for Laughlin wasn't as promising. Loren longed to get the project under way and over. She'd questioned Adam's motives before; the questions loomed larger now. And she intended to get some answers.

At five minutes before six, the black Geo glided up to the front of the Icarus hangar. Loren noted with relief that Adam was alone. Had Daphne brought him, she'd be free to stay at the airport or come back later. With the car here and Daphne at Los Arboles, Loren felt much better about leaving.

At least she felt better until Adam climbed out of the car, a jaunty smile on his face. Watching him walk toward her was like experiencing a sudden drop in altitude. Her ears rang and her stomach flip-flopped.

"I didn't pack a lunch today," she said, searching for some mundane detail to dilute the effect of him. "We should be back before noon."

"That's what I told Daphne. Which was fine with her. She plans to sleep till then."

Good, Loren thought.

Adam walked toward the hangar where Walt and Josh were working. "How's the plane look?"

"Not bad," Walt said, easing his head out from under the cowling and wiping his hands on a rag stuffed in the pocket of his coveralls. "Want an estimate before you go?"

"No. Just do whatever you think needs doing. If you're trusting me with your plane, I can certainly trust you with mine."

"Just don't let the top sergeant there bother you," Walt said. "See you in a few hours, Loren." With that he ducked back under the cowling.

"Bye, Dad," Loren called. "Bye, Josh."

Josh didn't respond.

Stung, Loren turned to Adam. "Let's go," she said more abruptly than was polite.

"You'd better sit up front with me at first and make sure I don't screw anything up," he said as they walked over to the Icarus plane.

"Fine. You can tell me about your divorce on the way to Laughlin."

He shot her a quick look, then muttered something under his breath.

She could feel her blood pressure rise. "Hey, if you wanted to keep it a secret, you should have informed your daughter."

"I didn't want to keep it a secret," he retorted. "I just wanted to tell you in my own way."

"Oh? And what way was that?"

He paused and lowered his voice. "I wanted some privacy to—"

"Privacy?" She turned to face him, hands on her hips. "Okay, Adam, let's get a few things straight, shall we?" She was tired of beating around the bush. "What exactly did you have in mind when you hired me for this job?"

CHAPTER FOUR

ADAM HADN'T EXPECTED to explain himself so early in the game, and he felt ill prepared for this inquisition. "Because I needed the work done and because I wanted to see you again."

"Why?" Her dark glasses concealed any emotion that might have lurked in her eyes.

To find out if there's any hope for us was the most honest reply, but something in her stance made him hesitate. There were things a guy just didn't say to a woman whose eyes he couldn't see, a woman who challenged him with chin lifted and feet braced apart. Before he could come up with a more appropriate answer, she jumped into the fray.

"Pick up any self-help book and you'll find out it's a mistake to go running back to an old girlfriend when a relationship ends."

He groaned and glanced away. He'd be wasting his breath to try to convince her of anything now. They still had the whole morning ahead of them, provided they got off the ground. He looked at his watch. "You're probably right, and it's getting late. Ready to go?"

The muscles tightened in her jaw, but she nodded.

She didn't, however, sit in the copilot's seat. Damn. Josh had probably told her about the divorce last night, so she'd had several hours to form her opinions. Unless she'd changed a lot in the years they'd been apart, it would take hours to alter those opinions. Or days. He completed the preflight check of the plane, put on his headset and contacted the tower. As the plane's wheels left the runway, he realized he was finally alone with Loren. And she didn't want to have anything to do with him.

THAT LITTLE GLANCE at his watch and remark about the time had really frosted her. So he was interested in efficiency, was he? Was that what this little stunt of his was all about? Ditch the wife, pick up the old girlfriend without missing a beat? Can't be without someone to warm our bed, now, can we?

Loren cleaned the camera lens with such vigor her arm ached. If he had the least notion she'd been pining away, patiently waiting for him to show up in her life again, he could kiss that idea goodbye. She had a fine life, thank you, and she didn't need Adam to mess it up for her. And he would. Adam took risks that broke hearts; she'd learned that twenty-three years ago.

Somehow she'd get through this morning's assignment, present him with his damn pictures and eliminate any more reason to be in his company. She glanced out the window at the horizon, sawtoothed with mountains. Gray clouds nestled against the peaks, and as she watched, they slowly advanced toward the plane like a distant tidal wave. She prayed Adam would beat the clouds to the river.

He didn't.

"I can't see a blasted thing," Loren muttered into her microphone as Adam maneuvered through the grid pattern above the construction site. "Take it down another hundred feet."

"After I get clearance, of course," Adam snapped.

"Of course." Her response dripped with false sweetness. "But I wouldn't worry about running into anybody. Who else would be dumb enough to cruise around in this soup?" Frustration had frayed her patience, and Adam's, too, apparently. Seconds after they'd reached the target area, the cloud ceiling had dropped drastically. They'd wasted valuable time and fuel searching for the bottom edge of it. Loren was beginning to believe the dense cloud had settled about ten feet off the ground. And it didn't seem to be going anywhere.

Adam contacted the Bullhead City airport, located just across the river from Laughlin. "Bullhead City tower, this is 206 Whiskey Foxtrot requesting permission to drop to five hundred feet."

Whiskey Foxtrot, Loren thought, hearing the Cessna's call letters differently now that Adam spoke them, instead of her father or Josh. Her father had chosen the two letters of identification because they were his and Fran's initials. Loren tried to remember what letters had been stenciled on Adam's Cessna 414. A picture of the plane's fuselage appeared in her mind, along with the letters AR, Alpha Romeo in radio code. Or Adam Riordan. Or even Anita Riordan.

"Anything?" Adam's voice came through the earphones.

She jerked from her preoccupied daze and peered through the lens. "No."

"That's it, Loren. I can't take it down any more unless we get pontoons on this baby. What now?"

An unladylike epithet escaped her lips.

"Ditto."

She whipped off her headset and stared out the window in defeat. Why did everything have to go wrong on this particular assignment? Just one hour of clear, even moderately clear, weather was all she needed. Was that asking too much?

With a resigned sigh, she replaced her headset. "We have two choices," she said. "Actually, three. First, we can abort and head back to Sedona, maybe try again tomorrow morning. Second, we can abort permanently and you can try this with some other photographer out of Phoenix next week."

"That's out. I don't think I have that long to catch this guy in the act. What's the third choice?"

"We could land in Bullhead City and wait it out. It means getting back later than we'd planned, but this front's supposed to be gone by this afternoon, according to the Prescott Flight Service."

"Let's get it done today. I'd rather go back late than be on time and have to tell Daphne I'm flying again tomorrow."

"Then I guess you'd better contact the tower and request permission to land." Loren took off the headset again and glanced at her watch. By now they were supposed to be on their way back to Sedona. She didn't want to spend extra time with Adam. Didn't want to find herself looking into those blue eyes any more than necessary. Every minute spent with him chipped away at her common sense. Fortunately, she had a lot of common sense. With luck, she'd have enough to last until the weather cleared.

She hoped Adam had his instrument rating—it was a little late to ask—because that was the only way he'd be able to land the plane. The leap of faith an instrument landing required had always bothered her, which was why she wasn't much of a pilot. But Adam accepted the task with equanimity. The runway didn't appear in front of them until the wheels were almost touching it. The sensation of the ground suddenly materializing right below them when she'd had the illusion of being high in the air made Loren's stomach jump, as usual. Adam settled the plane on the runway as if it were made of Waterford crystal.

"Not bad," she murmured, knowing he couldn't hear her with his headset on.

He taxied to their assigned tie-down spot, turned off the engine and removed his headset. "It's raining."

"I noticed." Across the river from the airstrip, the lights of the Laughlin casinos glowed eerily in the fog and rain. Years ago, the only way to get across from the airport to the casinos had been by boat, but now a concrete bridge arced over the river. The population explosion in the neighboring cities was the reason Adam's bridge was under construction farther south.

"Feel like gambling?" Adam asked.

"No, thanks."

He turned in his seat. "Anita and I went to Vegas once. Have you ever been up there?"

"Once." Jack had thought it would be great fun. She'd spent the whole time thinking of how she and Adam had planned to get married there.

"Anita liked it, but I..." He looked into her eyes. "I didn't."

"Stop it, Adam."

He lifted his eyebrows.

"Don't pretend you don't know what I'm talking about," she said. "Bringing up Las Vegas, giving me that look. Whatever you're trying to do isn't going to work. I'm not the same person I was, and neither are you. Don't sort through the embers looking for a spark. There isn't one."

He rested his chin on his fist and studied her without speaking.

Her face grew warm under his scrutiny. "I mean it, Adam. This was not a good idea. And why you roped your daughter into this trip is beyond me."

"She asked to come. My relationship with her is pretty fragile right now, so I didn't want to turn her down."

"Then I suggest you concentrate on that fragile relationship and leave me out of the picture."

"Permanently?"

She felt a catch in the vicinity of her heart. But she mustn't leave the door open, not even a crack. Once he'd smashed her heart like a papier-mâché piñata, and she didn't want to find out if he could do it again. "Permanently."

His eyes grew hooded, his expression remote. "I'd never force myself on a woman."

"Good." The catch in her heart had become a persistent ache, but it would go away once Adam went away. Until then, she'd just have to deal with the pain. A man embroiled in a midlife crisis was never a safe bet. Everyone knew that.

He pushed himself erect. "Now that we have that settled, how about going across the river for something to eat?"

She considered the suggestion. Walking around a casino full of people was probably a better idea than staying cocooned in this plane with Adam. She'd made her stand, but that didn't cloak her in immunity. Just glancing at his capable hands or the firm line of his chin weakened her resolve. "Sure. We can pick up a courtesy car at the terminal and drive across the bridge."

"By the time we tie this baby down and run to the terminal, we'll be so wet we might as well swim across the river."

"That's the thing about private planes. No jetways." She couldn't keep the sarcasm from her voice. "But considering you're the client, I should probably go get the car and drive over to pick you up here."

He grinned, apparently ready to ignore her prickly mood. "Would you do that?"

"No."

"Didn't think so." He reached for the door handle. "Let's go."

Rain lashed them as they shared the job of securing the wings and tail with cables to the hooks imbedded in the tarmac. True to Adam's prediction, they were soaked by the time they reached the terminal. Loren asked the gas attendant to top off both the plane's tanks and Adam picked up the keys for the courtesy car. Then she and Adam plunged out into the downpour again.

He unlocked her side of the car first, and out of habit she leaned across and unlocked the driver's door.

"Thanks," he said as he climbed in. He started the engine and switched on the wipers before gazing at her with a faint smile. "You remind me of how you used to look after we went down Slide Rock."

Loren pushed back her damp hair and glanced away from that seductively soft gaze. Slide Rock. Hot, sunny days when they had put on their oldest cutoffs and T-shirts, taken coolers of sandwiches and soft drinks, and sailed down the wide, smooth sandstone where water sluiced in a constant current. They'd slide until they were drenched, then find some secluded spot higher up the canyon, where their passionate embraces heated their wet clothes until they were nearly steaming from the erotic friction of their bodies.

Adam moved the car into light traffic. "We had some good times," he said.

"Yes, I suppose we did." She waited to see if he'd suggest they could have good times again, but he didn't. Apparently, he'd accepted her decree. Setting him straight had been fairly easy. Maybe too easy, warned an inner voice.

When they'd crossed the bridge, Adam parked the car in front of the nearest casino and they ran through the rain into a buzzing, jangling, flashing world of slot machines, roulette wheels and blackjack tables. People crowded around the machines and gaming tables, eyes totally focused on the play. Weather didn't matter inside the casino. The air-conditioning made Loren, in her wet clothes, shiver.

"You're cold."

She shook her head. "It doesn't matter. I'll dry out in a little while."

"Listen, these places all sell T-shirts and stuff. Let me buy you something dry to put on before we eat."

"N-no, that's not necessary."

"Dammit, Loren," he said in a low voice. "You've made it obvious you don't appreciate my hiring you for this job, so I'm already carrying a load of guilt about that. We're not adding a case of pneumonia to it because of some idiotic pride on your part."

She glanced up and evaluated his determination. From the set of his jaw, he looked ready to continue the argument until she gave in or they created a scene. She *was* cold, and a dry shirt would be heaven. And why should she pay for a shirt she'd never wear again in her entire life? "You're right," she said. "I could use a dry shirt. Let's find the gift shop."

Fifteen minutes later, armed with T-shirts and running shorts emblazoned with the casino's logo, they separated to go into their respective rest rooms and change.

Inside a stall, Loren discovered that her denim shorts had kept her panties pretty dry, but her bra was as soaked as her tank top. She had the choice of leaving it on, in which case her T-shirt would have two wet circles in the front in short order, or going braless.

After deciding the T-shirt material was thick enough to protect her modesty, Loren left the rest room.

Adam was already standing there, his shirt and slacks in a bundle under one arm. Immediately, her gaze went to the firm length of his thighs and his muscled calves. How she'd once loved the movement of those powerful legs under tight football pants as Adam had sprinted down the field for yet another touchdown. She didn't think he'd gained an ounce of fat since those days.

"And I won't even charge you extra for the show," he said with a smile.

She felt her face grow hot. "I—"

"Hey, forget it." He took her elbow and guided her toward the restaurant. "My battered ego appreciates the fact you looked."

"You misunderstand me. I just..." But she couldn't come up with a plausible excuse.

He grinned at her. "Yeah. Me, too." He glanced at the hostess. "Two for nonsmoking. Put us over in that corner booth if you can."

An intimate little corner, Loren thought as she followed the hostess to the table. The pulse beating erratically in her throat told her that Adam was getting to her. He was directing her thoughts into all the wrong channels, channels still electrified with curiosity. Had they made love—complete, satisfying love—all those years ago, she'd have a different kind of problem.

She sat in the booth, and he placed himself at right angles to her, his knees occasionally brushing hers. He picked up a menu. She followed suit, trying to concentrate on the list of items as her mind cavorted in its own private playground with the charged subject of Adam. Curiosity had always been her triumph and her downfall. Curiosity had put her behind the lens of a camera early in life. Curiosity had led her to try marijuana at a friend's party, and it was there she'd met Jack.

And now she was still curious about Adam, about what making love to him would be like. Perhaps the experience would be anticlimactic. Most probably it would be anticlimactic, considering the level of her expectations at the age of eighteen. She'd probably discover Adam wasn't any better at lovemaking than Jack had been. Or Stewart, the man she'd had a disappointing interlude with three summers ago.

That was her other problem, besides curiosity. High expectations. Perhaps no man could live up to them.

"I'll have the beef stew, salad with Italian dressing and a cup of black coffee." Adam folded the menu and put it on the table. "If you don't mind ordering, I'll call your dad and tell him we've been delayed."

Loren set down her menu and stared at him. She'd totally forgotten about her father and Josh. Of course they'd start to worry soon. She'd better get hold of herself, and fast, or she was liable to do any number of irresponsible things. "I'll call," she said, rising from the booth.

"Have you decided what you want to eat?"

"No."

He put his hand on her arm and gently pushed her back down. "Then let me." He stood. "Besides, I want to ask Josh if he could take the Geo back to Daphne. It isn't fair to leave her stranded all day.''

Loren tensed. She hadn't anticipated all the ramifications of waiting out the storm. Now Daphne would be back in contact with Josh. Her gaze met Adam's.

"From that stony glare, I assume you don't approve of that plan. Do you have a better suggestion?" he asked mildly.

"Maybe my father could . . ."

"Oh, come on, Lor. You act as if you can't trust your own kid."

"It's not Josh I'm worried about."

His eyes narrowed. "Meaning that if they get into some sort of trouble, it will be all Daphne's fault? Even your father isn't that unfair."

"We're not talking about *fair*. She's a big-city girl. That puts Josh at a disadvantage."

He braced both hands on the table and brought his face close to hers. She could smell the spice of his after-shave, see the pattern of his eyelashes as they framed his blue eyes, which at the moment snapped with impatience. "You're overreacting, Loren. I talked to Daphne about yesterday. She understands Josh's responsibilities at the shop. And she's not a bad kid, despite what you may think."

Her gaze flicked from the intensity in his eyes to the movement of his lips. With a guilty start, she looked back into his eyes, her heart hammering. "So you vouch for her behavior? But you've admitted you haven't been very close to her."

Anger flared in his eyes, making him look slightly dangerous. "I'll vouch for her."

His closeness was making her very nervous. "Okay," she agreed, just to end the debate and separate herself from him. After all, Walt would be at the hangar this afternoon. Daphne couldn't get Josh in too much trouble with Walt around. Adam pushed himself away from the table and she took a shaky breath.

"I'll also get an updated weather report from Prescott," he said.

"Fine."

She watched him walk away and her heart lurched in the old, familiar way. Oh, she was skating on thin ice. She forced herself to concentrate on the menu, and when the waitress arrived, Loren placed Adam's order and chose a French-dip sandwich for herself.

Adam returned to the table as the busboy delivered two glasses of water.

"Did you reach everyone?" She tried to sound casual.

Adam nodded as he slid into the booth. "Walt says not to worry. I assume that's his code phrase to tell you he'll keep Josh out of my daughter's clutches."

Loren ducked her head to disguise her relieved smile.

"And I called Daphne. She wasn't too happy with the news, but I promised her a long excursion tomorrow. It was the best I could do. I only hope I can deliver."

Loren's head shot up. "Why is that?"

"I checked with Prescott, and the front isn't moving on as predicted."

Loren swallowed. "But surely it will clear up in a few hours, won't it?"

Adam gazed at her, his expression enigmatic. "Not necessarily. They're saying the bad weather may last all night."

Loren felt a stirring in the pit of her stomach. "We aren't staying here overnight."

"I'm glad you have that under control."

She seemed to be sinking into the depths of Adam's blue eyes. With effort, she broke the connection and glanced around. The restaurant had no windows, and she needed to look outside and reassure herself that there would be a break in the weather. There *had* to be a break in the weather. "Excuse me," she said and slid out of the booth. "I'll be back in a minute."

As she walked past the tables, her attention was drawn to the large number of couples—a woman smiling into the face of a man, a man squeezing a woman's hand, a man and woman leaning across the table toward each other, expressions intent, arms touching, fingers brushing. She'd never noticed before that Laughlin was a hangout for lovers, but now the place seemed filled with them.

She hurried out of the restaurant and through the clamorous rows of machines toward the bank of windows facing the river. The rain had lessened, but the clouds boiled overhead, and a new element had been added. Jagged lightning bolts flashed like hammered silver hieroglyphics against the dark horizon. And the message was clear. Beware.

Heart pounding, she turned away from the window and searched for a public telephone. She finally found a row of them near the registration desk. Picking up the receiver of the nearest one, she pulled off her shoe and took out the quarter she kept there. Then she punched in the series of numbers she'd memorized so she always had access to long-distance information.

The Prescott Flight Service report was even worse than she'd imagined. In addition to the storm already hovering over Laughlin, a warm front was moving into the area with terrible weather behind it. She set the phone back in its cradle. She was trapped.

CHAPTER FIVE

As LOREN WALKED toward him, her expression that of a person mounting the gallows, Adam's heart twisted. He'd had such hopes for their reunion, but she was obviously petrified of him and the potential havoc he might introduce into her life.

She moved her bundle of wet clothes, setting it firmly between them before she sat down. Their food had arrived while she was gone, but he hadn't touched his. "You should have started," she said, positioning her napkin on her lap.

"No rush." He picked up his fork and shoved the prongs into his salad.

She grimaced. "No, there certainly isn't a rush. I called Prescott again."

He paused with the bite of salad halfway to his mouth. "Didn't trust me to give you the truth?"

Her glance was swift, skittering away before he could catch it. "I just wanted an update."

"Every five minutes?"

"Okay, so I wanted to hear it for myself."

He was irritated enough to push it. "Because you thought I might have lied to you."

"No! I just...didn't want it to be true, thought it might change."

"And did it?"

"No." She wouldn't look at him, just kept swirling her sandwich in the cup of broth and watching the bread disintegrate.

He ate his salad, not tasting it.

"Damn." She put down her sandwich and picked up a french fry. She didn't eat that, either. "I want this assignment to be over."

His stomach knotted and he gave up all pretense of eating as he pushed his salad plate aside. He folded his arms on the table and gazed at her. "I know you do. Believe it or not, so do I. Daphne will never believe that weather kept us pinned down in Laughlin. I haven't the foggiest idea how I'm going to make this up to her."

She looked at him, her gaze softening a little, then looked away. "We'll have to call them, won't we?"

"Let's not do it yet. Maybe a miracle will happen and the weather will clear."

"Maybe."

He sighed and pulled his plate back in front of him. "We might as well eat this stuff. If the weather clears, we won't want to worry about food."

"I guess you're right." She took a bite of her soggy sandwich.

They ate in silence, until he couldn't stand it any longer. "Look, I'm sorry I got you into this, Lor. I didn't mean for it to turn into such a mess."

She brought her napkin to her lips. When she met his gaze again, he caught his breath at the compassion in her eyes.

This time she didn't look away. "I'm sorry, too," she said. "Divorce is hell. I ought to know that much at least, and I haven't been much help. I think it's a bad idea for us to get involved again, but if you need to talk, we seem to have some time on our hands. I'm willing to listen."

He was still for a moment. She was inviting him to talk about his divorce, but he found that wasn't the subject uppermost on his mind anymore. "I do need to talk," he said carefully, "but not about Anita or the divorce."

Wariness flickered in her eyes.

"I've been waiting for twenty-three years to find out why you never answered my letters."

The wariness turned to apprehension as she straightened in her seat. "That was so long ago, Adam. Let's leave the past in the past."

"It may be long ago to you, but it's like yesterday to me. Sending those letters off, one after another, and waiting for mail call the way you might wait for your lottery number to come up. And it never came up."

"Adam . . ." She glanced nervously around the restaurant and he realized he must have raised his voice.

Picking up the tab from the table, he tossed down a tip. "Let's get out of here."

"And go where?"

He stood. "I don't know. But this isn't where I want to discuss this."

She slid out of the booth. "I think it's better if we don't discuss it at—"

"Come on." Without giving her a chance to protest further, he headed for the cash register. After paying the bill, he led the way through the casino and out the door. A brief overhang protected them from the rain, but the space was too confining for him.

He glanced out at the covered boat dock floating in front of the hotel. Every casino had one, and skiffs shuttled people from one gambling opportunity to another. But the rain had discouraged most of the casino-hopping and the dock was empty.

"Let's go down there," he suggested, taking her hand. She didn't withdraw it as they ran through the rain and down the steps to the dock. Under the canopy, Adam found a dry section of bench and sat down, putting his bundle of clothes next to him.

Loren disengaged her hand and sat several feet away, her clothes on her lap. She remained silent, as if unwilling to reopen the conversation.

He took a deep breath. "Well?"

She stared out at the swift current of water for a long time. When she spoke, her voice was so soft he had to strain to hear it over the gurgling water. "I tore up your first few letters unread, because I wanted to hurt you." Her grip on her clothes bundle tightened until her knuckles showed white. "You'd chosen that damn war over me."

"That's not true."

She offered him nothing but her profile. "Isn't it?"

"No." He cocked his knee on the bench so he was facing her. "I chose the person I wanted to be, instead of the one *you* wanted me to be."

She met his gaze. "Meaning I wanted you alive and you wanted to be dead?"

"Meaning I had to go and I knew you'd never agree with that. But I thought, in time, you might understand if I explained it. So I wrote the letters." How he'd labored over them, while the other guys in the unit smoked grass and told him he was an idiot for writing to a commie war protester. "Did you read *any* of them? The later ones, maybe?"

She looked away and swallowed. "No. I destroyed them all without opening a single one."

"Damn you! I poured my guts out in those letters!"

Her words seemed forced past a constricted throat. "How could I read them? By the time each letter got to me, you could have been dead. I couldn't stand to think about you over there, so I pretended you weren't. If I'd read the letters, I would have had to face what was happening to you."

He stared at her, his heart a sodden weight in his chest.

She turned her head and her dark eyes glistened with tears. "I loved you so much, Adam."

A lump lodged in his throat. *Loved.* Past tense.

LOREN'S WHOLE BODY ached, as if the dredged-up memories had invaded every part of her system with pain. "I told you we should leave it in the past," she whispered, wiping at her eyes.

"I can't." He halved the distance between them, and her senses flashed a warning. "Being cut off from you all these years was like being cut off from a part of myself. So many times I thought of coming to see

you, but you were married. You married Jack before
I came home.''

"I know." She accepted the accusation in his tone,
knowing he was right to accuse her. She'd acted out of
malice and fear.

"Couldn't you have waited? I came home two
months after you married him. Two *months,* Loren.
Were you so desperate to have him?''

"Yes." From the way he recoiled, she knew she'd
cut deep. "He was the exact opposite of you. He was
like a talisman I could hold up to protect myself from
you."

"You didn't have to protect yourself, for God's
sake!''

"I thought I did. I'd backed myself into an ideo-
logical corner. I'd denounced what you did by going
over there, but I didn't trust myself to stay away from
you if you came back.''

"What would have been so bad about that?''

"Don't you see? I thought it was a test of my character to reject you on principle. Jack was a reminder
of those principles.''

Adam's jaw worked and he looked away. "If he was
so damn wonderful, why did you divorce him?''

She hesitated, a little ashamed, even now, of how
poor her choice had been. "He refused to take any responsibility for me or Josh," she admitted. "He said
it was because he had a responsibility to the anti-war
movement and didn't have the time or energy for a
paying job.''

Adam sucked in his breath but said nothing.

"So I worked and supported all three of us while I finished my degree." Her basic honesty forced her to tell it all. "But a funny thing happened. The war ended, and Jack found another cause that required sign-carrying and passing out leaflets. I finally figured out he was just lazy."

Adam turned to her, his eyes ablaze. "And that's the creep who took my place?"

"You shouldn't be surprised." Sadness filled her as she remembered all the rifts created during those years. "People chose up sides back then. Jack was on my side. You weren't. Black and white, right and wrong."

"God, Loren. It was never that simple."

"When you're young, it seems simple."

"I guess it does."

"And by the time I let go of my need to be right, by the time you and I could have had a reasonable discussion about our differences..."

"I was married," he finished wearily.

She nodded. "And judging from Daphne's age, you didn't take very long to do it, either."

"Yeah." He sighed. "Such a cliché. I married her on the rebound, got her pregnant on our honeymoon. It was as if I had to show you, too. But I still wished you'd have called me. It would have helped so much knowing what was going on in your head."

"Be honest, Adam. Would seeing each other then have helped anything for us?

He gazed at her for a long while. "I suppose not."

She gave him a small smile. "And you left me, remember? Then you married someone else."

"So did you!"

"True, but just because my marriage was a mistake didn't mean yours was. I had my pride, Adam. I wasn't about to call you up and admit that my life was in chaos because of bad choices. What if I discovered that yours was just peachy? Then what?"

"But it wasn't." He touched her cheek. "I needed you, Loren."

As his fingers caressed her cheek, she told herself to move away, to put more distance between them. But the tenderness of his gaze still had the power to hold her captive.

His fingers trembled slightly as he cupped her jaw. "When I got home and discovered you'd only been married two months, I made Jim tell me where you lived. I almost came storming over to that little trailer."

She looked into his eyes, mesmerized as always by the sound of his voice, the whisper of his touch. The telltale quickening of her heartbeat sounded a warning, but she was helpless to heed it.

"I figured if you'd only been married two months, I could get you to leave him." His thumb brushed her lower lip.

"By then, I was already pregnant."

"I thought of that." He drew her subtly closer. "I didn't care."

Her blood fizzed in her veins, awakening long-dormant yearnings. "You'd take a woman carrying another man's child?"

"If that woman happened to be you." He leaned down, his breath warm against her mouth. "Would you have come with me?"

"I don't know," she whispered.

"I do."

And so did she the moment his mouth covered hers.

No one else had ever kissed her like this. His lips settled softly, with a deceptive lightness that teased her into a frothy cloud of warmth. She felt wrapped in shades of pink and gold as he coaxed her mouth open with a playful caress that seemed to invite her on a pleasant adventure.

Deceiver. "Pleasant" was not what he had in mind, yet she remembered too late how his Pied Piper song would always change, how the chords would ripen, the shades of color deepen to red. Gentleness gave way to passion, coaxing gave way to demand.

And she gave.

Gave as she had the first time Adam had kissed her, and her world had changed forever. Gave with the fervor of a caged animal released into the wild. With a sob, she opened her mouth to receive the thrust of his tongue, buried her fingers in his hair and rode the whirlwind.

When at last he released her, they were both gasping. He gazed at her, his eyes wild with longing. "My God, Loren."

The sound of a boat engine edged into her consciousness, and she remembered they were on a dock. And she remembered other things—things she would do well not to forget. She struggled out of his embrace, stooped to grab the bundle of clothes that had fallen to the floor and stood, glancing toward the skiff coming alongside the dock.

"You folks need a ride?" called the captain.

Loren straightened her T-shirt. She didn't trust herself to look at Adam. "No, thanks," she managed to say.

"Okeydoke." With a spin of the wheel, the skiff's captain pointed his craft toward the next casino dock several yards away.

"Loren."

She turned in time to sidestep Adam's attempt to gather her close.

"Loren, what—"

"That was a dumb thing to do." She took a deep breath. "I'm as much at fault as you, but let's not allow that to happen again."

He stared at her in disbelief. "You're joking."

"Absolutely not."

"You're going to disregard what just happened?"

"I'm going to take it as a warning that we're playing with fire. The timing's not any better for us now than it was back then. You're in no psychological shape to start a relationship, not this soon after a divorce."

"That's crap! You have no idea what psychological shape I'm in."

"And there's your daughter. I refuse to help drive a wedge between the two of you any more than I unwittingly have already."

He looked desperate. "I'll talk to her, explain things."

"Like what? That you never loved her mother and were pining for me the whole time you were married? That should be a big hit with Daphne."

With a muttered oath, he turned away and studied the darkening sky. The wind came up, whipping the river into whitecaps as rain blew under the canopy, pelting them with cold drops. He swung back to face her. "How do you expect us to get through a night together after what just happened?"

"By exercising restraint. Surely you haven't forgotten how?"

His laughter lacked humor. "Where you're concerned, it's the only thing I've ever known." He gestured toward the sky. "I guess we'd better call Sedona and get it over with. And book a place to stay tonight."

"Two rooms."

"Is two rooms safe enough? Maybe we should choose two different hotels."

"Don't be ridiculous."

He flung her a heated gaze. "The way I feel right now, it's not ridiculous."

CHAPTER SIX

"LET'S BOOK the rooms first," Adam said once they reached the casino lobby. "I'd rather not call Daphne with slot machines jingling in the background. It will be a difficult conversation, anyway, without reminding her I could be here having the time of my life."

"Okay."

"Is here all right?"

Loren shrugged. "Doesn't matter."

"Here, then."

At the reservation desk, the clerk automatically gave them adjoining rooms. Loren started to protest, but then realized a protest might sound as if she couldn't bear to be near this person she was registering with.

"Luggage?" the desk clerk asked.

"None," Adam replied smoothly, picking up both keys and heading for the elevators.

"This feels really strange," Loren admitted as they stepped into the bright interior of the elevator.

"Tell me about it." He handed her a key. "Here. You have the power to lock me out, just in case you were worried."

Not about you. When she looked at him, she experienced a craving that seemed dredged up from the bottom of her soul. But she distrusted that craving; it was a siren song to heartbreak.

They entered their rooms separately to make their respective calls. The adjoining door was closed. Loren flipped on a light against the gloom and walked over to the window. She had a view of the parking lot and more casinos across the street. Oh, well. She wasn't here for the view. She was here because her job had brought her here. The knowledge that Adam was in the other room, would be for the rest of the night, must be erased from her mind.

The room wasn't anything out of the ordinary. A quilted flowered bedspread covered the king-size mattress, and a Monet print of a garden hung over the bed. Against the window wall, a round wood-veneer table flanked by two chairs held an ashtray and matches. The television set sat on a double dresser opposite the bed.

In the bathroom, she found shampoo and lotion. She'd been stuck on assignment before, usually without even these amenities. Maybe she should pick up a comb, she decided, running a hand through her hair as she glanced into the wide bathroom mirror.

With a shock, she saw the eighteen-year-old she'd once been staring back at her. The eighteen-year-old who'd come in from a day at Slide Rock, her face washed free of makeup by the creek, hair soaked and allowed to dry as it lay. Even her lips were the same, reddened from Adam's kiss, and her chin glowed pink from the friction of his stubble. When she was eighteen, she'd imagined her mother hadn't known what she and Adam had been doing all afternoon. Of course she'd no doubt guessed.

Loren flushed at the knowledge that the desk clerk, too, might have guessed what the two of them had been doing this particular afternoon. She should never have succumbed to the hypnotic effect of Adam's touch, which allowed him to dare still more. His kiss was everything she remembered, a fiery prelude to the lovemaking she'd never known. Would never know. It was too dangerous.

A rapping sound made her jump. Flipping off the bathroom light, she walked toward the adjoining doors where Adam was knocking. "Yes?"

"Have you called?"

"Not yet. I—"

"Good. Daphne wasn't at the resort, and I'll bet she's at the hangar with Walt and Josh. I don't have that number. Besides, when you call, I'd like to be there so I can talk to her."

"All right." She unlocked the door and opened it. Had she really expected the doors between their rooms to stay closed?

Adam walked in, and immediately the atmosphere of the room became electric. "Nice place you have here."

She made a brave attempt at humor. "Wait'll you see the view."

He smiled, and she wondered if she dared ask him to stop doing that. His smile made her heart squeeze.

"My view's just as great," he said. "All those cars. I could sit and watch them for hours."

"We didn't even think to ask for the river side." She hadn't been capable of thinking much at all while they'd registered. "I suppose it doesn't matter."

Adam walked to the window and pulled back a flowered drape. "A view is a funny thing. We're told that a river is beautiful and a parking lot is ugly. But if you look at the lot as a mosaic of colors and constantly changing patterns, if you look for pictures in the asphalt instead of pictures in the clouds, why couldn't you enjoy a view of the parking lot?"

She doubted he'd said that to produce any effect in her. It was just a typical Adam remark, but she'd forgotten how much she loved his way of seeing the world. They'd had sexual tension between them—and it still existed—yet the strengthening bonds had been woven of remarks like this one, and her delight in them. They'd built their young love on mutual respect. He'd appreciated her gift for capturing beauty on film, and she'd cherished his inquisitive mind.

"You make me wish I had my camera," she said, her voice a little husky. But she wouldn't take pictures of the parking lot, although it was a unique idea. She'd focus on Adam and try to capture the soft gray light that picked out the prominent features of forehead, nose and chin, while feathering over his cheekbones and daubing shadows below the bone, across his eyes, and in the creases beside his mouth. But then for her peace of mind she'd have to destroy the pictures, so what was the point?

He turned, his face fully illuminated by the lamp on the bedside table. "Are you still doing landscapes?"

"Some."

"Remember that sunrise shot at Red Rock Crossing?"

Her heart rhythm seemed to falter. "Sure." She wished he hadn't mentioned that picture. A print of it still hung over her father's fireplace. Her dad wouldn't hear of taking it down, so she'd taught herself not to look at it. Adam had been with her that morning beneath an opalescent sky that had gradually blushed pink, then shaded to robin's-egg blue.

Cathedral Rock dominated the buttes that surrounded the crossing. With the sun rising behind it, the sandstone had remained in shadow, its dark spires backlit in gold. Oak Creek had lain wide and shallow at their feet, its gently rippling surface mirroring the buttes and the unfolding brilliance behind them. *This is where we'll be married,* Adam had said. *At sunrise.* And she'd believed him with all her heart.

He gazed at her now, as if trying to bridge the long span of years.

Resolutely, she turned toward the telephone on the bedside table. "We'd better make our call." They could never get back those years. They were gone forever. That Loren and Adam were gone forever, too. Taking a steadying breath, she picked up the receiver. "I'll talk to Dad first."

She dialed and glanced over at Adam. He still faced her, hands in his pockets, but his head was bowed. Perhaps he, too, had had a glimpse of the vast chasm. One passionate kiss didn't eliminate all the years of unshared experiences. Once they'd known nearly everything about each other. Now they knew almost nothing.

Her father answered the phone.

"Hi, Dad."

"Thought it might be you. The weather hit here about an hour ago. Had to close the hangar door, it was blowing so bad."

"A second front is right behind that one, so batten down the hatches."

"Will do. You and Adam are staying put, I trust?"

Adam was gazing at her now.

"Yes, we're spending the night in Laughlin," she said, keeping her tone businesslike. "Fortunately, they had a couple of rooms left."

Adam smiled. He probably guessed she'd made that last statement on purpose.

"As long as you're with Adam, I'm not concerned."

You should be, she thought. "We won't take any dumb chances. The weather should clear up by morning, so we'll get the pictures then and head on home. We'll be back before noon."

"Sounds like a reasonable plan. We're fine here, so don't worry about a thing. The plane okay?"

"Last time I saw it. We tied it down good and tight. Listen, Dad, is Daphne there, by any chance?"

"Yes."

Loren looked at Adam and nodded. He started toward her.

"Daphne's been helping us this afternoon," Walt told her. "Said she needed something to do, and she seems to know quite a bit about airplanes."

Great, Loren thought. Josh must be thoroughly smitten by now. "Adam wants to talk to her and explain the situation," she said. "He thinks she might be a little disappointed that he's not coming back tonight. This was supposed to be a father-daughter vacation, as well as a business trip, and it's not turning out the way he planned."

"I'll get her."

Loren held the receiver out to Adam and moved away from the bedside table. She walked over to the window and gazed out at the parking lot. It *was* a mosaic of color, and the rain had turned each roof into a polished sheet of stone.

"Hi, Daphne."

Adam's voice, so resonant and filled with affection, pushed past Loren's defenses and tapped into a wellspring of longing that frightened her with its depth. She wanted him to use that tone with her, to hold her again, to kiss her... No! She forced herself to concentrate on the cars and pick out a pattern that would resemble a face or a common object. She had no luck.

"Well, we ran into some trouble with the weather," Adam said, obviously answering a question of Daphne's.

"In the morning," he said after a pause. "Probably before lunch."

Loren abandoned all attempts to ignore the conversation. Somewhere along the way, she'd become invested in Adam's attempt to reconnect with his daughter.

"This isn't what I expected, either, Daphne." He sounded frustrated. "But the pictures are important to me." Another pause. "Because Scorpio Steel's involved in the bridge project. You knew that."

Loren winced. She understood that Adam hesitated to explain his underlying reasons for wanting to get the pictures, but without that reason, his explanation made it sound as if he was putting his business ahead of his daughter.

"Daphne, I'm sorry about this, but—" After a short silence, he swore and glanced at Loren. "Tell me the number for the hangar."

"What happened? Were you cut off?"

He gestured with the receiver. "Daphne hung up on me."

Loren's chest tightened and she crossed the room. "Adam, maybe you'd better tell her your suspicions about the diverted steel. She needs to know this isn't an ordinary business matter."

"No."

"Why not? What harm can it do now that you're ready to catch the guy red-handed?"

"Daphne knows him and likes him. She'd never believe he'd do something like this, so I don't want to say anything until I have real proof. If she's really ticked off at me, she might even call and warn him."

Loren shook her head in disbelief. "You plan to incriminate one of Daphne's friends on this trip, and she doesn't even know about it? How do you ever expect to win her trust with maneuvers like that?"

With a groan, he dropped the receiver into its cradle and massaged the back of his neck. "I shouldn't have brought her, but she practically begged to go. She hadn't asked me for anything in a long time. Turning down this request would have seemed like a rejection." He glanced at Loren. "I realize I should have refused, but...after the divorce it seemed as if it would be so easy to lose Daphne. I was afraid I'd wake up and discover she'd simply slipped out of my life."

Loren took pity on his anguish. "Maybe it's not so bad. How close is she to this guy?"

"She thinks he's about to become her stepfather."

Loren was momentarily speechless. "Anita's engaged to the contractor for this bridge?" she said at last. "How did that happen?"

He grimaced. "I suppose I set it up. When I found out he was the contractor and my company was supplying the steel for this project, I decided to renew the acquaintance. I invited him over for dinner to meet the family. He obviously enjoyed himself."

Loren studied his face, reading between the lines. "You never told me the grounds for divorce."

"Incompatibility."

"A catchall phrase. What really happened?"

"Less than a week after that dinner, I walked in on them."

"Oh, Adam." Everything clicked into place. No wonder he considered Haskett capable of pirating steel, but that didn't mean the man was guilty of it. This whole escapade with the pictures might be some sort of vendetta. "Are you sure he's diverting the steel? There couldn't be bookkeeping errors, or perhaps someone in your own company who's embezzling from you?"

He frowned, his gaze assessing. "You think I'm trying to nail him because I'm the jealousy-racked husband, don't you?"

"Maybe."

"I didn't love her enough to be jealous, unfortunately."

She wanted to believe that. "But your pride certainly is involved."

"Pride, hell! The guy's cost me half a million bucks. That's how much the steel he's stolen is worth."

"That much?" Loren was floored. If Adam could lose half a million dollars and not be bankrupt, then he had a more profitable business than she'd realized.

"That much," he said with a sigh. "I make a lot of money, and that was my appeal for Anita. If I hadn't been such a terrific wage earner, she might have looked for greener pastures and taken Daphne with her. But even when she'd stopped caring for me, she'd fallen in love with the money."

Loren didn't welcome the empathy that flooded through her. It only made her more vulnerable. But money had been Jack's motivation for staying, too. "If you knew she was that mercenary, why did you stay?"

"For Daphne. Just listening to her singing 'Sesame Street' songs when she was little or watching her swim like a dolphin in the pool was worth suffering through Anita's indifference. I'm crazy about that kid. I wouldn't have won custody so..."

Loren nodded. "Depriving Josh of a father was no picnic. Josh loved his daddy. He hated me for a long time."

"I'm pretty sure Daphne blames me for the divorce. She knows her mother wasn't very happy with me—and perhaps with good reason—but she doesn't know anything about me finding Barnaby and Anita together, and I don't want her to know. But it's tough, sometimes, always being the bad guy."

"You'd better call her back, try to smooth things over."

He picked up the receiver. "If she'll even talk to me."

"You have to try." Loren recited the number while he punched buttons on the phone.

"Walt? This is Adam again. Is Daphne still there?" He waited for an answer. "Yeah, I'm sure she is upset. Would you try and get her to the phone, please?" He waited, hand massaging the back of his neck.

Then he paused, and his shoulders sagged. "I was afraid of that. Listen, I have a big favor to ask. Would you or Josh sort of watch out for her? Maybe there's a good movie in town, or something. I hate like hell to leave her on her own tonight, but we don't have much choice."

Panic rose hot and fast, pushing out Loren's sympathy. It was one thing to understand Adam's pain. It was quite another to approve the use of her son as a Band-Aid. She shook her head violently at Adam. Daphne wasn't some little Munchkin singing her ABC's anymore, and tonight she was staying in a resort, unchaperoned. Loren wasn't sure if Walt would remember Daphne's circumstances. Walt wasn't much of a night owl, and she could just imagine him sending the "kids" off to a movie, never suspecting they might end up in Daphne's room.

"Just a minute, Walt," Adam said. "Loren's trying to tell me something." He covered the mouthpiece with his hand. "What's the matter?"

"Don't put Josh in charge of amusing Daphne while we're gone."

His eyes narrowed. "I wasn't putting *Josh* in charge. I was asking both of them to—"

"My father's nearly seventy. He doesn't stay up past nine-thirty. Who do you suppose will be 'watching out' for Daphne after that? And where do you suppose they might end up? A romp in the resort Jacuzzi, perhaps? And then what?"

"Whatever you're implying is stupid. They barely know each other."

"I've seen your daughter, and I don't think I'm being the least bit stupid."

His gaze hardened. "And what's that supposed to mean?"

"Let me talk to my father."

He hesitated, then with a disgusted snort handed her the phone.

"Dad? Hi. Listen, I'm a little concerned that Josh could get in over his head with Daphne." She didn't look at Adam, but she could sense his anger. Tough. She was protecting her son.

"Like how?" Walt asked, amusement in his voice.

"Well, for example, if you bail out of the evening early."

"Which I might. These young people have a lot more stamina than I do."

"But I worry that Daphne might invite Josh back to the resort. I don't want him going there alone with her."

"Hmm. I guess you have a point." Walt hesitated and lowered his voice. "But the boy is almost nineteen. He knows the facts of life."

"Basically, but Daphne's..." She turned away from Adam and lowered her head. "She's more worldly, if you know what I mean," she said softly, not able to bring herself to explain that she believed Josh was still a virgin and she'd bet Daphne was not. "I'd hate for Josh to have a bad experience. Why don't you invite Daphne over for a barbecue or something? And try to stay awake until she leaves."

"I'll do what I can, but I can't chain the boy to the house."

"I know. But if you get a chance, talk to him. He thinks he can handle himself around her, but I'm not so sure."

Walt chuckled. "This from my daughter who married some long-haired weirdo? How does it feel to be on the receiving end of parental worries?"

She was stunned. "You never told me you thought Jack was weird."

"You married him before I got the chance to tell you. Then it was too late, and now for Josh's sake I don't say much. No reason for him to be ashamed of his father, even though his father deserves it."

Loren drew a long, shaky breath. "I always thought you were kind of neutral on the subject."

"I hate to butt in. You know that. But as long as we're having this conversation, I'll cast my vote for the man standing next to you."

"But—"

"He did the right thing years ago. I know you hated it, but he did the right thing. The fellow has character. And he's not a bad pilot, either."

She stood clutching the receiver, speechless before these revelations.

"Okay," her father said. "That's enough butting in to last the rest of my life. I'll be quiet now. And I'll do my best with this other business. You can't protect your children forever, though. I learned that early on with you."

Loren swallowed. "I know, Dad. Thanks. Take care." Slowly she replaced the receiver.

"So you think my daughter is some wicked woman who will lead your poor innocent son into the depths of depravity."

She turned to confront the fury in his blue eyes. "That's putting it more harshly than I meant it."

"Oh, I wouldn't say so. I'd say that about sums up your thoughts. Your son is too pure for the likes of my swinging daughter."

"He's shy, Adam. And she's... not."

"It's the shy ones I worry about!" He laughed bitterly. "Come to think about it, I should be questioning you about your son's moral fiber. Daphne's the more vulnerable, because she could get pregnant if they decide to play around. But I haven't questioned you. And you know why? Because I trust that you've raised him to be responsible."

She folded her arms. "Which I have."

"Bully for you. Well, let me tell you something about Daphne. She may be a bit materialistic, a bit spoiled, but she's never missed a curfew, never been busted for drugs, or alcohol, either. She's outgoing, intelligent and funny. The guy who ends up with her will be getting a wonderful deal. And I resent your implication that she can't be trusted alone with your son!"

Loren threw back her shoulders and met his anger head-on. "And I think you have blinders on. Daphne's not a cute little five-year-old anymore, in case you hadn't noticed."

"And I doubt Josh is the angel you paint him to be, either. Not if he's got Montgomery blood in him."

"And what's that supposed to mean?"

"Why do you think you're so suspicious of Daphne? Could it be that she reminds you a little bit of yourself at that age?"

"No way."

"Really? I haven't told you about the interesting conversation I had with Sherry a few months after I got back from Nam. She told me you threw away the birth-control pills the night we were supposed to elope."

She stared at him, her face aflame.

"That was probably overkill, Loren. Once I'd made love to you, I wouldn't have been able to leave, baby or no baby. I craved you the way a bee craves honey. That's why I enlisted without telling you goodbye. I put all that in a letter. Several times."

"Adam, I—"

"None of it matters now." He turned and headed for the door. "I think I'll get some air."

CHAPTER SEVEN

ADAM STEPPED into a deserted hallway and rode an empty elevator to the casino. The main floor, however, overflowed with people. People looking for magic, he thought. Pull a lever and your dreams will come true. Had he imagined life would become that easy once he saw Loren again? Yes, dammit. What a fool he'd been.

Shouldering his way through the crowd, he headed for the door leading to the river. Once outside, he took a deep breath of cool night air and stood quietly, hands in the pockets of his running shorts. The rain had stopped, although clouds still draped the sky in funereal black.

He lost track of how long he stood there while Loren's suspicions about his daughter twisted in his gut. And to make matters worse, the animosity cut both ways; Daphne considered Loren a threat, too. After this debacle, he'd be lucky if he could restore any of the goodwill he'd been cultivating so carefully with Daphne. He'd brought her because he hadn't wanted to hurt her feelings. What a laugh. Bringing her along on this trip might destroy their relationship altogether.

And for what? Loren didn't want anything to do with him. Years ago a kiss like the one they'd shared on the boat dock would have swept away all problems between them. Apparently, a kiss no longer held that kind of power, although for a moment, as she'd softened against him, and then matched his ferocious need...

Gamblers coming through the door jostled him out of his preoccupation. He moved away from the entrance and walked down toward the river where large catfish undulated through the shallows near the water's edge. The marshy scent of the riverbank stirred memories of muddy rivers halfway around the world, of slogging through them in camouflage gear, his rifle held over his head.

The only reason he'd stayed alive in that dank, primitive world was so that he could come back and explain to Loren. Now it didn't seem to matter anymore. Maybe she'd been right all along, and years of erosion had destroyed the solid ground upon which they'd once built a bridge between them.

He directed his gaze across the dark water. Multicolored casino lights reflected on the surface, transforming the current into a river of jewels. A shuttle boat sliced the water, destroying the illusion. Adam watched until the skiff moved down the river and the current repaired itself, becoming a fantasy of lights again. A raindrop splashed against his cheek. Another followed, and soon the rain pattered all around him. With a sigh, he turned and headed inside.

He debated the wisdom of going upstairs, returning to her. His anger had eased enough that he might be able to reestablish civil communication if she'd join the effort. They still had a job to do in the morning, and he didn't want their personal feelings to get in the way of that. Yes, he'd go back upstairs and try to smooth things over.

On the way to the elevators, he stopped off at the gift shop to pick up the latest issue of *Flying* magazine. Might as well have something constructive to do tonight, he thought. As the clerk rang up his purchase, Adam's glance fell on the display of condoms. He sure wouldn't be needing those, he thought with a bitter smile. She'd kissed him as if she wanted to make love, and since then she'd handed him a laundry list of all the reasons that making love was an ill-conceived and foolish idea.

But he remembered the implied promise in that kiss. She'd meant every bit of it at the time. Was it possible that things might change between them before morning? Absolutely impossible, he decided, given the circumstances and their personalities. No chance at all, he told himself, even as he took a package from the rack and tossed it on the counter to be added to his bill.

He shared the elevator with a bellman delivering a dinner cart. As the small space filled with the scent of steak, Adam's stomach rumbled. He should probably suggest that he and Loren have a meal sent to the room. They wouldn't even have to eat together, but it was his responsibility to buy her dinner, regardless of their differences of opinion.

He stepped off the elevator and soon became aware of the bellman rumbling along behind him as he walked down the hall. When he stopped at his room, the key in his hand, the bellman paused outside Loren's door. Adam glanced at the cart.

There were a hell of a lot of covered dishes on it. Plus wine in an ice bucket and a red carnation in a bud vase. And two wineglasses. Apparently, she'd ordered dinner for both of them, preempting his idea. Curious to find out for sure, he opened his door and walked in before she had a chance to answer the bellman's knock.

The connecting doors were still open. Tossing his package on a bedside table, he sauntered over and leaned against the doorframe between the rooms. He concluded that the arrival of dinner had covered the sound of his entrance, because she seemed unaware of him as she supervised the laying of the table, tasted the wine the bellman offered her and signed the check. The bellman wheeled the empty cart toward the door, and she turned in his direction.

Her eyes widened. "Adam! I didn't hear you come in."

"Expecting company?" He angled his head toward the table, quite obviously set for two.

She looked uncertain, an unusual expression for her. She gestured toward the table. "I'm afraid this will appear on your bill, but when we get back, I'll reimburse you. I'd like to offer it as—" her glance wavered, slid away from his "—an apology."

And a very sedate one, he noted. This wasn't on a par with throwing herself into his arms and begging his forgiveness. Or begging for his love. This apology suited damaged friendships and business relationships. He didn't change position. "What does this apology cover exactly?"

She steepled her fingers together and brought them to her mouth, tapping gently against her chin. Her gaze was troubled. "Perhaps I have been too quick to judge Daphne. All I can say in my defense is that Josh is the most important person in the world to me. I'd do anything to keep him from getting hurt."

"Then you know how I feel about my daughter," he said quietly.

Her fingers pressed together more tightly. "Yes. Yes, I do."

"We have that in common, at least."

She nodded.

He realized she was waiting for him to accept her gesture. What the hell. They had to eat. "Thank you for ordering dinner," he said, starting toward the table. "But I certainly don't expect you to pay for—"

"Oh, yes, I will."

He glanced at her rebellious expression and almost laughed. "So, are we now going to fight about who pays for the dinner?"

"Not unless you insist on playing the macho big shot."

Now he did laugh. "Heaven forbid. Come on, Lor, let's eat."

He thought of holding her chair and canceled the impulse. With the problems that stood between them, he'd be better off keeping his distance, because coming too close to Loren made him think of that kiss on the boat dock. And thinking of that kiss made him long for what he couldn't have.

"Wine?" She held the bottle poised over his goblet.

He hesitated. Wine usually made him feel romantic. Not a good idea right now. "No, thanks."

She lowered the bottle to the table. "If you don't like this kind, we can order something else."

"There's nothing wrong with the wine."

"You're still furious with me, aren't you?"

"No." Furious wasn't the adjective he'd have chosen. Disappointed, frustrated, confused, but not furious. Not anymore. She'd obviously taken his rejection of the wine the wrong way. She didn't know how wine affected him. How could she, considering the only alcohol they'd ever consumed together was a glass of champagne at her graduation party?

He shrugged. "What the heck. Sure, I'll have a little wine."

She visibly relaxed and filled his glass with the ruby liquid. "I ordered your steak medium. I hope that's okay."

He liked it rare these days, but again, she couldn't have known. Another of the endless things they didn't know about each other. He'd imagined long, satisfying conversations as they filled in the lost years. Oh, well. "Medium's fine."

"Good."

They ate in relative silence after that, with only occasional comments. He mentioned that his steak was tender, and she asked if she could use his sour cream, if he didn't want it. When he passed it over, their fingers brushed, and she glanced into his eyes. The speed with which she broke eye contact and the intensity she lavished on the task of spreading the sour cream on her potato told him she was strung as tight as he.

"Did you gamble when you went downstairs?" she asked as if to cover up the moment. But her tone was breathy, and he wasn't fooled.

"No. Just walked down by the river."

"Oh."

Outside, the wind whipped up, blowing rain against the window and emphasizing the coziness of their setting. Adam took another sip of wine and settled back in his chair.

He had nowhere much to look except at Loren, and that was dangerous. In a T-shirt, with her face washed free of makeup by the rain, she looked very much like the teenager who'd won his heart. His gaze lingered on her mouth, the curve of her cheek, the sweep of her eyelashes.

He remembered how she'd tasted that afternoon, how her lips had opened for him, how she'd moaned softly, a special moan that sounded like no one else's. Desire returned to taunt him with unattainable images. With an effort, he glanced away, which only made matters worse. To her left was a far-too-inviting stretch of mattress. He put down his wineglass. Enough of that.

Except he'd had only half a glass. Not enough to explain the persistent ache gaining momentum every time he looked at her. He shoved back his chair. "Have you checked to see what's on TV tonight?"

She paused, her glass halfway to her lips. "No. Have you?"

"No." He stood, glad for a chance to move. The room was too small, too intimate. Crossing to the television set, he reached for the movie guide and read the selections aloud, omitting the x-rated ones. That was all they needed, a porno flick. "Anything sound good?"

"I suppose we could watch the Billy Crystal one. Josh keeps pestering me to see more movies, but I'm always so busy."

"I haven't gone to many, either. Well, maybe this is the night to see a movie." He figured it was a good middle ground, not as abrupt as stalking off to his own room and closing the door, yet less perilous than lingering over another glass of wine and gazing across the table at her.

"Actually..."

He looked up from the television guide. She sat swirling the remaining wine in her glass and gazing into the tiny maelstrom she'd created. His heart beat heavily in his chest. He waited.

"I was wondering if you'd tell me what was in those letters."

He caught his breath, amazed that she'd volunteered a tentative step onto very treacherous ground. And now that she'd asked, could he satisfy her request without stirring up emotions better left alone?

He could cut her off. He knew his line and the exact way he should deliver it. *It's not important anymore, Loren,* he should say in a bored, worldly tone. *Billy Crystal would be a lot more entertaining than that old story.*

"I can understand if you don't want to," she continued. "But after we take the pictures tomorrow, I don't think we'll be seeing each other again. This is probably my last chance to find out why you changed your mind about leaving. Our last chance to clear the air between us."

Oh. So she didn't expect the conversation to serve as an opening. She wanted closure. Pain stabbed his heart. "Does it matter?"

She met his gaze. "It matters to me."

He hadn't been able to resist that look of supplication twenty-three years ago, and he couldn't resist it now. He put down the television guide and returned to the table. "All right. Where shall I start?"

"From the beginning, from the time you left my house that night. Did you stop off at Jimmy's?"

"No." He pushed his plate aside and leaned his forearms on the table. "After I left you, I went home and sat in the family room, and sort of stared off into space, trying to adjust to the fact I'd just agreed to marry you."

He looked into her eyes. Big mistake. They'd turned soft as a fawn's. He remembered that look, too. It used to mean good things were about to happen between them.

She put down her glass and left her hand resting beside it. "Go on," she murmured.

He noticed the short distance between his hand and hers as they lay on the table—a miniature no-man's-land that neither dared cross. He didn't move his hand closer, but neither did he retreat. "I feel a little like an actor on opening night. I've practiced this speech hundreds of times, but I've never given it to the intended audience.''

"Then maybe you should now."

"Maybe I should." His gaze drifted to her mouth. Mentally he traced the deep bow of her upper lip and the seductive lushness of her full lower lip. A generous mouth, so capable of giving. With an effort he looked away. "So, I was sitting in the family room. My folks had a copy of *Life* magazine lying on the coffee table. I picked it up, and there was a story about this little village in Nam."

She stayed absolutely still, all her attention trained on him, just as he'd imagined she might listen. Her complete absorption gave him goose bumps.

"The people seemed just like my next-door neighbors, except for one thing. They never knew from one day to the next if they'd all die. All that kept that from happening was their wits and the protection of American soldiers."

Her throat moved in a convulsive swallow. "And you left me to go and protect them?"

"They seemed to need me a whole lot more than you did."

Pain flashed in her eyes. She opened her mouth to deny his words.

"It's true, Loren," he said gently. "You were—are—one of the most self-sufficient people I know."

Her throat worked again. "You left me because I could take care of myself and they couldn't?"

"No, not just that."

"Then what else?"

His universe narrowed to the expressions playing across her face. They reflected a depth of emotion that mirrored his. His pulse rate climbed. "I wasn't strong enough to give you up on that kind of logic." A flicker of passion lit her eyes and he focused on it, coaxing it into a brighter flame. "You had me in the palm of your hand."

"But you left," she whispered.

His gaze didn't waver from hers. "I also went through my yearbook that night, seeing friends who'd since lost arms or legs, some who'd died. Most of them had girlfriends, wanted to live a normal life, but they went." His throat tightened as it always did when he thought of the ones who'd sacrificed so much more than he.

He glanced down, taking a moment to get a grip on his emotions, and realized with a jolt that her hand had crept closer to his. He looked into her eyes and wondered if she even realized it. "So I had to go, too, Loren," he said.

"But we could have gotten married first like we planned," she said in a throaty murmur.

He shook his head, let his gaze sink into hers. "Once I'd made love to you, I wouldn't have been able to go away. You knew that, didn't you?"

She hesitated, her color high. "Yes," she said at last. "That's what I was counting on. But the plan didn't work."

"Because I never gave it a chance to work."

With sheer strength of will, he kept from reaching for her. He wouldn't make the first move. It had to be her. He held his breath, willing her to touch him.

When at last the tips of her fingers brushed his, he closed his eyes. Her tentative caress felt like butterfly wings against his skin.

Her touch was sweet, so sweet. And it was driving him insane. At last his control snapped. In one swift movement, he captured the butterfly in a fierce grip. She gasped and tried to pull away, but he held her fast. Slowly, he opened his eyes, finally allowing her to see the beast of passion that had slept within him for twenty-three years. And the beast had been awakened.

BARBECUING HAMBURGERS on the deck with Walt and Josh was more fun than Daphne had expected. The deck was partially covered, and to escape the rain they'd moved the grill and picnic table under the overhang. Fortunately, the wind was hitting the front of the house, so they kept dry. Smelling the smoke from the grill as she sat looking at Oak Creek rushing along just beyond the deck made Daphne think a little bit of camping, especially with the kerosene lantern Walt had just lit. Probably her dad hadn't meant what he'd said about camping, either.

"Ready for another one?" Walt asked, coming across the deck with a steaming patty balanced on his spatula.

"Sure, why not?" She dug out another bun from the package on the table and slapped it open on her plate.

"I don't even have to ask Josh." He returned to the grill for another patty.

Josh came through the sliding door carrying a re-filled bowl of potato salad and more ranch-style beans. "Was somebody taking my name in vain?"

"Your grandfather thinks you eat a lot," Daphne said, laughing.

"Whoa. News flash. Call Peter Jennings." Josh grinned and set the food on the table. Then he lifted an eyebrow at Daphne's plate as she layered on to-mato slices, lettuce, onions, pickles, ketchup and mustard. "You're packing it away pretty good your-self."

"I'm just trying to be polite." She pressed the bun top down on her four-inch sandwich.

"Yeah, sure. I told you Gramps cooks the best burgers in the West."

"Mesquite chips," Walt said, sitting down to his second hamburger. "That's the secret."

"You should tell my dad." Daphne bit into her hamburger and juice dribbled down her chin.

"Does he cook out a lot?" Walt asked.

"He never does. But I wish he would. Besides, we're going camping this summer. He'll cook out then." She could pretend it would happen, anyway.

"There are some great camping places around here," Josh said. "Mom, Gramps and I used to go out a lot, but once I started college we sort of slacked off. If you need a tent, though, we've got one. And lots of other camping stuff."

"Thanks. Dad'll probably buy everything." She didn't dare accept the offer of a tent, because, when she never borrowed it, they'd know her father hadn't taken her camping, after all.

After dinner, she helped clean up and then they all sat at the picnic table and played rummy. She was having a blast until Walt said it was time for him and Josh to hit the hay.

"Maybe Josh would like to come to the resort and sit in the Jacuzzi for a while," she said, flashing Josh a seductive look. "The rain's slowed down."

Josh's eyes lit up and she figured she'd have company for at least a few more hours.

But Walt shook his head. "I'd rather he didn't. He's got a tight schedule tomorrow. Has to be up by five. I don't want him working around machinery if he's not well-rested."

Daphne noticed Josh's frown of resentment, but he didn't say anything to contradict his grandfather. She should have known he'd be the kind to toe the line.

"Thanks for the offer," Josh said. "Maybe another time."

"Maybe." Daphne put on her bright and breezy look. "Anyway, there was a guy hanging around the pool this morning. He asked me if I'd planned to go to the lounge for some dancing tonight. I told him I might. That sounds like more fun than soaking in hot water. See you later. Thanks for the meal."

She made a quick exit, smiling all the way out. Then she put the top down on the Geo and zoomed away into the night. She drove as fast as she dared on the slick, winding roads. The wind in her hair helped. The radio turned up loud helped. She hoped they'd believed the story about some guy who wanted her to go dancing.

Her mood of defiance lasted until she opened the door of her quiet, solitary room. The door to her father's room was still open, and she slammed it shut.

After wandering around the room for a few minutes, she picked up the phone and punched in a number. She got the housekeeper at the house in Fountain Hills. "Georgia? Listen, what's the number in Aspen where Mom is? Yeah, I'm pretty sure she was going to stay there a few more days before she went on to Reno, but give me that number, just in case. Thanks." She pressed the disconnect button and punched in the Colorado area code and the number of the Aspen spa where Anita Riordan had gone to shed a few pounds before a planned rendezvous with Barnaby in Reno.

The spa switchboard operator connected her with Anita's room and she answered on the second ring.

Daphne felt tears pressing against the backs of her eyes. "Hi, Mom. It's me."

"Daphne. Are you having a good time with your father?"

"No."

"Why not?"

"Because he didn't really come up here to have a vacation with me, that's why. He's all hot to get some aerial pictures of some stupid bridge."

Anita sighed. "I've been telling you this for years, Daphne. His business comes first. That's why I finally left him. But I'm sorry it isn't working out. Would you like me to speak to him?"

"You can't. He's not even here."

"Not there? Where is he?"

"Over in Laughlin, where the stupid bridge is. And that's the other part that stinks. He's got a thing going for this aerial photographer, Loren Stanfield. He's over there with her, supposedly trying to get pictures of the bridge. But I have a pretty good idea what he's really doing."

There was a brief pause. "Well, I've warned you about this before, Daphne. He's never taken much of an interest in you. I've tried to make up for it as best I could."

Daphne swiped at her tears. "I know. I appreciate it. But I just wish—"

"It does no good to wish with a man like Adam." There was another pause. "I'd have you come up here, but—"

"No, Mom. That's supposed to be your getaway. You deserve it."

"Something you said interests me. Isn't that bridge the one Barnaby's company is putting up?"

"I don't know. I've never paid much attention to that stuff."

"I wonder why Adam's taking pictures of it?"

"I think it's just an excuse. It's this Loren person he's after." Daphne had hoped for a little revenge by seducing Loren's precious son, but Walt had foiled that plan.

"I'm really sorry, Daphne. Are you sure you'll be all right?"

"I'll be fine."

"Okay, then. Good night."

"Good night, Mom." Daphne decided she'd just have to figure out some other way to sock it to Loren Stanfield. And her father.

ANITA HOPED she hadn't sounded too interested in the bridge pictures or hustled Daphne off the phone too quickly. Being careful of her new manicure, she used the eraser end of a pencil to push the buttons on the bedside phone.

"Barn? Hi. I'm fine, but Adam's doing something strange, and I thought you'd better know about it immediately. He's hired a woman in Sedona by the name of Loren Stanfield to take aerial photographs of the bridge site...."

CHAPTER EIGHT

LOREN'S PULSE leapt at the blaze of primitive need in Adam's blue eyes. Perhaps she'd known all along they'd come to this moment.

His grip on her hand tightened a notch. "You don't plan to see me again after tomorrow," he said.

Her chest felt tight and breathing was difficult. "I think it would be best that way."

"For you."

Her lips were dry. Heart pounding, she moistened them. "For everyone."

His glance flicked to her mouth. "All right. We won't debate it." His gaze recaptured hers. "But that's tomorrow, isn't it? Several hours away."

Her body began to quiver in response to the look in his eyes. She had no doubt where this conversation was leading. "Yes," she whispered.

Without relinquishing her hand, he stood. Then slowly he drew her to her feet. "Then give me tonight."

She pressed the back of her hand to her mouth to prevent a moan as she shook her head. "We'll hurt each other," she said tightly.

The demand lurking in his eyes was relentless. "We already have. We've already proved we can take it."

Pain clogged her throat. "I don't know if I can."

"Yes, you can." His voice was ragged, his grip on her hand almost painful. "So can I. We're tough."

She watched him through swimming eyes, in an agony of indecision. He wasn't the man for her. He had serious family problems and he still had the idealism and the potential for self-sacrifice that had driven them apart before. Should she trade a few hours in his arms for a lifetime of heartache? Should he?

"A long time ago you asked me for one night. The tables have turned." His voice grew husky. "Give me this, Loren. Give me this before you go."

Her heartbeat thundered in her ears. "And what if the tables have turned in another way? What if I'm the one who can't leave afterward, even if I know it's the wisest decision?"

"I guess you'll have to take that chance."

"You didn't. You ran away."

"I'm not running now."

She'd never wanted him this much, not even at eighteen. His story of Vietnam had left her vulnerable, needing to hold him and be held. Instinct shoved away logic, making the choice. "Neither am I," she whispered.

With a groan, he pulled her roughly into his arms, the movement rattling the dishes on the table next to them. His lips came down on hers with a ferocity that took her breath away. Then he deepened the kiss, and her heart wrenched. She could taste desire and frustration, perhaps even anger. And overlaying every emotion he gave her, the salt of his tears.

This time he didn't lead her gently toward passion, he hurled her into the inferno, stoking the fire within her until she blazed with a matching heat. When he reached under her shirt, he sucked in his breath at discovering she wore nothing beneath it. And then, as ravenous as he'd seemed before, his mood changed to tenderness, almost to reverence. As his hand closed softly over her breast, he shuddered.

He caressed her with such gentleness tears escaped from her own eyes. His touch was so perfect, so right. He'd been the first to stroke her like this, and her body had never unlearned him. She moaned against his mouth as her body tightened and arched into his, seeking his answering tension, begging for connection.

His mouth left hers and kissed her wet cheeks, her eyelids, her throat. "Don't cry," he said, his own voice rough with tears.

"I won't if you won't."

"It's a deal. Oh, God, Loren...Loren." Gently he pushed up her T-shirt, uncovering both breasts. She lifted her arms, and he pulled the garment over her head and tossed it aside. Catching both her hands in his, he stepped back.

She flushed under the warmth of his gaze.

"Thank you," he murmured, looking deep into her eyes.

Her breasts tingled, needing his touch once again. Her breathing quickened and her lips parted, wanting...wanting. With a soft smile of awareness, he stepped forward and scooped her up. She held his gaze as he carried her through the connecting doors to his room, where no light shone except that spilling from her room. He placed her on the bed and stepped away, reaching for the back of his T-shirt to pull it over his head.

"Wait, please."

He paused.

"If tonight has to last me a lifetime, I want more light."

Without speaking, he walked to the bedside lamp and switched it on. His voice was soft. "Is that enough?"

"Yes." She quivered with longing. "Stand right there. In the light."

He pulled off his shirt, revealing a jagged white welt down his bicep.

She gasped and reached out toward it. "What is that?"

"Nothing." He kicked off his shoes.

"But—"

"A sniper with poor aim. Other people died. This was just an inconvenience."

Her stomach churned at the thought of a bullet ripping through his arm. Poor aim. The sniper had meant the bullet to rip through Adam's heart. And Adam would have died in the jungle....

He pushed his thumbs under the waistband of his shorts and stripped away shorts and briefs in one movement. She braced herself for more scars. But no, he was perfect—lean, strong, his manhood thrusting from a swirl of dark hair. He had lived. Her Adam had lived. And for one night, he belonged to her again. Gratitude filled her, and she held out her arms.

Adam exhaled slowly. He couldn't believe that she was here. Loren had been the subject of his fantasies from the time he'd been old enough to have fantasies. An hour ago, he'd been prepared to give her up, but now she was smiling at him. Wanting him. After so long.

Yet she'd agreed to only one night. The beginning might also be the ending.

"Adam?"

He slid down beside her, cradling her face in both hands and brushing his thumb across her lower lip, swollen from his kisses. "I'm here."

"You looked so fierce."

"I guess I did." He tasted her lips, then raised his head to look into her eyes, heavy-lidded with desire. "Dreams of a lifetime don't come true every day." His breath mingled with hers as he leaned toward her again. "I'm possessive about this one."

As he savored the kiss, the pounding promise of what was to come, he realized she hadn't asked him about birth control. His heart quickened at the possibility that she didn't care. But he did. He wouldn't burden her with a child now any more than he would have twenty-three years ago.

She slid her fingers through his hair, and he closed his eyes at the sweet caress. "I love touching you," she murmured.

"Then do."

Tentatively at first, then with more confidence, she ran her fingers over his chest. Then her explorations moved lower, and he clenched his jaw as she grasped his heated shaft, her fingers cool and supple.

Her touch was heaven and hell, testing every ounce of control he possessed. All the times he'd dreamed of this moment hadn't prepared him for the reality. His blood roared in his ears as she fondled and stroked, caressing his thighs, his stomach, but always returning to the aching center of his need for her.

At last he had to make her stop, had to grasp her hands and guide them upward to clasp around his neck while he pulled himself back together. "Enough," he murmured into her ear. "Or I'm liable to disappoint you."

"You couldn't."

"More of that and I might." The night was long, he told himself. He would have more chances to invite that sort of bliss. He'd matured as a lover since those nights in Oak Creek Canyon, and he wanted to give her everything he'd become.

Her skin was smooth and hot, her breathing shallow. He remembered that sound—short, quick breaths that told him passion had claimed his Loren. His Loren. He'd never thought of her as anyone else's, marriage or no marriage.

He'd promised himself if he ever earned the right to love her again, he would cherish every moment. He ran his knuckles down her cleavage as he gazed into her eyes. Her pupils widened when he cupped the weight of one breast and spread his fingers, pressing, remembering.

He could feel her heartbeat racing in time with his. Sweet moisture gathered on her skin like dew, making her glow in the light from the lamp. He caught her nipple between thumb and forefinger, teasing it to erectness. "There were nights I would have given years of my life to touch you like this."

"When you left, I thought it didn't matter to you."

"It mattered." He lowered his mouth to her breast. "It still does."

His blood sang at the sweetness of her, the shape of her on his tongue, the sound of her soft cries as he suckled, the pressure of her fingers against his scalp.

He left the heaven of her breasts to recapture her lips and pull her tight against him. Stroking her back, he slipped his hand beneath the elastic of her panties and shorts. Her bottom curved beautifully against his hands, and lower, between her thighs, the moist center beckoned.

Reaching behind and beneath, he touched her there. When she gasped, he plunged his tongue into her mouth and absorbed her moan as he probed deeper and found the wellspring of her response.

Urging her onto her back, he pulled her shorts away quickly, but took his time with her damp underwear, kissing her sensitive inner thighs as he slowly, erotically slid the elastic over her skin. He kissed her knees, her calves, the arches of her feet. Then he tossed the panties on the floor and gradually, inevitably, retraced his steps, parting her thighs as he drew nearer to his destination.

When he tasted her, she cried out his name, and it was the most fantastic sound he'd ever heard. And then, for the first time in his life, technique blended with love. The result nearly shattered his control as he coaxed her higher and higher, then higher still.

She thrashed beneath him and dug her fingers into his shoulders. And ultimately surrendered. He thought his heart would burst as she cried out his name again. He held her until the quaking stopped, then slowly eased up beside her, pushing the damp hair from her forehead, feathering her lips with a kiss.

"Oh, Adam, that was..." She sighed, as if unable to find the words.

He gazed into her eyes, reading the pleasure she couldn't describe and exulting in it.

And now.

He rolled away from her, finding the package and tearing it open.

When he turned back, he found her watching him, her eyes bright, her face flushed.

He moved between her thighs, kissing her breasts, her lips. He could hold back no longer. With one swift thrust he was inside her, and he closed his eyes against the wave of sensation that nearly carried him away. Not yet. He'd waited too long. Please not yet. He schooled his responses and slowly opened his eyes. The look in her eyes made his heart turn over.

"You're a magician," she murmured, lifting her hips to lock him more tightly against her. "This is..." Fresh tears slipped from the corners of her eyes. "This is magic," she said, her voice choked with emotion.

"We made it," he said, leaning down to kiss her. It was the way he'd always imagined, being buried deep inside her. The rightness, the completeness, washed over him, and pressure built behind his eyes. He blinked away the moisture and knew he couldn't say the words ready to tumble from his mouth. They would only make the end more unbearable. He and Loren could take a lot, but they couldn't take the devastation of those words hovering between them when they said goodbye.

Maybe the words didn't matter. He eased back and pushed forward again. Maybe all that mattered was holding her like this, absorbing the excruciatingly sweet pleasure surrounding him. "Ah, Loren," he breathed. His throat closed as the rhythm claimed him, but he kept his gaze fastened on her face, knew the moment she caught fire by the sudden widening of her eyes.

Yes. It took all the control he'd learned, but he slowed imperceptibly to give her time to catch up. With this woman, he could do anything. When she matched him gasp for gasp, he increased the tempo. He felt her tighten around him and arch her hips. It was all he needed to catapult him over the edge, and her cries mingled with his as they held tight and rode the whirlwind. Together.

WALT HAD NEVER SEEN Josh like this. He hardly knew him. The Josh he knew wouldn't have picked a fight about Walt's decree that he needed a good night's sleep. And he damn sure wouldn't have stormed out of the house headed for the resort and a sexy young girl.

Walt paced the floor and finally picked up the phone. Hastily he dialed the number scribbled on a pad beside it. Loren would want to know that her son had gone berserk.

The phone rang four times before she picked it up. "Hello?" she said, sounding funny, sort of breathless.

"Loren? Am I catching you at a bad time?"

"Of course not, Dad. What is it?"

"I thought I'd better warn you. I tried to do what you asked and thought I'd succeeded. Then after Daphne left here, Josh tore into me about treating him like a baby because I said he needed his rest and shouldn't go over to the resort with Daphne."

"Oh, God."

"I tried to smooth things over. I even explained that Daphne seemed like someone to stay away from. She really is hungry for attention, Loren."

"I know that, Dad."

"But Josh wouldn't listen. We wrangled awhile and I tried to convince him not to go over there. Finally he said, 'By God, I'm old enough to make those decisions for myself,' and took off. I assume he went to the resort."

Loren sighed. "Great."

"Look, I know you can't do anything about it, stuck there like you are, but I wanted you to be aware of the situation before you came home. I'm not sure what sort of mood Josh will be in, if he'll even be here."

"Dad, I'm sorry you had to deal with this."

"He just startled me, that's all. He's never been the type of kid to act like that."

"And it's pretty obvious why he's acting that way now."

"Guess you're right. Well, we'll probably be able to straighten everything out when you get home."

"Let's hope so. Call me if anything else happens."

"I will. Good night, Loren."

Walt hung up the phone hoping he'd done the right thing by calling. Of course Loren would spend most of the night worrying, but she would have been upset with him if he hadn't notified her. She'd always wanted to know everything that pertained to Josh, even when the knowing didn't make much difference to the outcome, like now. Walt understood that preoccupation. Children had the power to hold your heart hostage.

CHAPTER NINE

LOREN REPLACED the receiver and stood by the phone, her whole body clenched. She was wearing only Adam's T-shirt, which she'd grabbed reflexively and pulled over her head on the way into her room to answer the piercing ring. Adam stood just behind her—she could sense his presence—but she didn't want to turn, didn't want to deal with the next few minutes.

"What is it?"

She fought the heavy weight of disappointment and anger settling in her chest as she slowly turned to face him. He wore his running shorts and nothing else. His hair lay in a tousled wave over his forehead and his gaze was still soft with the aftermath of passion.

Moments ago it had seemed so right for them to give in to their needs, to take this night for themselves and enjoy the pleasures they'd denied themselves for so long. Not now. What had been so beautiful between them had soured and curdled in the space of one phone conversation.

"Loren . . ." He stepped forward as if to take her in his arms.

She backed away. "That was my father. It seems your daughter has lured my son over to the resort, just as I was afraid she would."

His jaw tightened. "Wait a minute. *Lured?*"

"What else would you call it?" She moved past him, wanting more space, and he didn't try to stop her. "She asked him to come over, and my father said Josh needed his rest. Normally, that would have been the end of it, but after she left, Josh told my father he'd make his own decisions about needing rest and took off after her."

"Good for him."

She whirled, fury igniting like dry kindling. "What?"

"A boy his age doesn't need his grandfather telling him when to sleep."

She closed her hands into fists. "I *asked* my father to keep an eye on things, remember? He wasn't trying to tell Josh when to sleep. He was trying to prevent what's just happened!"

Adam's gaze never wavered as he rested his hands loosely on his hips. "And what exactly has happened?"

His stoic acceptance of the situation inflamed her even more. "They're alone together at that resort, doing God knows what. I'd appreciate it if you'd call and talk to your daughter."

"Absolutely not."

"Adam, don't you even care? They could be—"

"I care a great deal." Although his voice remained steady, there was an undercurrent of anger. Loren welcomed it. She wanted a fight. "And that's why I won't call," he continued. "I'd consider it an invasion of her privacy."

"Oh, come on!"

Adam didn't respond immediately. She'd have thought he was in complete control, except for the muscle twitching in his jaw. "Daphne's a flirt. So are most girls her age. That doesn't mean she's determined to jump your son's bones, although I can see you're paranoid about the possibility."

"I'm just using common sense, Adam."

"Are you? Or are you letting what's been going on between us color your perception of those kids?"

In one stroke he'd pierced to her secret bubble of shame. The emotion flowed unchecked, heating her skin, making her unable to look at him. Her protest was feeble. "That's a crummy thing to say."

"And maybe it's the truth. I'd guess that Daphne's just lonely, and Josh is somebody to talk to."

Desperate to wound as she'd been wounded, she lashed out. "Oh, she's lonely, all right, but I don't believe all she wants to do is talk."

His gaze turned hard. "That's enough, Loren. I won't have you making those kinds of statements about my daughter."

"Oh, you won't?" Cleansing anger fizzed through her veins. "Well, let me assure you, Josh would never have defied his grandfather if Daphne hadn't given him the come-on."

"For God's sake, Loren, wake up!"

His explosion made her back up a step, but she wouldn't surrender the field. "Me? You're the one who's asleep! You refuse to acknowledge how seductive your daughter can be!''

"And you refuse to acknowledge that an eighteen-year-old boy—a young *man*—can't be controlled by his mother and grandfather.''

She clenched her back teeth. "We never had a problem until Daphne showed up.''

"Then maybe it's about time someone like Daphne did blow into town.'' His voice was edged with steel. "People have to learn to make their own decisions, their own mistakes. You have no right to think for that kid, just like you had no right to think for me twenty-three years ago.''

She gasped, feeling as if she'd been punched in the stomach. "What is *that* supposed to mean?''

"Do you realize what would have happened if all your scheming had worked out?''

"Of course.'' She wrapped her arms around herself to control her shivering. "I would have become pregnant and you would have stayed. We'd be married now, with two children. Now, doesn't that sound terrible?'' She loaded the question with sarcasm.

"It's all I ever dreamed about,'' he said quietly.

"And you threw it away!''

"Because I had to.''

"Oh, really? Because you're some sort of superpatriot?''

"No, dammit! If you'd succeeded, you'd be married to a man you could manipulate. And you would have lost respect for me, as well you should!'' He swung away from her, his jaw working. His voice dropped to a resigned murmur. "We would have torn each other apart in the end."

She choked back a sob. "That's great. So you saved us from that so we can tear each other apart now?"

He turned to face her again, the sorrow in his eyes bottomless. "I guess that about sums it up." Then he walked into the other room and closed the connecting door on his side.

DAPHNE HAD SEEN every pay-per-view movie available on the resort's closed-circuit system, but decided to stay up all night and watch them over again. Or at least she'd leave the television on so the movies would be charged to her father's bill.

Then she inspected the contents of the courtesy bar and unloaded crackers, cheese spread, cookies and an assortment of juices. She wasn't able to eat much after two hamburgers and a mound of Walt's potato salad at dinner, but she sampled just about everything, including a two-serving bottle of Chardonnay.

When the phone rang, she thought it might be her mother, urging her to come up to Aspen, after all. If it was, Daphne had decided to say yes. The first time her mother had asked, she'd felt obliged to turn her down, realizing her mom didn't really want her hanging around.

But this time, if her mom insisted, she'd go, even knowing she'd be in the way, even knowing she'd have to eat tofu and sprouts for a few days. Anything was better than being alone, or worse yet, watching her father make a fool of himself over some old girlfriend. She'd thought Josh might be a good distraction, but he'd wimped out on her.

She put down the wine bottle she'd been sipping from and reached across the bed to pick up the receiver. "Hullo?"

"Hi, Daphne. It's Josh."

"What? You're allowed to make phone calls after nine o'clock? You have more privileges than I thought."

"Cut it out, Daph. I'm in the lobby. Where's your room?"

"Well, now." A thrill of happiness ran through her at the prospect of company. "How do you know I'm not fooling around with that guy I told you about? Maybe this isn't a convenient time."

There was a long pause and she wondered if she'd overplayed her hand.

"Are you with somebody?" he asked finally.

"Actually, no. He was *trés* boring."

"So?"

"So maybe you won't be." She gave Josh directions to the room, then ran around picking up cellophane wrappers and sweeping crumbs off the bed. She screwed the cap onto the small bottle of wine and stuck it back in the refrigerator. Then she turned off the television and switched the FM to a rock station. Last of all, she kicked her fuzzy bear-paw slippers under the bed.

When he knocked, she let him in with a slow smile. "Did you bring your swimsuit?"

He shook his head.

She gave him an arch glance. "Then just wear a towel and go in with nothing on. Lots of people do that late at night."

He shifted his weight uncomfortably and didn't look at her. "I didn't really come here to get in the Jacuzzi with you."

She paused and studied him. "Well, now."

His ears turned red but he didn't look away this time. "And I didn't come for that reason, either."

"Whoa." She spread her arms. "Go ahead, stomp all over my ego while you're at it."

"Daphne, you're beautiful, but—"

"Did you take vows for the priesthood, or something?"

He shifted his weight again and she took pity on him. In two days of being around Josh, she'd learned that he wasn't a speech-maker. "Then why did you come?"

"Partly because Gramps said not to," he admitted.

Daphne punched a fist in the air. "Yes! I knew there was some spunk hidden under that halo you keep polishing all the time."

Josh grinned. "Oh, I'm no angel."

"I was beginning to wonder. So did you tell the old guy off or sneak out?"

"I sorta told him off." Josh looked unhappy. "I hated to, in a way, but he had no right trying to run my life like that."

"Right on, Joshua. You have potential, boy."

"Thanks."

"So now that you're here, what do you want to do?"

"I don't know." Josh looked around. "This place isn't bad, Daph."

His use of a nickname and his approval of the resort delighted her, but she gave a negligent shrug. "I guess it's okay."

"What were you doing before I got here?"

"Honestly?"

"Yeah, honestly." He eyed the rumpled bed. "There wasn't really a guy here, was there?"

Daphne gave an exaggerated sigh. "Okay, Mr. Truthfulness, there was no guy. If you must know, I was just hanging out watching movies and cleaning out the courtesy bar."

"The what?"

Daphne shook her head. "Your education is sadly lacking, Joshua. Look here." She crossed to the small refrigerator and flung open the door.

Josh hunkered down and peered inside. "Not bad. That stuff comes free with the room?"

"Oh, no. It's all extra and costs a pretty penny, which is why I'm eating it. When I get through with this one, I'll hit the one in Dad's room."

"That's kind of a bratty thing to do."

"I know. Care to join me?"

"There's a lot of booze in here."

"You can have that. I tried some of the wine, but I'm not into drinking."

"I'm not, either." Josh stood.

"So we can pour that down the sink."

He glanced at the price list on top of the courtesy bar and whistled. "You really are ticked off about him deserting you on your vacation, aren't you?"

"I haven't even started on my room-service order."

"Sure wouldn't want you getting mad at *me*. I couldn't afford it."

"Dad can. Besides, I don't get mad." She winked at him. "I get even."

He chuckled and stooped down to grab some cookies and chocolate milk from the bottom shelf. "Then what are we waiting for?"

An hour later, they sprawled on a bed littered with crumbs and empty cartons while they laughed at the latest Billy Crystal comedy.

Her mouth full of crackers, Daphne glanced over at Josh. "Hey, you said you came partly because your grandfather said you couldn't."

He grinned and tossed a pillow at her. "I can see chewed crackers. That's gross."

She deliberately opened her cracker-filled mouth wider and he laughed. She liked making him laugh. "So what was the other reason you came over?"

His gaze was open and uncomplicated, unlike the look any other boy had ever given her. "I thought you might need a friend," he said.

Tears sprang to her eyes and she turned away. "Thanks," she mumbled as Billy Crystal's image blurred.

ADAM HAD SAID they were strong enough to take it. Loren guessed he was right so far, because somehow she'd made it through the night. She'd spent hours battling her twin demons: fear of what might be going on with Josh, and a guilty desire to creep into

Adam's room, beg his forgiveness and spend the rest of the night in his arms.

At last the sky had lightened, setting her free from the imprisoning and tempting darkness. But the long night alone was child's play compared to what lay ahead—a morning spent with Adam, an afternoon assessing the damage to her son.

She washed her face and finger-combed her hair. Her clothes had dried during the night, but as she started to dress she couldn't find her panties. Then she remembered where they were.

She put on her shorts. Then, taking a deep breath, she tapped on his connecting door. Hers had stayed open all night; his had stayed closed. Had he been inclined to come to her, she hadn't wanted any barriers. But he hadn't been so inclined, it seemed. "Adam?"

After a moment, he opened the door. He was fully dressed in the clothes he'd worn the day before. One quick glance into his haggard, unshaven face and intense blue eyes nearly undid her. She looked away before that haunted gaze could draw her in. "I, um, need my panties," she said. "I'll come in and check, if you—"

"Here they are."

She gazed down at his outstretched hand clutching the lacy garment, and her stomach plunged as if she were staring over a precipice. She remembered the way he'd eased the panties down the night before, and how he'd—

"I figured you'd want them."

"Thanks." She grabbed them from his hand and escaped, closing her door. She stood still, catching her breath as if she'd been running, the panties balled in her fist. "I'll be ready in a minute," she called through the door.

"Fine," he called back.

But she was shaking so badly it took more than a minute to remove her shorts, pull on her panties and put her shorts back on. As she fought for composure, she wondered how in hell she would take pictures today. Maybe he'd changed his mind and she wouldn't have to. Maybe they'd be able to fly directly to Sedona and end this agony.

Surely that would be his decision, she told herself as she struggled with the button on the waistband of her shorts. They needed to find out what was happening with Josh and Daphne. Even though Adam had insisted nothing was going on between the two teenagers, he might have doubts he'd been unwilling to let her see.

If they left for Sedona immediately, they could minimize the pain of being together with the wreckage of a doomed relationship scattered around them. Adam might be tough, but everyone had limits. She was very close to reaching hers.

Finally, she was dressed and ready. She walked to the door with more confidence, half-convinced he'd tell her the picture-taking session was off.

She opened the door. He was sitting by the window reading a magazine and didn't look up. While he read, he pinched his earlobe. The familiar gesture reminded her of all the times they'd studied together— or tried to. She'd teased him about his habit of manhandling his earlobe while he read. He'd said he was a tactile person, and suggested if she was worried about his ear, he'd much rather work on various parts of her body, instead. It had become a joke between them, one she'd forgotten until now.

She swallowed the lump in her throat. "Ready to go?"

He glanced up and closed the magazine. "Sure."

When he stood, she faced him with brisk efficiency. "We can be in the air within a half hour. I'm sure you'll agree we should skip the photo session and go straight to Sedona."

He rolled the magazine into a cylinder. "No, I don't agree."

Her heart began to thud with more force. "But...the kids. You need to get back to Daphne. We should find out what—"

"I do need to get back to Daphne, and I will. But if we don't get those shots today, I may not get them at all. Haskett must have realized that once the divorce proceedings were over, I'd start paying more attention to the steel shipments. He'll wind up his operation any day now. I have to act or he'll get away with his scam."

She stared at him. So the nightmare of pain would continue.

His gaze gentled a fraction. "We're only talking about a couple of extra hours. It shouldn't make that much difference with the kids. What's done is probably done. Our arriving home a little earlier won't change much."

"I guess not."

"Are you too upset to take pictures? Is that the problem?"

Pride reared up in her, refusing to allow him to be the stronger one. "If you can fly the plane, I can take the damn pictures."

An emotion flickered in his eyes; a ghost of a smile touched his lips. "Then let's go," he said quietly.

As they left the hotel, the sky arced over them like newly fired pottery with only a slight chip of white marring the rim. Loren knew that by afternoon that chip on the horizon could spawn a whole bank of angry clouds, but by then she and Adam would be back in Sedona. Sedona, where Josh and Daphne waited. Where she'd watch Adam walk out of her life forever.

They worked together silently and smoothly readying 206 Whiskey Foxtrot for takeoff. As Adam taxied the Cessna onto the runway, Loren began cleaning the camera lens. Her exhaustion complicated the task, but she was glad the job took all her concentration. She was better off paying no attention to Adam.

She'd made the mistake of glancing toward the cockpit as he gunned the engine and sent the plane hurtling skyward. With his eyes hidden behind aviator sunglasses, his chin stubbled with a day's growth of beard and his expression grim, he looked like a renegade. If he'd ever feared she could manipulate him, he had nothing to fear now. He looked like a man nobody should provoke, a man who would be dangerous if aroused.

And he is, she thought, her wounded heart aching.

CHAPTER TEN

THE PLANE'S FLIGHT PATH followed the river, glittering like a strip of aluminum foil in the glare of the sun. Loren lifted her headset over her ears as the bridge site appeared, with construction equipment crawling over the riverbank and derricks swinging steel beams into place. She peered through the camera lens as they drew closer. "Tell me what you want," she said into the mouthpiece.

There was a brief hesitation, and she closed her eyes. Bad choice of words.

"A normal grid, to start with," Adam said finally.

"Right." Her reply was too curt, but she couldn't help it. Although his words were innocent enough, the mere sound of his voice coming through the earphones conjured up images of their lovemaking, warming her skin and quickening her breath. No, dammit. She would not do this to herself. It was over.

"The Scorpio trucks are red," he continued, "so look for cabs of any other color. When we find one loaded with steel, we have our evidence. If you see one like that start to move, tell me."

"Okay." She willed herself to forget everything but the job she had to do. "Start with the southeast corner and work your way north. And keep it steady."

"I will."

She shivered. Listening to that voice in her ear for another hour would be torture. She wondered how he was taking it. His profile revealed nothing. Maybe he really was stronger than she and had already closed himself off from her.

She focused and started snapping. As the work began to absorb her, she was gently released from her preoccupation with Adam. Gradually, the identity of the pilot was pushed to the back of her mind, and she began issuing instructions automatically, without thinking who she was commanding. "That's good. Like that. Perfect. Now, again."

His sharp intake of breath brought her crashing back to reality. She froze, missing part of the grid. He wasn't closed off, after all. The radio connection that allowed them to murmur into each other's ears was bothering him as much as it had bothered her. The thought shook her so much she almost missed seeing the truck.

She noticed it just in time. "There!" she called, pressing the shutter button. "A different-colored cab. Deep blue. Pulling a flatbed loaded with steel."

"Did you get it?"

"Yes." Barely.

"Was it moving?"

"I think so. We'll know when you come back across— Okay, there! Yes, it's moving."

"I want a shot of whatever markings are on that truck." His voice resonated with excitement.

"Forget the grid?"

"Yes. Just get that damn truck."

She fought to keep calm. She didn't want to participate in his mood. Emotions could explode beneath her like land mines today, blowing her control to bits. "We should pick them up on the next pass. They're moving north. This time go in lower, bank the plane and I'll take an oblique shot." She gasped as he dived beneath the five-hundred-foot limit. "Adam! Not—"

"Take the pictures."

She took two shots of the side of the truck before he swooped up again.

"Get it?"

"A little lower and I'd be able to count the bugs on his windshield. Dammit, Adam, you—"

"Then hang on. I'm going to act like I'm some crazy guy out for a joyride."

"Shouldn't be too hard. You've already scared the daylights out of—" She swallowed the rest of her sentence and held her stomach as he dived again, banked and dived. The river rushed up to meet them and then she was staring into the cloudless sky again, adrenaline pumping through her. It wasn't really fear she felt. It was excitement, a stimulating rush, a curling tension not unlike desire. She suspected it had a great deal to do with the pilot, who was demonstrating that he flew with the same sense of daring as he made love.

"Now let's gain some altitude and find out where our fellow is taking my steel."

He'd said this in a conversational tone, but Loren picked up the controlled anger beneath the words. She wouldn't want to be in Barnaby Haskett's shoes when Adam confronted him. No doubt his days as a contractor were ended.

"Can you see the truck?" he asked.

She looked through the viewfinder and spotted it pulling a rooster tail of dust as it inched along a dirt road. "Yes. Heading for Highway 68."

"Guess we'll hang around up here for a while. When he gets close to the intersection, so we can identify a direction, we'll take a shot of that. Then we'll follow him as far as we can."

She panicked. He was extending the time they'd have to be together. "I don't think that's necessary. We've got the incriminating shots."

"I do think it's necessary. If I know where he's hauling the stuff, the authorities may be able to arrest a whole network of crooks. I doubt if I'm the only one who's had steel pirated."

He made sense. How could she argue, when a little detective work now might help bring criminals to justice? But the wire of tension within her was tight and humming. She needed to get away from this man as soon as possible.

"Did you catch the name on the side of the cab?" he asked.

"Ace Trucking. Has a big wind foil on top."

"Are you sure? Trucks that pull flatbed trailers don't usually have wind foils."

"This one does."

"Then it probably means the driver's free-lancing, somebody hungry for some quick money with no other connection to the operation. That's okay. We have photographic proof that steel is leaving that site. If we can find out where it's being delivered, that, along with the shortages Haskett's been calling in, should be enough to nail him.''

Loren wondered what would happen then. With Haskett exposed as a thief, maybe Anita wouldn't want to marry him. Maybe she'd beg for Adam's forgiveness. And maybe Adam, for Daphne's sake, would grant it. If Loren had harbored any doubts about her decision to keep far away from Adam, they disappeared with that thought.

"Truck's at the intersection," she reported, giving him the coordinates. He circled, guiding the plane lower. She took a shot of the truck making a right turn.

"Might be headed for Kingman or Vegas," Adam said.

"Or Seattle," she reminded him. "We may not be able to follow it all the way to its destination."

"I know. I'll keep track of the fuel gauge."

"That would be nice. Running out of gas at ten thousand feet leaves a lot to be desired." She sounded bitchy. Too bad.

"I haven't run out of gas since that time you and I got stranded at the Flagstaff Observatory."

Damn, he would have to bring up that particular night. Nobody had believed they'd really run out of gas, which in fact they had. But they'd also lingered in his Capri for quite a while before trekking to the gas station. She tried to stem the memories that flooded through her, but it was no use. She felt the strength of his arms, the hunger of his mouth, the urgency of his caress, old memories forming tributaries from the torrent of passion he'd given her last night.

She grasped at the only distraction available, and peered through the camera lens, looking for the truck. She found it. "Our guy's approaching the next intersection."

"Give me the coordinates."

She did, and then snapped a picture of the truck turning left toward Las Vegas.

"I'm taking us up to about seven thousand feet," Adam said. "If I throttle back to about sixty, we can follow him right down the road."

She didn't like anything about that plan, but she didn't have much choice except to go along with it.

"You okay back there?" he asked.

Just terrific. "I'm fine."

"We won't need any more pictures until he delivers the steel somewhere, so you can take off the headset and relax awhile if you want."

"Thanks. Guess I will." Relax. Sure. She took off her headset and got to her knees to gaze out the side window. Beneath her, mountains rumpled the landscape like love-tossed sheets. A few innocuous white clouds settled against them like feather pillows strewn over a bed.

She looked away, cursing the sensuous images. While she was at it, she cursed the capricious weather. If they'd had a morning like this yesterday, Josh and Daphne wouldn't be a concern. On the other hand, Adam wouldn't have made love to her. And despite the pain, she wouldn't want to erase that memory. If she could go back in time and change the weather, change the outcome, she doubted she would.

FOR ANOTHER HOUR, Loren monitored the progress of
the dark blue truck while Adam cruised above the
highway. Eventually, the road slipped into the crevice
that snaked toward Hoover Dam. Even from the air
the dam was imposing, fitting into the canyon like a
giant ax blade, cutting side up.

To the left of the dam stretched the subdued Colorado River, its harnessed waters supplying electricity
to cities as far away as Los Angeles. To the right, held
in place more than seven hundred feet above the
riverbed, the waters of Lake Mead flashed like liquid
silver poured into the copper mold of surrounding
canyon walls.

Traffic slowed to a crawl going across the dam.

"Keep an eye on him," Adam called over the drone
of the engine. "I'm taking us up to seventy-five hundred feet so I won't have to deal with air-traffic control in Vegas."

Using the camera lens as a monocular, Loren did as
he asked. There seemed little doubt that the truck was
headed for Las Vegas. Once out of the twisting canyon, the road widened, becoming a main artery into
the city, and keeping track of the semi became more
difficult. Both she and Adam put their headsets back
on for more effective communication. Adam slowed
the plane as much as possible, yet they outdistanced
the truck twice and had to double back to pick it up
again.

"What we need is a chopper," Adam said. "This
thing doesn't hover worth a damn."

"Can you fly one?" Loren wondered if he'd done that in the war. She kept her attention focused on the road below them.

"Not very well. Is your dad still certified?"

"Yes." She thought how the vehicles moving beneath them looked like colorful bits of debris on a conveyor belt. She was about to mention the notion to Adam, then kept silent. They didn't need to connect on that level. Finally, she picked out the dark blue cab with its elaborate wind foil crowning the roof. "He's approaching the Strip, Adam."

"See if he turns down it. That steel could be going into a new casino."

"Or a new office building in Seattle," she reminded him.

"Yeah, but I can't picture Haskett making that kind of long-distance connection. Selling the stuff to a builder in the nearest big town, which this is, makes more sense for a two-bit criminal like him."

"The truck's moving into the right lane," she reported. "And there he goes onto the Strip. Either he plans to gamble or you've guessed right."

"Hot damn." Adam swept the plane in another circle over the canyon of hotels lining the Las Vegas Strip.

Loren focused on the carnival-like street, where even during the day hotels glittered with millions of lights as marquees flashed the names of entertainers, bargain dinners and recent jackpot winners. "There he is." Despite her determination not to become involved in the excitement, her heart beat faster. "He's turning into a construction area. You've got him."

"*We've* got him. Now let's take his picture."

"From here?" She readied the camera.

"No. I'm going down."

"What about air-traffic control?"

"I'll be fast."

"Adam, if there's a fine—"

"I'll pay it."

"Just how close are you planning to get?"

"Very."

A jolt of guilty excitement shot through her. Darned if she didn't like being bad with this man. "If you take us below a thousand feet you're going to be in megatrouble."

"If I get caught, I'll say the altimeter went haywire for a while. See how this pass looks to you, and then we'll go in for the kill. I'd love to know how much of that building is being held up by Scorpio steel."

"When we print the pictures, we may be able to blow them up enough to see your company ID on the girders." The skeleton of the casino rose beneath her lens. "Wings steady, Adam. That's it. Good. I've got the truck in one of the shots."

"Now I'm taking the same flight line at five hundred feet."

"Five hundred feet? Have you lost your mind?"

"No, I've lost my steel," he said evenly. "You'll only get one try at this altitude, so make it count."

"Who do you think you are, Luke Skywalker? You could lose your license!"

"I'll take that chance. Get ready. We're coming in."

"So I see." She snapped frantically as the structure loomed beneath her. the spires of steel seeming to reach for the plane like bony fingers. Then she saw only sky as Adam shot upward. She pulled off her headset and listened to the chatter on the radio, head pounding, expecting any minute to hear a barking challenge from the tower. None came.

She took a deep breath and replaced her headset. "You are one lucky cuss, Adam."

"Sometimes." When they reached seventy-five hundred feet once more, he banked the plane and pointed it southeast, for Sedona. "Did you get the pictures?"

"Yes."

"With good detail?"

"Well, I don't know," she said wryly. "There was a fly on one of the girders, and I'm not sure if we'll be able to count the hairs on his little legs. But we might."

"Want to go back for another look?"

"Don't even joke about it. You are positively crazy."

"I just did what the situation called for, Loren," he said quietly.

And do you always know what that is? she wanted to ask. But that would open a line of inquiry best left closed.

They'd worked well together, she thought. Mission accomplished. She'd been aiming for that goal for the past three days. Now it was achieved, and the sense of adventure and excitement drained away, leaving her emptier than she'd ever felt in her life.

AN ATTENDANT BROUGHT the cordless phone to Anita Riordan as she lay on a massage table having her skin buffed with a mixture of oils and crushed pearls. She lifted her head, grown heavy from the deep massage she'd had prior to the buffing process. With effort she placed the phone to her ear.

"Just letting you know we spotted a suspicious plane over the bridge site this morning," Barnaby said. "Then we got a call from one of our drivers about some nut buzzing the casino site. Same color plane. I figure it was Adam and his aerial-photography friend."

Anita's facial muscles contracted as she frowned. She made a conscious effort to relax them. "So what are you going to do about it? One more delivery and we're finished. It would be a shame to—"

"Don't worry. I'll deal with it."

Anita swore under her breath. She should have dragged out the divorce proceedings another few months, but she'd become so tired of the endless haggling, and Adam hadn't seemed the least suspicious about the steel shortages. But he was suspicious now. And she was far from convinced that Barnaby could handle him.

"How will you deal with it?" she asked.

"I'll get the film. Without pictures he won't be able to prove anything."

"And you think he'll just hand you the film?"

"Don't worry, Anita. I'll get it."

She felt a headache coming on. She'd have to have her shoulders remassaged. "See that you do," she said, and punched the disconnect button on the phone before handing it to the attendant and repositioning herself on the table. She wished she had more confidence in Barnaby's mental capacities. And less fear of Adam's.

CHAPTER ELEVEN

HE'D ACCOMPLISHED his objective, Adam thought as red spires appeared in the distance and he contacted the Sedona tower for landing instructions. He had the evidence he needed to put Haskett behind bars. Of course, in the process he'd ruined his chances with Loren and alienated his daughter, but who said life was perfect? He gritted his teeth in frustration.

Well, he might as well tie up the loose ends with Loren and get on with pacifying Daphne. He hoped to hell she hadn't slept with Josh, not that he planned to ask that question. As he'd told Loren last night, he believed Daphne had a right to her privacy, just as he had a right to his.

Anita had announced to him during Daphne's senior year that their daughter was on birth-control pills and sexually active. He'd pushed himself into one awkward conversation with Daphne about requiring boys to use condoms, and she'd informed him loftily that she knew all about the spread of AIDS and wouldn't dream of risking her life so some guy could have a better time.

So he wasn't concerned about Daphne, but he didn't relish the idea that his daughter might have initiated Loren's son into the mysteries of sex. Josh probably needed to be initiated—Adam just didn't want his daughter to be the one doing it. The real kicker would be if Josh and Daphne started dating in earnest. He didn't even want to think about that possibility.

No, he needed to cut things off clean with Loren, because that was what she wanted. He wasn't sure how he'd find the strength to walk away after what they'd shared the night before, but he would find it.

So he'd just take his pictures and go.

And then it hit him. They weren't pictures yet. Terrific. He'd been so caught up in his personal turmoil, he'd neglected to figure in the film processing. And he wanted those prints right away.

"Do you use a photo lab in Sedona?" he asked.

"No. I mail the film to Phoenix or take it down if I'm in a rush."

Damn.

"I might be able to do that for you today," she said. "Then I'd have the prints back later tonight. It all depends on whether I can talk the lab people into working overtime on it."

He imagined her driving alone to Phoenix with the film. He didn't like it. He doubted they'd been identified today, but there was always the possibility.

Besides, he didn't really want the film out of his possession for long. If the lab had been in Sedona, he could have subtly kept tabs on the film. But he couldn't let Loren take the risk of driving down to Phoenix with it by herself.

God, this would really louse up his standing with Daphne. But he couldn't see a way around it. "I'm going to drive you to the lab this afternoon."

"No, you're not."

"Yes, I am. Now, if you'll excuse me, I have a tricky landing to make." He could imagine how she looked, her mouth compressed into a determined line, her chin jutting forward in defiance. But he figured she was probably more frightened than angry at the prospect of spending more time with him.

If he could have spared her that, he would have. If he could have spared Daphne the disappointment, he would have. It seemed no matter what he did, he ended up the bad guy. Good thing he had broad shoulders.

He throttled the plane back as they swooped in toward the black swath of runway perched on a mesa. The wheels touched down with a sweet gliding motion. He enjoyed flying such a well-maintained aircraft. He and Walt got along just fine, and he liked Josh, too. For all any of that mattered now.

As they approached the hangar, he saw the black Geo parked in front of it, and as they drew closer he took in the tableau. Josh had his head stuck under a cowling as usual, but Walt glanced up at their approach. Daphne stood by the door of the hangar in a pair of borrowed coveralls. She held a wrench and was tapping it into her palm as she gazed at them. She looked as if she'd like to hit somebody with it.

Adam turned off the engine. Time to face the music.

"You are absolutely not coming with me to Phoenix," Loren said.

"I need the film developed now and you're not going alone. It's possible we attracted some attention, and I'm not sure who we're dealing with. I'm riding shotgun on the way to Phoenix."

"You're being melodramatic."

He turned in his seat. "Look, I know you don't want me along. I know Daphne will hate it, too. But I'm not putting your life at risk so everybody can be happy. Please don't let stupid pride get in the way of your safety, Loren."

He watched the taunt take effect, as he'd guessed it would. He added another. "You can handle the trip with me, can't you?"

Her brown eyes gleamed with defiance. "Of course. I just thought I'd free you up to be with Daphne."

"That can't be done right now. I'll talk to her."

"And tell her the whole story."

He desperately wanted to, but she could still contact Haskett and warn him. He'd be a fool to trust her in her present frame of mind. "Not yet."

"Okay." Loren shrugged. "Your funeral."

His smile felt tight. "Yeah, that is the way it looks, isn't it?"

"And for God's sake, don't come around and help me out of the plane," she warned.

"Wouldn't dream of it." He opened his door and hopped down.

Walt approached, wiping his hands on a grease-smudged rag. "Get some good pictures?"

"Exactly what I wanted." Adam glanced at Daphne, who hadn't left her sentry position. Josh continued to look absorbed in his work. "How's everything here?"

"Okay." Walt nodded. "At breakfast Josh asked if Daphne could help around here today. I said she could."

"That was decent of you, Walt," Adam said. He was glad to hear that Josh had at least been home for breakfast and that Walt wasn't the sort to bear grudges against either Josh or Daphne. "Guess I'll go say hello to my daughter."

He liked the effect of the coveralls, and not just because they were more modest than what she usually wore. With them on, she looked more serious about life and her place in it. If only she'd accept Loren, and Loren would accept her, all sorts of possibilities would open up. But Daphne didn't look open to any possibilities at the moment.

"Hi, Daph," he said.

"Looks like you could use a shave, Dad." It wasn't delivered as a teasing remark.

He tensed for the battle. "As you know, I hadn't expected to stay overnight."

"Or so you said." She slapped the wrench against her palm.

"You're a pilot. You knew what the weather was like."

There was no give in her. "I think you flew into that weather hoping to get stuck."

Adam sighed and ran a hand through his hair.

"So what happens now, Dad?" Smack, smack went the wrench. "Are you going to spend the rest of the vacation with her?"

"No." He met his daughter's rebellious gaze. "Loren and I are not involved with each other." At least not anymore, he amended silently.

"Could've fooled me."

He resisted the urge to pull the wrench out of her hand. The rhythmic slap of it against her palm was getting to him. "However, I'm taking her down to Phoenix this afternoon so we can get the film processed and developed."

"Are you really? I suppose she needs you to show her the way down there? I mean, since you're not involved, or anything, that's the only explanation."

He expelled a breath of air in one sharp puff. "I need to personally supervise the processing of the film."

"Sure you do." The wrench slapped against her hand harder.

"Daphne, dammit, I—" He struggled with his anger. "You're welcome to come with us if you want," he said in desperation.

Her laugh was harsh, echoing against the corrugated metal walls of the surrounding hangar. "Now that's an offer I can hardly bear to refuse." She balanced the wrench across two spread fingers. Finally, she looked up. "But I will refuse," she said. "You see, Josh and I have plans."

His stomach clenched. "To do what?"

"There's an outdoor rock concert in Flagstaff tonight. I sort of figured you wouldn't want me hanging around, so Josh and me, we made plans to go."

"Daphne, I do want you around. Once this film's developed . . ." He paused. Once the film was developed, he'd want to deliver it to the authorities, which meant they'd have to leave Sedona in the morning. His "vacation" with Daphne was officially over.

"Yeah, just as I thought," she said, her eyes suspiciously bright. "Mom sure has you pegged. She warned me not to expect you to give up business for me. But as usual, I had to find out for myself."

He felt as if she'd been slapping him on the side of the head with the wrench. He could make her a promise that after he finished with this problem, they'd take a trip together. She wouldn't believe him. His credibility had never been very good, especially with the digs Anita had been getting in. Now it was shot to hell.

"Have a good time at the concert," he said with a sigh. "How's the money holding out? Do you need any more?"

"I don't need anything from you, Dad." She turned and walked into the hangar.

"SO THEY'RE GOING to a rock concert together," Loren said as she sat in the passenger seat of the Geo headed for Phoenix, the film in a canister at her feet. They put the convertible top up against the possibility of rain, and it fluttered occasionally in the wind.

"Walt said Josh was there for breakfast this morning." Adam took a curve a little faster than she would have liked, but she decided not to comment. She had other fish to fry.

"That only means Josh didn't stay with Daphne until sunrise." She crumpled up the wrapper from the hamburger they'd grabbed at a fast-food outlet and stuffed it into the carry-out bag. "That leaves a whole lot of hours unaccounted for."

He handed her his empty soda cup and she added that to the bag. The crunch of the paper sack as she shoved it beside her seat seemed unnaturally loud.

Adam tapped his thumb against the steering wheel. "Did you ask him about what happened last night?"

"There was no chance." Besides that, she'd been thinking about what Adam had said about privacy. Her parents hadn't quizzed her when she was that age. Once they were sure she understood about birth control, they'd left her alone to make her own decisions. Maybe that was what was bothering her. Taking stock of those decisions, she wasn't terrifically happy about the outcome. Not that she'd trade Josh for the world, but . . . last night had shown her what she'd missed by being pigheaded.

"But you believe they're having sex," Adam said, breaking into her thoughts.

"Don't you?"

He frowned. "I'm not quite as ready to assume it as you are. But if you're sure, I hope your son carries condoms."

She decided not to dignify his remark with a response.

"Well, does he?"

"I haven't the foggiest idea!" she snapped. Her indignation gave her the courage to ask a question that had been eating at her for hours. "And speaking of that, how come you were so well prepared for our 'spontaneous' behavior last night?"

He grimaced. "I was wondering if you'd call me on that."

"Consider yourself called." When he didn't answer right away, she glanced sideways at him.

He caught her glance and gave a little shrug. "I don't have a good answer. I was buying a magazine and telling myself we didn't have a chance in hell of making love. The condoms were there by the counter. I picked them up on impulse. I really had no idea I'd use them. I felt dumb getting them, to tell the truth, like someone buying sunscreen on a rainy day."

She thought about his explanation while she stared out the window at storm clouds boiling up from the southwest. They mushroomed as if attached to a helium tank. How appropriate that she'd meet Adam during the most volatile season of the year.

"I suppose you don't believe me."

"Actually, I do."

"Well, that's something." His sigh was deep. "Now, if only Daphne believed that I didn't set out to hurt her."

She wondered if he realized how vulnerable he sounded just then. She didn't want to feel sympathy, wasn't even sure he deserved it, but her heart ached at this evidence of how much he agonized over his daughter. "I still think you should tell her about Haskett and the steel shipments. The sooner the better. How can you expect her to understand if she doesn't have the facts?"

He gripped the steering wheel. "Why can't she just trust me without having all the facts?"

Maybe because you haven't built a relationship with her, Loren thought, but she didn't say that. "Because she's eighteen," she said. "Hard to take things on faith at that age."

"That may be part of it." His voice grew bitter. "The other part is she doesn't think much of her father."

Loren didn't know what to say to ease his pain. Perhaps there was nothing to say. As she glanced out the window, she noticed how fast the Geo was hurtling across the mesa, and she leaned over to check the gauges on the dash.

He frowned at her inspection. "What?"

"You're speeding."

With a muttered oath, he slowed the car. Then he unexpectedly swerved onto an exit that led to a viewpoint area. One other car was there, and all three occupants were madly snapping pictures.

"Where are you going?"

"Just give me a minute. I'll be fine." He parked the car, opened the door and got out. Then he walked over to a low rock wall and stood, his hands in his jeans pockets.

She sat there, debating the wisdom of getting out, of involving herself further in his torment with his daughter. It was unwise. She and Adam had achieved some distance between them, and that was the way she wanted to keep it. But he looked so alone, so desperate for answers.

She unfastened her seat belt and climbed out of the car. The camera buffs had left. Beyond the wall shimmered layers of shadowed canyons etched in purples, blues and grays. Storm clouds cushioned the horizon. Adam stood facing them, the hot summer breeze ruffling his hair.

She stood beside him, not touching him, directing her attention to the same distant point on the horizon. He didn't overtly acknowledge her presence, yet she was sure he was aware of her.

"She didn't even ask me to teach her to fly," he said.

"What do you mean?"

"She hired somebody else to teach her. God, I would have given anything to..." He swallowed.

Needing to do something, Loren put a hand on his arm. "You should tell her that, too."

"I don't...I don't know how."

Her heart wrenched. "Just tell her," she murmured. "It doesn't matter how you do it. Just tell her. Don't worry about your pride or your image." She rubbed her hand along his arm, offering comfort. "Let down your guard, let her see that you need her, and you'll be fine."

Slowly he turned to her, his eyes unreadable behind the sunglasses. Then he took them off, and she saw a dark flame burning in their blue depths. "Do you have any idea...?"

Her mouth went dry and she couldn't speak.

"God, Loren." Without preamble he pulled her into his arms and his glasses clattered to the pavement.

There was nothing gentle about the embrace or his kiss. They seemed forged of a molten substance within him that had escaped the taming influences of civilization. A wildness born of all they'd shared in the past two days took hold of her, too, and with a moan she deepened the kiss and pressed her body against his.

The heat of the afternoon seared them, bonding them together. His beard rasped against her face as she ran her hands over his back, across his buttocks, down his thighs. He crushed her closer, his tongue delving into her mouth again and again.

When he released her, they backed away from each other, both gasping.

He took a long, shuddering breath and ran his hand through his hair. "I guess it would be better... if you didn't touch me anymore. I know you were only trying to help, but my emotions are pretty raw right now, and I..." He didn't finish the sentence, but the primitive glow in his eyes finished it for him.

She brought the back of her hand to her bruised mouth.

He leaned down and retrieved his sunglasses. "Let's go," he said softly, replacing the sunglasses and covering, temporarily, the blaze in his eyes.

CHAPTER TWELVE

THEY RODE the rest of the way to Phoenix in silence, sliding down out of the mountains into the sunbaked outskirts of the city. There was nothing to say, nothing to do but get through this the best way they could, with the least amount of pain. Adam was right, Loren thought. Her touch had been an offer of friendship, but it was too late for that. They'd destroyed any hope of mere friendship the night before.

The concrete freeways sluiced them through Phoenix traffic along with hundreds of other cars as rush hour wound to a close. Midway through town they left the freeway and Loren gave Adam directions to the photo lab. She'd called before they'd left Sedona and sweet-talked Bill, the lab technician, into a rush job that would mean his having to work overtime. Adam had agreed to any price Bill wanted to charge.

Bill greeted Loren with a broad smile and looked questioningly at Adam. She introduced him as a client and Bill looked pleased with the information.

"Just give us a couple of hours," Bill said, taking the canister of film.

A couple of hours. Loren realized she'd forgotten about the block of time they'd have to fill until the prints were ready. How in hell would she and Adam get through another two hours together with nothing to do and tension still thick between them?

She thought quickly as they returned to the Geo and climbed in.

"Where to now?" he asked, not looking at her as he pushed the key into the ignition. Apparently, he had no ideas, either.

She thought quickly. They needed to be around other people, but she wasn't hungry, and strolling a mall window-shopping sounded like a particularly inappropriate way to spend time. Lovers did that sort of thing. Finally, she latched onto a possibility. "Does your plant operate around the clock?"

"Yes." He glanced at her. "Why?"

"How about a tour?"

He looked startled. "I doubt you'd find it very interesting."

"You'd be surprised what I find interesting. Besides, do you have a better idea?"

He gazed at her for a long time, a flicker of longing struggling for life in his blue eyes. Then it seemed he resolutely tamped it down. "No."

"Then let's go."

"All right." He drove toward an industrial area on the outskirts of town as the sun dipped behind the mountains to the west. Turning off the Geo's air-conditioning, he opened his window.

Loren followed suit. The rain that had threatened for most of the afternoon had never fallen, and she watched the blush on the swollen clouds deepen from peach to tangerine. As darkness settled around them, the brilliant sunset colors disappeared. Only a band of terra-cotta remained, etched by the jagged line of mountains as if it were a piece of Indian pottery.

The steelyard glowed in the distance, lit up by a circle of pole lights. As they drew closer, Loren heard the clank of machinery and smelled the metallic fumes of hot steel. Equipment and storage areas towered three stories high, dwarfing the masonry office building in front of the property.

They pulled into a parking spot marked Riordan. As Adam turned off the Geo's engine, metal gates to their right rolled back and a semi came through. The giant front grill glittered in the overhead lights, and the black scorpion logo on the door of the bloodred cab stood out bold as a pirate's flag.

The truck's air brakes gasped as the vehicle paused before entering the street. Loren noticed that the front wheel-well was nearly as large as the Geo. With a thunderous rumble, the truck moved into the street, giving Loren a view of the flatbed trailer it hauled. She recognized the pyramid-shaped load as a stack of ribbed reinforcing bars, except that she'd never before seen any as thick as a man's forearm and as long as telephone poles.

She turned to Adam, who was watching her with a bemused expression. "This is quite an impressive layout," she said.

"I guess it is." He didn't sound particularly proud of his accomplishments.

"You bet it is." She couldn't blame him for being disenchanted with his business success, but she hated to see him think it meant nothing. Perhaps this tour had been her instinctive desire to show him the value of what he'd single-handedly built.

Adam opened the car door. "Come on. Let's go in."

The main office was locked. Adam opened the door and flipped on an overhead light before ushering Loren inside. The receptionist's, secretary's and bookkeeper's desks were vacant, and soundproofing panels muffled the machinery noise. "When I said we worked round the clock, I didn't mean the office personnel, too," he explained. "Just the people in the yard."

"Oh. Of course." Yet that was exactly what she'd thought, and now they were in this very quiet office all alone, just what she'd tried to avoid. But a tour would include this part of the plant, too, and she couldn't insist he take her out of here, as if she were some scared little rabbit who didn't trust him—or herself.

"My office is this way." He led her to the back of the building and turned on another light. Then he leaned in the doorway and allowed her to explore.

The office was windowless and paneled in dark walnut. She walked over and put her hand on his massive desk, which held several stacks of papers. A framed picture was propped in one corner. Loren walked around the desk to confirm it was of Daphne, probably her high school senior portrait.

Then she glanced at the wall opposite the desk and froze. On the wall, in a position where Adam would have to see it every day, hung the shot she'd taken of sunrise at Red Rock Crossing, the same photograph hanging over her father's fireplace. "Where did you get that?"

His casual pose didn't change. "Your father had it made for me. I wrote to your parents after I came back from Nam and told them how much I loved that picture. Walt didn't bother asking you for the negative because he knew you wouldn't approve of my having this. He just borrowed the negative from your files and had the print made without telling you."

"And he still hasn't told me. I didn't know he was so good at keeping a secret." She stood there looking at the picture, unable to comprehend that, because of it, Adam must have thought of her nearly every day for more than twenty years. Her spine tingled, as if she'd seen a ghost. "Did you tell Anita where this picture came from?"

"Not exactly, but I think she guessed it had some deep significance connected with a woman. She started a campaign to redecorate my office and wanted to throw it out. I wouldn't let her and finally admitted I'd been there when a friend took the shot, although I didn't identify you by name."

Loren knew why he hadn't told Anita her name. It was the same reason she'd never spoken Adam's name to Jack, either, in some show of loyalty that probably made no sense at all. Each of them had wanted to keep their memories private.

"So you kept the picture."

"Yeah." His mouth twisted. "She gave up the decorating idea. In fact, she hardly ever came down here after that. I think she had the final piece of the puzzle that explained my behavior, but she never probed into it again. I guess she didn't relish the thought of what she might find out."

Loren felt a stab of pity for Anita, who'd tried to fight a phantom lover who seemed to have more hold over her husband than she had. "It's not so hard to understand why she might have turned to someone else."

"No." Adam looked sad. "I don't really blame her. And worse luck for her, she chose a crook for a lover. I dread the day she finds that out. But I can't just let him go because I feel guilty about the way I treated Anita."

"No, you can't just let him go." She glanced at the picture again. "I had no idea, Adam."

He studied her silently. "Someone came into the office once and said the picture had all kinds of power."

"Power? I admit it's a decent shot, but—"

"The technique's good, but it's the subject matter that's supposed to have power. I'm sure you've heard of the vortices that are said to exist in Sedona."

"I have, but I wouldn't expect you to pay attention to New Age mysticism." She remembered Jack had tried to convince her that there were centers of power in the red rocks surrounding the town. She'd been too busy working to support them all to pay attention to his fixations.

"I keep an open mind," Adam said. "Especially after this person told me Red Rock Crossing is supposed to be a vortex."

She was desperate to break the mood developing between them. They were too vulnerable for this. "It's just a picture, Adam."

He looked at her and his expression slowly closed down. "Yeah, I guess you're right. Ready to go on with the tour?"

It was either that or lock the office door and hurl herself into his arms. That wouldn't be fair to either of them. "Yes, I'm ready."

BARNABY HASKETT was having a bad day. First of all, Anita hadn't trusted him to handle this little glitch his own way. She'd gone and called their Las Vegas contact. Now Barnaby had to report in—like some little kid—to the Vegas construction office.

And the news he had to report wasn't wonderful. He found a pay phone in downtown Sedona and made his call while he wiped the sweat from his forehead with a bandanna. "Yeah," he said to the guy who answered the phone. "This is Haskett reporting in."

He waited while they transferred him to another line. He'd never been given names, just phone numbers. Checks with illegible signatures drawn on out-of-state bank accounts arrived in the mail regularly in return for the steel shipments. The checks had never bounced.

Barnaby had deposited them all in the account he and Anita had opened last year in the Bahamas. That money had been added to the hefty sum she'd received from Riordan in the divorce settlement. Once Anita sold the Fountain Hills house and added the proceeds to the account, they'd have more money than

Barnaby had ever dreamed of having. With Anita's expensive tastes, it might not be enough, but it was a good start.

Barnaby stared at the ruddy cliffs that rose across the street from where he stood. He'd always hated those damned red rocks looming over the town. The color was too intense. Made him nervous.

"What's the situation, Haskett?" barked a voice on the other end of the line.

"I've run into a few snags," he said.

"Like what?"

"I missed Loren Stanfield. She'd left for Phoenix by the time I tracked down Icarus Enterprises, which is her company. It's located in a hangar at the airport. I guess they repair planes there, too."

"Did you find out when she'll be back?"

"I couldn't go in there. Daphne Riordan, Riordan's daughter, was hanging around, and she'd recognize me. So I left and called you."

"Finally you're showing some sense. We don't want Riordan alerted any more than he already is."

"I know that!" Barnaby snapped.

His comment was ignored. "While you've been fumbling around, we made some inquiries," the contact said. "Loren Stanfield's divorced, with an eighteen-year-old son named Joshua."

Barnaby recalled the scene he'd glimpsed briefly in the airplane hangar before getting the hell out of Daphne's line of vision. "Yeah, that was probably him in there working with Daphne. Some older guy was there, too."

"Loren Stanfield's father, Walt."

"Could be."

"Keep track of the son," ordered the nameless voice. "We may need to know where he is."

Barnaby was confused. "Why? He doesn't know anything about this."

"Just keep track of him. And don't approach Loren Stanfield until we tell you to."

Barnaby mopped his forehead. "Look, I had a plan, okay? I was going to pose as a guy interested in hiring her, find out where she kept everything she was processing and go back tonight and take the negatives and prints. Simple."

His plan was greeted with brief, mirthless laughter.

"What's so damn funny?"

"Keep track of the son. That's all you have to do for now." The line went dead.

Barnaby held the receiver away from his ear and looked at it. "That's all you have to do for now," he mimicked in falsetto. He grimaced and slammed the phone into its cradle. "They act like I'm some friggin' robot," he muttered as he stalked to his car.

But he kept track of the son. An hour later, he reported that Joshua Stanfield, driving a 1981 green-and-white Suburban, had picked up Daphne Riordan at Los Arboles resort. The happy couple had made two stops, one at a McDonald's drive-through, and one at a gas station, before heading north up Oak Creek Canyon. While the Suburban took on gas, Barnaby had leaned against the station wall pretending to read a newspaper, which concealed his face. He'd overheard Daphne tell the station attendant they were going to an outdoor rock concert in Flagstaff.

As he reported all this, Barnaby felt quite proud of himself. He received no praise from the voice on the other end.

CHAPTER THIRTEEN

THE PRINTS WERE still warm from the dryer and
smelled of developing fluid when Loren and Adam
spread them out on the counter at the photo lab. Loren
sniffed appreciatively. She always associated the smell
with the excitement she felt every time she saw the results of her photographic efforts.

Bill hung around, looking curious as she and Adam
stood side by side at the counter, careful not to touch
each other as they started examining the grid pictures
and the first shot of the truck. Loren borrowed a
magnifying glass from Bill and compared that truck
with the one pictured at each intersection. The truck
appeared to be the same one she'd photographed in the
midst of Las Vegas traffic.

"You look," she said, handing the magnifying glass
to Adam.

He positioned the instrument over each print. "It's
the same truck, all right." His voice sounded controlled and unemotional. "Good job."

"Thanks." She cleared her throat and focused on
the prints. "Here are the shots I took over the casino
construction site." She pushed the others out of the
way and brought two pictures forward. In one, the
truck was small, but recognizable. Then she looked at

the shot taken from five hundred feet, with the girders of the high rise directly beneath them.

"Let's see that." Adam held the magnifying glass steady. "Well, that's all I need. Even if we'd missed the truck somehow, this picture takes care of everything. Look here."

He grew careless and their arms brushed. They both drew back as if burned. She calmed her racing pulse.

"See that double S etched at the end of that beam?" he said. "That's my mark. It's my steel, Loren."

She wondered if someone looking into her heart would find a similar mark there.

Adam examined the print again. "There's the proof. That bastard took my steel and sold it to whoever's building this casino."

She suspected he'd channeled some of his anger and frustration over their relationship into the steel theft. In any case, from the timbre of Adam's voice, Barnaby Haskett would soon feel the sting of Scorpio Steel.

"What next?" she asked.

He began stacking the prints. "Let's take all this back to Sedona. Negatives, film, everything. There's a wall safe in my room at the resort. I'll keep it there tonight and bring it back to Phoenix tomorrow. I couldn't get any action on these now, anyway."

Loren reached for the pile of prints. "Let me. Professional pride makes me want these stacked in order."

He relinquished the prints, glancing at them with satisfaction. "You really did a fantastic job," he said quietly.

"She's the best," commented Bill from the other side of the counter.

Loren looked up. She'd almost forgotten the technician was there. "So are you, Bill," she said with a smile. "I appreciate your agreeing to stay and do these tonight."

Bill nodded, which dislodged his glasses. He pushed them more firmly onto the bridge of his nose. "Sounds like it was important."

"It was," Adam said, reaching for his wallet. "Let me settle up."

While Adam paid, Loren finished arranging the pictures in order and placed them, along with the special ten-inch negatives, in a large envelope with a clasp. She and Adam thanked Bill again as they left.

"Here you are," Loren said, handing the envelope to Adam as they walked out the door into the warm July night. "After all we went through to get these, I hope you take good care of them."

"I intend to."

Silence settled between them as they began the return trip. They'd driven several miles before Adam broke it. "That lab technician has a crush on you." It sounded like an accusation.

"I'm aware of that."

"I just wondered if you knew is all."

"I knew."

"And? Have you gone out with him?"

She turned to him, her patience exhausted. "Adam, I do believe you're getting into matters that are none of your business."

He swore softly to himself in the darkness. "No, they aren't," he said at last. "Old habits die hard, I guess."

She didn't respond.

After a short while, he spoke again. "Listen, I'll bet you're hungry. Should we grab something to eat?"

"I'm not really hungry, Adam. Let's just get back."

ADAM BATTLED conflicting emotions as they rode in silence, leaving the myriad lights of Phoenix behind and climbing steadily up the sides of the darkened foothills toward Sedona. Once he glanced over at Loren. In the dim light from the dash, he could see her eyes were closed, her head back against the headrest. He didn't think she was asleep. Her body looked too rigid for that. So she was hiding from him and wishing their time together was over, no doubt.

And wasn't that what he wanted, too? But the closer they got to Sedona, the more he wondered if he did want that. Maybe it would be easier to drop her off at her house and drive off, but his heart rebelled at the idea. Like a condemned man, he searched for a way to buy time. It wasn't a logical need and would probably cause him more pain, but logic wasn't his long suit right now.

"Look, I hate our breaking things off between us so abruptly," he said into the void that had developed between them. "Why don't we both get cleaned up a bit, and I'll take you out for dinner?" In the silence, he heard her swallow hard. "I know what we've said before, about needing to get away from each other, but the fact is . . . that's not true for me. I'd like . . . a little more time.''

Her reply sounded strained. "Why?"

"I don't know. I realize it doesn't make sense, but then, nothing has recently. We've had a rough couple of days. Couldn't we just have a nice dinner and say goodbye like friends?"

"We can't be friends. We've established that, remember?"

"Loren—"

"You're prolonging the agony, Adam. Let me go. Let the idea of *us* go, too. Please."

He couldn't argue with that heartfelt plea, but panic grew in him as he envisioned a lifetime without Loren in it. But that's what she wanted, he reminded himself. Total silence between them. *No!* his heart cried. "I don't even know where you live," he said, his voice remarkably steady.

"Same place. With Dad."

"I wondered." He followed the familiar route to her house. Taking her home and leaving her there felt wrong, but he couldn't very well force her to spend the rest of the evening with him. "I'm a little surprised Walt kept the place," he said, wanting to keep her talking just to hear her voice.

"Because of me and Josh, I'm sure. I moved in when Mom got sick, to help out. Dad was good for Josh, so I just stayed on after . . . after she died."

"That must have been tough."

"It was."

Dammit to hell. He wanted the right to take her hand, to tell her how sorry he was that her mother had died so young. But he didn't dare.

The closer they got to her house the greater his distress. Just dinner. Was it so much to ask? Apparently. He couldn't bring himself to suggest it again.

Finally, he pulled into the gravel driveway. The house looked the same—a rambling log structure with a big porch in the back, facing the creek. The front door light was on in welcome, as it always had been when they'd been dating. Back in those days they'd always ended the evening with a few more passionate kisses as they postponed the inevitable parting. Tonight he wasn't even allowed to touch her.

He stopped the car and turned in his seat, but she was already halfway out the door. "Loren!"

"It's better this way," she said over her shoulder. "Goodbye, Adam." She swung the door shut.

He flinched, opened his mouth to call goodbye and couldn't say the word. He stared at her as she marched over the gravel, her loud crunching footsteps drowning out the soft babble of the creek nearby. He gripped the steering wheel to keep himself anchored inside the car. Then, his lips set in a hard line, he spun out of the driveway.

LOREN SQUARED her shoulders and wiped at her eyes before she entered the house. She didn't want her father asking any questions. Fortunately, he wasn't in the living room watching television, so she had a little more time to compose herself. He hadn't even bothered to turn on any lights in there, and the photograph over the fireplace was in shadow.

A light shone from the dining room, however. Maybe he was doing some Icarus paperwork at the table. Determined that he not be able to detect anything wrong, she pasted a smile on her face.

He wasn't doing paperwork.

A blond, beefy man sat across the table from him. The man looked bored. But her father... Loren knew she'd never forget the look on his face as long as she lived. The light from the wagon-wheel chandelier overhead revealed a faint sheen of sweat on his balding scalp. His eyes seemed sunken into his face, and the lines on either side of his mouth slashed his cheeks like wounds.

She put a hand to her chest, where her heart had begun to pound. Oh, God. "Is it Josh?" she whispered, the blood ringing in her ears.

"He's okay," her father said, but there was no inflection in his voice, no reassurance.

Her heart raced faster and she locked her gaze with his, probing the haunted depths. She forced her frozen lips to ask the necessary questions. "Was there an accident?" *Not Daphne. Please not Daphne, either.* "Was anybody else . . . hurt?"

"No," her father said. "Loren, this is Barnaby Haskett."

DAPHNE DANCED vigorously to the pounding beat, her gaze riveted on the stage of the outdoor arena, where the band played surrounded by towering ponderosa pines. Screaming out lyrics along with the crowd, she fed on the energy pulsing in the packed arena.

She coaxed Josh to dance, and once he let go, he wasn't bad at it. She began to reconsider trying to seduce him. For no matter how fast she danced or how loud she screamed, she couldn't erase the picture of the way her father looked at Loren Stanfield. So they'd gone off to Phoenix together with some excuse about processing film. Ha! Her father had chosen Loren over her.

Less than halfway through the concert, she nudged Josh. "Let's go."

"Go? I thought you liked this."

"I have a better idea." She started out of the arena, confident Josh would follow. He had a strong sense of duty. His responsible nature would work against her plan, but she should be able to overcome that obstacle.

Once they'd located the Suburban and climbed in, Josh turned to her. "Ready to go home, then?"

She grinned at him. "Absolutely not. I'm ready to party."

"But we were just doing that."

"Kid stuff," she said with a wave of her hand. "Let's do something really wild."

"Like what?"

She could tell he was nervous by the way he jingled the keys. "We could drive to Vegas," she said, making the suggestion sound like a treat to end all treats.

"Aw, Daphne, come on."

"I'm serious. Look at this." She dug in her tiny shoulder bag, found her fake ID and switched on the overhead light so he could read it. "I've never been questioned on this baby. Do you have one?"

His answer was hesitant. "Yeah."

"Great! Just think—we could gamble, have some drinks, maybe even see a late-night show. Josh, it would be such a kick!"

"There's not time. It'd take us four hours to get there, at least, and another five or so to get home. Even if we went there, turned around and came right back, we wouldn't be home until morning."

"So what?"

"Gramps and Mom would have a fit, for one thing. And your dad would probably go through the roof."

"Are you kidding? My father is so gaga over your mother, they don't even know we're alive. We could be gone for two days and they'd never know it."

Josh shifted uneasily in his seat. "Yeah, but what about Gramps? He's not gaga over anybody."

"We'll call him from Vegas and tell him not to worry. He didn't get mad about your coming in at four in the morning, did he?"

"No," Josh said with a laugh. "Surprised the hell out of me, too. I walked into the kitchen for breakfast expecting to be chewed out, and he just said, 'Good morning,' nice as you please, as if nothing had happened."

"That's because you stood up to him. He'll treat you like an adult from now on. But your mother is another story. She would have stopped you from coming to this concert with me if she could have managed it. She's still trying to run your life. And I wouldn't say she should be giving advice after the way she and my dad are acting.''

Josh shifted his weight again. "She's an adult. She has the right to do what she wants, I guess."

"You said last night she wouldn't let you go into the military, like you want to. When are you going to take charge of your own life, Josh?"

He glanced at her in the darkened cab, and his jaw tightened. "Come to think of it, I always did want to see Vegas," he said, and started the engine.

CHAPTER FOURTEEN

LOREN CLUTCHED the back of a dining room chair to steady herself as she looked at Barnaby Haskett, steel thief. His eyes were a pale blue and set close together. His complexion was florid, and tiny broken blood vessels across his nose suggested he overindulged in alcohol. This was the man who'd taken advantage of Adam's preoccupation with his divorce to embezzle half a million dollars' worth of steel.

She gripped the chair tighter and controlled the urge to march over and slap his face. "What do you want?"

"The negatives and prints from today," he said in a gravelly voice.

"I don't have them."

"Then I suggest you get them."

She glanced at her father to gauge whether the menace in Haskett's voice was something she should heed. He nodded almost imperceptibly. Why would her father want her to go along with this thug? "That would be difficult," she said as much to Walt as to Haskett. "I don't know where they are." *Not precisely, that is.*

At last her father spoke, his voice tight with strain. "I'm afraid you'll have to find out, Loren," he said.

"You see, they have Josh—" His voice broke and he looked away to collect himself.

Loren whirled and started for Haskett. "What does he mean, you have Josh?" she cried, reaching for his face, ready to gouge his eyes, tear out his heart, if necessary.

He caught her wrists and stood, holding her effortlessly. "We have him under surveillance," he said. "He's fine."

"What are you saying?" Her voice rose as hysteria crept in. "That he won't be fine if I don't get you those pictures?"

"Turn her loose," Walt said, rising. "Let go of my daughter."

"Tell her not to attack me."

"Leave him be, Loren," Walt said, sounding defeated. "He's just the messenger boy, anyway."

"I'm not!" Haskett said, shoving Loren away from him. "I'm in charge of this operation."

Loren faced him, trembling. "Where is he? Where's my son?"

"Last I heard he was at the rock concert, like he was supposed to be. You get me those pictures, and he'll come home, and everything will be just fine."

Nausea rose within her. "Who are these . . . people who are watching my son?"

For the first time, Haskett looked unsure of himself. "You don't need to know."

"The hell I don't!"

"Loren," her father said, "I don't think he even knows. He's got himself mixed up with people who play for keeps. If we don't turn the pictures over to this goon . . ." He didn't finish. He didn't have to.

Loren groped for a chair, pulled it out and sat in it before her knees gave way. She stared at the grain in the old maple table that had been in her family forever. Josh had done his homework sitting at this table. *Oh, Josh.* She gripped her stomach and fought the urge to be sick. She couldn't afford to fall apart. She had to think.

She glanced up at Haskett. "What about Daphne Riordan? She's with Josh."

Haskett looked a little confused, but he recovered himself and cleared his throat importantly. "She's being watched, too."

Loren's stomach twisted. "Then Adam needs to know about this."

"No, he doesn't need to know about this," Haskett said, a thread of panic running through his words. "He's not to be involved. You are to get the pictures without telling him anything, do you understand? Because if you tell him . . ." Haskett allowed the unfinished sentence to settle around her like a noose.

So it was up to her to protect both their children. "How much time do I have?"

"About three hours, I figure. By then the concert will be over and your son will start home. If I have the pictures by then, I'll make a phone call and he'll be allowed to return safely."

Loren had seen her share of gangster movies. "But my father and I know who you are, even if we don't know the other people. We can identify you."

"In twenty-four hours I'll be out of the country. Nobody will be able to find me. You'll have no one left to identify."

Loren wondered where that left Anita. But she couldn't worry about that. "If I somehow get the pictures and negatives and turn them over to you, what am I supposed to tell Adam?"

"That's up to you. You could say there was a terrible accident and they were destroyed. Of course you would apologize profusely for making such an unfortunate mistake."

She grasped at straws. "He could have others taken."

"No, he couldn't, fortunately. The operation's closed down. Once the photographs are gone, there will be nothing to show it ever happened. The word will get out that Scorpio Steel doesn't deliver as promised. Poor guy will probably lose a few contracts, may even go under."

"But his mark is on that steel! The authorities could—"

"Have you ever noticed how fast buildings go up in Vegas?" Barnaby interrupted. "By the time you convince somebody to investigate, if you could even do that, the casino will be nearly completed. Nobody will punch holes in the walls of a new high rise and risk being sued just to prove your theory."

He was right. Without her pictures, Adam had no case. "Adam will never believe I accidentally destroyed those negatives and prints," she said. "He knows me better than that."

"Who cares if he believes you or not? What's he going to do, press charges for negligence?"

Loren could almost hear the door of the trap click shut. Of course Adam wouldn't do anything like that. He'd drop the case and lose half a million dollars, perhaps even his whole company. But Loren stood to lose something far more valuable than that. And so did Adam. He'd have to take his chances on the business.

"I don't even know if I can reach him. We hadn't planned to meet again . . . before he left for Phoenix," she amended, unwilling to let their personal decisions be part of this nightmare.

"Try," Haskett said.

She struggled through the mental quagmire Haskett had created for her. She couldn't just call Adam and ask for the prints and negatives. The request had to seem more casual than that. Earlier he'd offered dinner. Perhaps he'd believe she'd had a change of heart.

Her legs felt like chunks of concrete as she walked to the kitchen wall phone. She opened a cabinet drawer and took out the phone book, her hands shaking as she paged through it looking for the number of Los Arboles. Finally, she dialed it and asked for Adam's room. Her heart pounded and her mouth grew dry as the phone rang. Mentally she rehearsed what she planned to say, but she had little confidence in her delivery. She was a terrible liar.

The phone rang countless times, until an operator interrupted. "He's not answering. Would you care to leave a message?"

Loren closed her eyes. He wasn't there. She grasped desperately at alternatives. "Do you have a paging service? He might be out by the pool, or in the bar." *Or driving aimlessly through the night. Please be there, Adam.*

"I'll check for you," said the desk clerk, a cheerful lilt to her voice.

Loren longed to trade places with her. How glorious to have nothing to do except cater to a hotel switchboard tonight. She fantasized about the young woman's life—single, childless, with the world still a bright, beautiful place to explore. She'd been like that once, too. She—

"Adam Riordan."

Her breath caught at the sound of his voice. "Hello, Adam."

"Loren?"

"I...wondered if it was too late to...to take you up on your offer of dinner."

"Of course not."

Knowing she was about to betray him, she winced at the note of anticipation that had crept into his voice. "You haven't eaten?" she asked.

"No. I've been sitting in the Jacuzzi. You can probably hear the bubbles."

He sounded so friendly, so eager to connect with her again, that she wanted to cry. "Yes, I can."

"I certainly didn't expect to hear from you. Just out of curiosity, what changed your mind?"

"I...I decided we're rational people who should be able to enjoy a last dinner together and part amicably.'' The speech sounded stiff and rehearsed. Would he question her further?

It seemed not. There was only a brief silence on the other end. "Okay," he said at last, not sounding quite as happy as before. "What time should I pick you up?"

She had three hours, until the concert was over. "I can be ready in fifteen minutes."

His laugh was tinged with surprise. "You must be a hungry woman."

She fumbled for a response. "I guess I am."

"I'll see you in fifteen minutes, then."

"Fine." She replaced the receiver, took a deep breath and walked slowly back to the dining room. She glanced at her father and looked quickly away. The emotions reflected in his eyes only increased her panic. "I'm meeting him for dinner," she said to Haskett.

"I don't care if you meet him for a game of boccie ball. Just get those negatives and prints."

"I haven't figured out how to do that yet."

Haskett looked at her with his pale, close-set eyes. "You're a clever girl. I'm sure you'll think of something."

ADAM GAZED across the candlelit table at Loren. She hadn't eaten much, despite her rush to have him pick her up. Her attempts at conversation seemed forced, and she acted as if she'd rather be anywhere but in this restaurant with him. So why had she called?

He'd tried several conversational gambits, but none of them had panned out. This last dinner together was turning out to be a very painful experience. So what was new? He was still glad to have a few more hours with her, awkward though they might be. "Did you mention the picture to your father?" he asked.

She jumped and spilled water from the goblet she'd been holding onto the pale green tablecloth. Her gaze was stricken. "What picture?"

"The Red Rock Crossing picture." Whatever had been bothering her, he seemed to have touched a nerve. "I thought you might have landed into him for making that print for me."

"No." She dabbed at the wet tablecloth with her napkin. "I didn't mention it."

"You're really jumpy, Loren. Is it that difficult just to sit across the table from me?"

She shook her head and attempted a smile. "I guess . . . I guess I'm thinking about Josh and Daphne on that winding Oak Creek Canyon road at night. We've had some rain and it's probably slick. That road has always worried me, anyway."

Concern for the kids on the wet road gave his gut a squeeze, but he didn't think the state of the Oak Creek Canyon road was what was bothering her. "From what you've said about Josh's sense of responsibility, I can't believe he's a bad driver."

"No, he's a good driver. A lot better than most pilots I know." She didn't crack a smile and he knew she hadn't been trying to make a joke.

"Then they'll be fine. I'll bet Josh has been up and down that road a million times since he got his license. Probably in a lot worse weather conditions than this."

"You're right, of course."

Adam talked to reassure himself as much as to comfort Loren. Daphne was in a rebellious mood, which didn't contribute to his peace of mind. Just before he'd left to pick up Loren, a bellman had come by and suggested he might want to hang on to both courtesy bar keys from now on. With a little probing, Adam had discovered that every bit of food and drink had been cleaned out the night before, presumably by Daphne and Josh.

Adam had considered telling Loren about the incident, but she seemed so preoccupied and worried that he was afraid the information would only make things worse for her. It didn't much matter, anyway. He could afford the extra charge, and he'd confront Daphne about it later.

He'd already decided that when she came home tonight, he'd show her the pictures and tell her about Barnaby Haskett. He had to trust her with the information sometime, and if he handled the whole thing right, she wouldn't call her mother. He couldn't predict what Anita would do if she was given the information that her lover was about to be arrested. She might write Haskett off or she might warn him. Adam didn't want him to be warned.

Loren picked up her wineglass, stared at it and put it back down, untouched.

"Ready to go?" he asked gently.

She nodded. "I'm terrible company tonight. You're probably sorry you offered this dinner."

"No," he murmured. He'd take what he could get.

"I suppose it's the exhaustion from all that we've been through."

"I'm sure it is." Adam motioned to their waiter. After the check arrived, he left money on the table and helped her from her chair, although he was careful, as he had been all evening, to keep touching to a minimum. She'd worn a simple gauze dress belted at the waist with a full skirt that skittered around her bare calves as she walked. It reminded him a little of the white chiffon graduation dress she'd worn twenty-three years ago. He wondered if she'd thought of that. Probably not.

Outside the restaurant he paused, uncertain what to suggest. He was quickly running out of excuses to be with her. The rain-fragrant night beckoned, but he couldn't think of any acceptable way they could enjoy it together.

"You know, I just thought of something," she said, her voice a tad too brittle, too bright.

He gazed at her. *In a pig's eye.* Intuition told him he was about to hear the real reason she'd agreed to this dinner.

"You'll be presenting those prints to the authorities in Phoenix tomorrow, right?"

"That's right." He went on full alert. So this whole strained evening had something to do with the pictures they'd taken.

"Well, I could get some exposure out of your doing that."

"I'd be glad to give them your card," he said easily. And waited.

"That would be great, except the prints aren't prepared the way I normally prepare them, and I'd kind of like them to be."

"I don't understand."

She laughed, but it sounded false. "Oh, I wouldn't expect you to. You probably don't remember, but all the prints I've sent you in the past were stamped with the Icarus logo. I haven't done that with these. It may seem like a small point, but when people are confronted time and again with the same logo, it sticks in their brain, and I get more business."

"I suppose so." He couldn't believe it, but maybe, just maybe, she was doing this in order to find a graceful way to go back to his hotel room with him. It seemed way out of line for her, but he was having trouble coming up with an explanation for her strange behavior. "The prints are in the safe in my room," he said carefully, watching her face. "Would you like to drive over there now and get them?"

"That would be great."

His heart began to pound. There was a feverish, eager light in her eyes. Maybe, just maybe... but he was still very confused. Despite his hopes, he couldn't imagine Loren's wanting to make love in a room adjacent to his daughter's, especially when they didn't know when Daphne would be back. Even he'd be uneasy about that, although he could always lock the connecting door. He decided to play out the hand and see where it led.

BACK AT THE RESORT they walked past perfumed flower beds on the way to his room. "Why do flowers always smell sweeter at night?" he asked, more to break the silence than to get an answer.

"Maybe it's an illusion," she said. "Maybe they smell just as sweet in the daytime, but we're so bombarded by the brilliance of daylight colors, we don't use our other senses as much."

"Maybe." He hesitated, then decided he didn't have much to lose. "Or it could be part of a giant conspiracy to make people fall in love. A moon, a soft summer night, the scent of flowers in the air—what fool could resist all that?"

Had he imagined she'd say, "Not me," and snuggle against him? If so, he'd been way off the mark. She said nothing, didn't even look his way. He fitted the key in the lock.

During the war the commanders had used the phrase "acceptable losses" to describe the level of carnage the war effort, or the country, could tolerate. When Loren had refused to communicate with him years ago, he'd finally resigned himself to look at their parting as an acceptable loss. Painful, yes. Regrets had haunted him for years. But he hadn't been paralyzed. He wasn't sure he'd come out as unscathed this time.

He closed the door and turned toward her. She stood in the middle of the room, the expression on her face one of a woman purchased for the night. He'd tried that once in Nam, had hated the feeling that a woman came to him because she needed money, not love. What did Loren need?

"I'll get the prints," he said, crossing to the closet that housed the wall safe. If that was what she was here for, she wouldn't have to sleep with him to get them.

"You might as well give me the negatives, too."

He froze in midstep as an alarm sounded in his head. "Oh?" He forced himself to sound casual. "Why's that?"

"I want to make sure the prints are in the right order. I can't be sure I'm doing that unless I have the numbered negatives to go by."

Adam knew he had a decision to make, and only a fraction of a second in which to make it. In the end, it wasn't so hard to decide. She might not have even noticed his slight hesitation before he continued toward the closet, opened the door and punched in the wall-safe code. He pulled out the envelope and turned around.

She was right behind him, reaching for it eagerly. Much too eagerly. He handed it to her. "Thanks," she said, sounding breathless as she held the envelope close. "This will make for a much better presentation."

"I'm sure it will." He tried to hold her gaze, but it skittered away. The knowledge that she was keeping something from him stabbed with a pain sharper than he'd have thought possible. Something was terribly wrong, and she wouldn't confide in him. He glanced away, afraid he'd start asking questions and demanding answers. And that wasn't how he wanted to operate.

"I'll help you stamp and arrange if you like," he said, more to get her reaction than anything else. He didn't expect her to take him up on the offer.

What might have been panic flashed across her face for a moment. "Actually, I work much better alone when I'm doing something like this. I guess it's the artist in me coming out. Temperamental and all that.''

He glanced at the envelope. The negatives and prints inside were invaluable to him, and he had no idea what she was going to do with them. Certainly not what she'd told him. But she was more important than the contents of that envelope. She wouldn't trust him, but he would have to trust her. Otherwise, his life made no sense.

He tried one more time. "Loren, if there's any way I can help you, you only have to ask."

"That's nice of you." Her friendly tone was completely fake. "But I can handle this."

"Then I'd better get you home so you can get started."

He drove her back in silence. There was nothing more to say. She'd become a stranger.

He parked the car in the circular driveway and started to get out.

"I'll see myself in," she said, reaching for the door handle. "And I'll contact you tomorrow to return these. What time should I call? I wouldn't want to wake Daphne."

"Call anytime. Daphne would sleep through a four-alarm fire."

In the darkness, her smile looked more like a grimace. "Okay. Then expect a call about eight. You'll probably be anxious to get on the road."

"Thank you for having dinner with me," he said quietly.

"Oh! Yes! Thank you for dinner." She paused. "And for...trusting me with these." Her voice trembled.

She hadn't meant it to be a signal. He knew that beyond a shadow of a doubt. But in those trembling words he heard a faint cry for help, a cry she'd tried hard to repress. "I'd trust you with my life," he said.

"I know."

He read desperation in her gaze before she wrenched it away.

"Loren, what is it?"

"I'm very tired," she said, her voice choked. Then she flipped open her seat belt and got out of the car.

He watched her walk toward the darkened house, the envelope clutched in both hands. Sirens screamed in his head. There was danger here. And he would not leave her to face it alone.

As he circled the driveway, his attention was arrested by the reflection in his rearview mirror. Loren, her face illuminated by the porch light, looked petrified. What was going on?

He turned left and started down the road toward the resort. A glance back at the house convinced him she'd gone inside. He waited for oncoming traffic to clear and made a swift U-turn. A few yards before her driveway, he pulled to the shoulder, shut off the engine and got out of the car.

Instincts unused in more than twenty years took over as he moved forward in a semicrouch, keeping close to the foliage bordering the driveway. Clouds covered the moon and most of the stars, so he didn't have to worry about extraneous light. Adrenaline sharpened his senses to the sights and sounds of the night—the shrill rasp of crickets, the looping flight of a bat across the path of the porch light, the splash and gurgle of Oak Creek running behind the house.

Setting each foot down carefully, he edged toward the light spilling from the double casement windows at the side of the house. At a rustling in the bushes next to him, he froze. A raccoon scampered out of hiding and headed for the creek. Adam's armpits were damp and his pulse was faster than normal, but the concentration he'd learned in the jungle kept his movements steady.

Just beyond the reach of the double rectangles of light was a cluster of several lichen-covered rocks. Gripping the rough surface, he eased himself up high enough to see inside the window.

Loren and her father stood with their backs to him, Walt's arm around Loren's shoulders. They remained stationary, as if waiting for something. Then in unison their heads swiveled toward the kitchen. Someone was coming. Adam forced his breath to a normal rhythm, to be ready for whatever happened.

Haskett!

In spite of his effort at control, he gasped. Haskett held the envelope. That's why Loren had wanted it. For one mind-bending moment, he wondered if Haskett had bought her off. But if Loren could be bribed, then his world would collapse. There was some other reason.

He checked for signs of a weapon, but Haskett seemed unarmed. Then Loren cried out, and only Walt's restraining arm kept her from launching herself at Haskett. Adam balled his hands into fists. He wanted to go in there, but he'd have the advantage if he waited until Haskett came out.

Loren and Walt were arguing loudly with Haskett, but Adam couldn't understand what they were saying. Then Loren's tone changed to pleading. Adam ground his teeth. Haskett would pay dearly for making Loren beg. And whatever she wanted, the bastard wasn't giving an inch. Finally, Haskett shook his head and started toward the front of the house.

Loren ran after him, grabbing his arm. He shook her off as if she were a pesky child. A murderous rage engulfed Adam, propelling him toward the front of the house. He reached the front steps just as Haskett came out the front door.

CHAPTER FIFTEEN

WHEN LOREN HEARD an angry growl and Haskett's cry of fear, she thought Haskett had been attacked by a bear. She ran to the front door just as Adam grabbed Haskett by his shirtfront and hurled him down the steps. The man lost his grip on the envelope and it skittered across the gravel driveway.

"Adam!" she screamed just as his fist plowed into Haskett's midsection.

Haskett doubled over, but not soon enough to avoid Adam's uppercut to his jaw. He crumpled to the ground. Adam hauled him to his feet and cocked his fist.

"Adam, stop!" Loren hurtled down the steps, her father close behind.

Adam glanced at them and back at the dazed Haskett.

"Turn him loose," Loren said on a sob. "They have Josh and Daphne."

His face went white, and he released his hold on Haskett's shirt. Haskett wobbled for a minute before plopping down to a sitting position in the gravel. Slowly, Adam turned to Loren. "What did you say?"

She clenched her forearms across her stomach. Her teeth chattered. "They've k-kidnapped them, Adam.

Haskett said if I gave him the pictures, they'd come home s-safe, but..." She couldn't go on. She stared at him and rocked back and forth.

Adam's expression changed from disbelief to terror. Then terror gave way to fury. His eyes narrowed to slits and he leaned down to grab Haskett by his shirtfront again. "Where are they?" he said, a dangerous edge to his voice. "Where are they, you son of a bitch?"

Haskett's eyes widened with fear. "In Vegas. You'd better let me—"

"*Vegas?* What the hell are they doing there?"

"Don't ask me." Haskett's voice quivered. "All I know is they left the rock concert and headed for Vegas. My contact thought they might be up to no good, spying on the construction site for you, taking more pictures of the steel, or something. Anyway, they're being held captive there now."

"You're lying." Adam wrenched Haskett's shirt again and the material ripped. "If those kids are in Vegas, it's because somebody took them there."

"They were going there themselves, I tell you!"

Loren forced her vocal cords to work. "It doesn't matter." We just have to get them back safe and sound. If Haskett takes the pictures up there, Josh and Daphne will be released. So let him go." She started across the driveway toward the envelope. "I'll get the—"

"No!"

She whirled to face him. "Yes! I'm not taking any chances, Adam!"

"You're taking one right now," he said, breathing hard, "by believing a crook. Who says they'll release Josh and Daphne? If we give them the pictures, they don't have to do anything we say. We've lost all our bargaining power."

She gazed into his eyes, as frantic with worry as hers. She knew he loved Daphne every bit as much as she loved Josh. She'd never truly doubted it. His gaze pleaded with her to listen. She took a shaky breath. "What do you think we should do?"

"Deliver the pictures ourselves." He let go of Haskett's shirt and shoved him away with a look of disgust. "When we have the kids, they get the pictures."

Haskett gingerly touched his swelling jaw. "They'll never go for that."

"If we keep the pictures, they have no choice."

"Adam's making sense, Loren," Walt said.

"Look, Riordan, you don't know these guys." Haskett staggered to his feet. "Just let me take them the envelope. I'll bring the kids back. I swear. You think I'm happy about this? Anita will be furious."

"No kidding. I'd say your little love fest with her is over." Adam glanced at Loren. "Better pick up the envelope. We're going to need it." When she hesitated, his tone sharpened. "Please, Loren. Be with me on this."

Her gaze locked with his. Then, as if the words had just streaked like a comet across the sky, she remembered what he'd said before he drove away tonight. *I would trust you with my life.* He was demanding no less. By trusting him with Josh's life, she placed her existence in the balance, as well. But his daughter's life was on the line, too.

She looked into his eyes and knew he would die himself before he'd let something happen to either of their children. Wordlessly, she turned and walked over to where the envelope lay in the gravel.

"I'm warning you, you shouldn't be fooling around with these guys," Haskett said as she picked up the envelope and hugged it to her chest.

"No, we shouldn't," Adam agreed, skewering him with a look. "And I will never forget you're the reason we have to. Okay, first of all, I want to talk to our kids."

Haskett blinked. "Talk to them?"

"That's right. Nothing you say holds any water with me, Haskett. For all I know, the kids are on their way home from the rock concert and this was a big bluff on your part."

"I'm not bluffing, I tell you."

"Then let's go inside and call Vegas."

Loren stared at Adam. The thought that Haskett was lying had never occurred to her. She'd based all her actions on an unquestioning belief that he was telling the truth. A rush of hope made her heart pound faster. "Adam, do you think maybe he is bluffing?"

"Let's hope so."

Walt led the procession into the house. Adam shoved Haskett into line after Walt and followed him in. Loren, holding the envelope as if it were a bomb, brought up the rear. If Haskett had been bluffing, she'd feel like a fool for handing him the pictures. But she'd gladly admit to being a fool if only Josh and

Daphne arrived home soon from the concert, healthy and whole and wondering what all the fuss was about.

Her stomach clutched as, without hesitation, Haskett went to the wall phone in the kitchen. Taking a slip of paper from his pocket, he punched in a number. If he was bluffing, he was too damn good at it.

"Yeah, this is Haskett," he said into the phone. "There's been a little problem."

Loren closed her eyes and prayed.

"Riordan showed up as I was leaving with the pictures. He wants to deliver them himself." Haskett paused. "He, um, sorta caught me by surprise. Anyway, he doesn't believe you have the kids. He wants to talk to them." There was another pause. "I don't know. Daphne, I guess."

It's not a bluff. Loren ached all over, as if someone had been pummeling her for hours. She opened her eyes and watched Adam take the phone from Haskett.

His knuckles whitened and he raised his eyes in anguish. Then he swallowed. "Hi, sweetie."

Loren moaned.

"Listen, don't be afraid," Adam said, his voice amazingly resonant. Loren marveled at the strength it must have taken for him to speak so normally. "All they want is the pictures Loren and I took today. I'll bring them up there and get you guys." He paused. "Well, because they were taking my steel shipments and the pictures show that. Don't worry. I'll give them everything they want and we'll have you home before you know it. I love you, too. See you soon. And Daphne..."

When he grimaced and didn't continue, Loren figured someone had pulled the phone away from his daughter.

"Yeah," he said, his tone rough again. "I'm convinced you have her. Now I want you to put Josh on, so his mother can verify his voice."

Loren's gaze flew to his. Could she do this?

He gave an almost imperceptible nod and handed her the phone.

Holding the receiver with both hands, she put it to her ear. "Josh?"

"Hi, Mom."

She felt dizzy. Adam put a steadying arm around her waist and she took a deep breath. "Are you okay?"

"Yeah, so far. Who are these guys?"

"I don't know, Josh." Her knees shook. Without Adam's arm bracing her, she might have fallen. "They have something to do with missing steel from the bridge construction in Laughlin. They're . . . keeping you until we give them the pictures we took."

"You mean we're hostages?"

"Well . . . sort of."

"When are you coming?"

"Soon. We'll be there soon. Josh, have they hurt you, or anything? Is—" The phone had been taken from him. She knew it immediately and stopped speaking. A clipped male voice asked to speak to Riordan. Choking back a sob, Loren handed Adam the receiver and stumbled toward her father. He enfolded her in his arms, gripping her so tightly she had trouble breathing, but she hung on. Maybe if they continued hugging each other, they could keep hysteria at bay.

"This is Riordan," Adam said into the phone. He paused. "No, I'm bringing the prints and negatives. Leave her out of it."

Loren stiffened. Were they asking him to have her deliver the pictures?

"No, I—" Adam was silent again.

Giving her father a parting squeeze, Loren left the shelter of his arms and walked unsteadily to the phone. If the kidnappers wanted her to deliver the envelope, she'd do it. She stood in front of Adam and mouthed, "Say yes."

He glanced at her and shook his head. Then he stared at the floor and ran his fingers through his hair while he listened some more. "Hoover Dam. Midnight tomorrow." A pause. "Because that's the way I want it." Then he looked at her again, and she almost could hear his mind clicking into overdrive. Finally, he sighed as if defeated. "All right." Another pause. "No, you've made yourself perfectly clear. We won't try to make extra copies."

He hung up the phone slowly and turned to Loren. "They want you to bring the prints and negatives."

"No," Walt said. "I'll go. They can't be afraid of an old man. Call them back, Adam. Tell them I'm almost seventy and feeble."

"I'll go," Loren said quietly, gazing into his eyes. "It'll be all right."

Walt came to stand beside them. "Don't let her do it, Adam."

Adam's glance flicked to Walt and came back to rest on Loren. There was loving concern in his eyes, but something else, too—a confidence that made Loren's heart swell. "You heard her, Walt. It'll be all right."

"What am I supposed to do?" Haskett asked.

Loren was startled. She'd almost forgotten Haskett was still around.

"You're supposed to take them a picture of Loren," Adam said. "They want to be able to identify her."

"That's it?"

"That's it." Adam glanced back at her. "Do you have a recent picture? A snapshot or something?"

"I don't like this at all," Walt grumbled, rubbing the bald spot on his head and gazing up at Adam from under his eyebrows. "Thought you had more sense, Riordan."

"I'll get a picture," Loren said. The prospect of facing the kidnappers frightened her, but it also gave her a sense of purpose. As her father continued his protest, she left the dining room. Shelves lined the wall on each side of the fireplace, and one held a row of photograph albums. She pulled down the most recent and switched on a lamp beside the couch.

Standing with the album braced against her hip, she opened it to the first page. Josh grinned back at her, his safety goggles pushed to the top of his head, making his thatch of blond hair stick up behind them. One hand rested on the wing of 206 Whiskey Foxtrot, and the other was raised in a victory sign. The picture blurred. Loren wiped at her eyes with the sleeve of her dress and kept looking, but the shot wouldn't stay in focus.

Finally, she gave up and held the open album pressed against her heart, rocking it like a child, while tears dripped onto her arms and hands.

She heard her father call her name. She gulped back a sob. "Be right there," she called, hoping she didn't sound as shaken as she felt. She laid the album on the end table next to the lamp and wiped her eyes again. Her fist pressed against her mouth, she turned the pages until she found a picture of her alone, standing in front of her favorite ice-cream shop, a triple-dip in her hand, a silly grin on her face.

Josh had taken the picture, she remembered, earlier in the summer when he'd accused her of losing her zest for life. "When was the last time you had a triple-dip cone?" he'd challenged. When she couldn't remember, he'd insisted they go into town for just that. He'd taken the picture to serve as a reminder to her to put more fun in her life.

She slipped the picture out of its plastic sleeve. She'd be willing to sacrifice everything—her business, her home, even her ability to take pictures—if she could share a triple-dip cone with Josh right this minute. Her chest tightened and she gasped as a new wave of grief hit her. Holding on to the edge of the table, she struggled for control.

When she was sure she had it, she closed the album and walked back to the dining room. "Here." She handed the picture to Haskett.

Walt still looked disapproving, but Adam nodded.

"You know," he said, addressing Haskett, "I'd love to know how you discovered we took these pictures."

Haskett looked smug. "I just bet you would."

"Not even my secretary knew I'd hired Loren, and my trip to Sedona was supposed to be a vacation. Even if somebody at the bridge site spotted the plane, there was no link to me."

Haskett smiled, then winced and touched his bruised jaw. "For a smart guy, you can be pretty dumb."

"So enlighten me." Adam's tone was deceptively casual, but Loren noticed the muscle twitching in his cheek.

"Not a chance."

"I'll find out."

"Yes, I think you will."

Adam dropped the casual pose. "Get out of my sight."

"With pleasure." Shoving Loren's picture into his hip pocket, Haskett headed for the front door.

Adam watched until the door closed behind him. "I want to make sure he leaves," he said in an undertone, heading for the kitchen door that opened onto the back porch. "Lock this door and the one in front in case he circles back. He might still try to steal the envelope. If I'm not back here in fifteen minutes, call the police." Then he slipped soundlessly out the door and melted into the shadows of the porch.

"You lock that one and I'll get the front," Walt said. In a moment, he returned to the kitchen. "Are you keeping track of the time?"

Loren nodded and fought her growing panic. She'd kept it under control as long as Adam was there, but now he was gone. She was terrified she wasn't up to the challenge despite Adam's confidence in her. And if she didn't succeed, what would become of Josh and Daphne?

She stood by the back door staring at the jerky motion of the kitchen clock's second hand. Each time the hand moved, she made a bargain with herself that she could last one more second before the hysteria that was working its way up her windpipe had to be released.

When the knock came, she cried out and backed away from the kitchen door.

"Loren, it's me," Adam called from the other side of the door. She wrenched it open. He took one look at her and pulled her into his arms. "It's okay," he murmured into her hair as she shook and gasped for breath. "You're the bravest person I've ever known. It's going to be okay."

Finally, the tremors lessened and he gradually released her. He held her by the shoulders and peered into her face. "Better?"

She nodded and glanced away, feeling weak for having rushed into his arms like that. She stepped back out of reach. It wouldn't happen again.

"Adam, I don't want Loren to do this," Walt said. "It's too dangerous for her to deliver those pictures alone and you know it."

"I know," Adam said, his gaze remaining on Loren's face. "That's why you and I are going with her, Walt."

"Going with me?" Loren asked. "How?"

Adam gave her a rueful glance. "I'm not sure yet. That's why I set the exchange for midnight tomorrow." He walked over to gaze out the kitchen window, his hands braced on the sink. "They wanted you to start up there tonight and meet them at four this morning at Hoover Dam."

"What?" Loren met his gaze in the reflection from the window, her pulse racing. "You turned down a chance to get the kids back right away?"

He faced her. "You have to stop believing they'll do what they say. We should expect them to lie and make our plans with that in mind."

"But Adam, a whole extra day? We don't know if they're hurting those kids. We don't know if they're being fed, if they're—"

"You think I like it any better than you do?" He paced in front of the sink, rubbing the back of his neck. "I don't want them up there a minute longer than necessary, but I needed to buy some time."

Walt cleared his throat. "How about the police?"

"No!" Loren said, expecting Adam to echo her.

Instead, he sighed and glanced at her father. "I've been asking myself that for the past hour, Walt. If we did call the police, I'm sure they could eventually catch these guys. But to have them there during the exchange at Hoover Dam, with all the inevitable gunpower..."

"No, Adam," Loren said again. "If you call the police, we lose all control. If these people are based in Las Vegas we could be talking about Mafia. The police might see it as a chance to nab the guys, when all we want is our kids back safe."

Adam was silent for several moments. Finally, he turned to her. "How about this. At first light, let's take a plane—yours or mine, doesn't matter—and fly over Hoover Dam. We won't have time to take pictures and get them processed and developed, but we can still study that sucker from all angles."

"Good idea," Loren said, her confidence in him growing.

"If we can find a way for Walt and me to come in as backup, we'll consider pulling this off ourselves. If we can't, we'll call in the police."

"We'll find a way." Pride surged through her at the answering flash of agreement in his eyes, and she felt more hope than she had since Barnaby Haskett had first made his demands. In her mind, she and Adam stood shoulder to shoulder, as they once had years ago, ready to take on the world.

"I don't know," Walt said. "I'd feel better if we called the police tonight."

Adam flicked a glance toward Walt and gave him a ghost of a smile. "You'll have to forgive us, Walt. Loren and I grew up in the sixties. We question authority."

over. Move over, Dean. We won't have time to take pictures and get them developed and delivered, but we
can still send that snuff from a—"

"Good idea," Louie said, her eyes livid. "Do it
again..."

"We can bring Sam and Samantha down here to come in
as backup, we'll make sure I don't get overzealous. If
we can, we'll call in the police."

CHAPTER SIXTEEN

DAPHNE AND JOSH ransacked the bedroom and bathroom where they'd been locked in, searching for
something to identify where they were. The towels had
no laundry stamp, and there were no matches or ash-
trays. They pulled the sheets off both double beds
looking for some evidence of a name.

"But we're definitely in a hotel," Daphne said,
holding up the Gideon Bible she'd pulled from the
bedside-table drawer.

"That's the only thing normal about this room,
though," Josh said, keeping his voice down. "And
you have to wonder why they left it here."

Daphne shuddered. "You mean like we should be
praying, or something?"

"Let's hope not, but that metal thing that locks over
the window is creepy. I'll bet they've held prisoners
here before."

Daphne gripped the Bible and stared at him. Her
voice dropped to a whisper. "You think they're Mafia, don't you?"

Josh nodded.

She glanced away and bit her lip until the urge to cry
eased up a little. "It's my fault," she said at last, still
not looking at him.

"The hell it is. You didn't know anything about this. Your father should have told you."

"Or your mother should have told you!" she retorted hotly, glad for a chance to be angry.

"There's such a thing as client confidentiality, you know. But your dad brought you up here supposedly on vacation, when he was really investigating this whole thing with missing steel. You had a right to know that."

"Oh, yeah?" Daphne shook the Bible at him. "If your mother had done her job, instead of seducing her *client,* the pictures would've been taken a long time ago, and we never would have gone to that dumb rock concert, because I would have been doing all sorts of fun things with my dad!"

Josh's face reddened with anger. "You don't know anything about what happened that night. Gramps said they had two rooms."

"That proves zip!"

"It proves a lot in my book! Just because you have a suspicious mind, doesn't mean they—"

"Pipe down in there!" yelled a man from the other side of the door. "Or we'll do it for you."

Daphne and Josh each froze in their belligerent stance and looked at each other. After the fake police car had pulled them over just outside Las Vegas, they'd been tied, gagged and blindfolded, then brought here, where the restraints had been mercifully removed. Daphne rubbed her cheek where the duct tape had irritated her sensitive skin. She never wanted to be gagged again.

"That's better!" shouted the man.

As far as Daphne knew, he was the only one out there, but he was enough. She called him the Incredible Hulk in her mind. Besides that, he had a gun.

Then in the silence, she heard somebody talking to him. She knew that voice. Hurrying to the door, she pressed her ear against it. Yes, it was him! They were saved!

"Barnaby!" she shouted, banging on the door. "Barnaby!"

Josh crossed quickly to the door. "Who?"

"I know the other man out there!" She laughed as tears of relief poured down her cheeks. "Barnaby, let us out!"

"Pipe down, I said!" growled the Hulk, slamming his fist against the door so hard the jolt knocked Daphne a foot away.

Her mouth sagged open in disbelief. She strained to hear Barnaby's voice again, but now there was only silence.

"Who's Barnaby?" Josh whispered.

They weren't getting out. The acute disappointment made Daphne sick to her stomach. "My...my mother's fiancé."

"Your mother's fiancé was out there?"

She nodded, sure she hadn't been wrong.

"Daphne, what—"

She waved him to be quiet and sank cross-legged to the floor. "I have to think." She propped her head in her hands and let her hair fall around her face in a protective curtain. Resolutely, she blinked away tears and focused on the problem. Barnaby Haskett. He was a contractor, or something. She struggled to remember things that hadn't mattered to her at the time. Her father had so many deals. But Barnaby Haskett had been the contractor for one of them. That's how her mother met him. Was his deal this dumb bridge? *Think, Daphne!*

The gentle weight of Josh's arm settled on her shoulders. He didn't say anything. She liked that about Josh. When they weren't fighting, he seemed to understand when to talk and when to be quiet.

The bridge had to be it, she decided. Barnaby was in on this. That's how the Mafia guys had known to pick up her and Josh, because Barnaby gave them a description of them and their car. Her mother was going out with a horrible crook and didn't even know it. Fear spun like a whirlpool in her stomach. Her mother could be in danger, too, and there was no way for Daphne to warn her.

She shoved a length of hair behind her ear and glanced over at Josh. "I hate to tell you, but this is a bigger mess than I thought. My mom's fiancé is the contractor who was taking steel for the Mafia from my dad's shipments."

"Do you think your mom knows?"

"No way. That's what has me worried. She's supposed to spend a week with him in Reno. I have to warn her."

"My mom and your dad will get us out. Don't worry. My mom's really smart."

"So's my dad." Her laugh was hollow. "I mean *anybody's* smarter than the ape-man out there, right? If he's any example of the brain power of this operation, my dad'll run right over them."

"Yeah." Josh squeezed her shoulder. "We'll be out of here in no time."

"Yeah. In no time." The implication of Barnaby's actions were beginning to sink in. Once this was over, Barnaby would be out of the picture. She could definitely testify in court that he'd been in that room with the Hulk. And if her dad turned out to be a hero during the rescue, then her mother would see that he cared more about his family than his business. Then maybe her mother would forgive him, they'd remarry and everything would be okay again. If that happened, this whole nightmare would be worth something.

She smiled at Josh. "Let's ask ape-man to order us a pizza. I'm hungry."

ADAM WAS RELIEVED Loren agreed to wait before bringing in the police. If both she and Walt had insisted, he'd have given in, but he wanted to try it another way first. He already had some ideas about how they could get the kids safely out of the hands of the enemy. For that was what they had become in his mind. He'd deal with the kidnappers the same way he'd dealt with the Vietcong. You had to outthink them. He was alive today because he'd become an expert at that.

"We should try and get some rest," he said, evaluating the lines of exhaustion in Walt's face. Loren looked as keyed up as he felt, but Walt was sixty-eight and looking years older at the moment. Adam figured he might need Walt's expertise tomorrow night, and he wanted him alert.

Walt shook his head. "I don't think I can sleep."

"I don't, either," Loren said.

"Do you have anything in the house you can take to help both of you sleep?"

"I think there's something in my medicine cabinet," Walt said, "but I don't—"

"Then you'd better get it."

Walt shrugged and walked toward his bedroom, but Loren's chin came up in defiance.

Adam smiled at her. "What?"

"You know what. You sound like a top sergeant."

"That's exactly what I mean to sound like. I'm treating this like a military operation."

"And we're just two of your recruits?"

He crossed to her. "You're not *just* anything, and you know it. But I'll want you to take orders when the time comes. We can't all be chiefs or we'll have mass confusion."

Her brown eyes flashed. "I'm not used to taking orders, Adam."

He considered whether or not to lay it on the line and decided he might as well. "That's because you've never been through a war. This is a lot like war, Loren. Can you concede that I've had that experience and you haven't?"

Her expression became grim. "Yes, unfortunately."

"And because of my experience in that war, I understand some things that you don't?"

"I—"

"Here's the stuff," Walt said, returning with a small cardboard box. "But it really knocks you out. I don't like the idea that I might not hear some commotion."

"Don't worry. I'll hear it," Adam said. "I don't think we'll be bothered by anyone tonight, but I'll wake you both up if necessary."

"All right." With a resigned sigh, Walt took a capsule from the cardboard holder inside the box. "I hate to admit that I'm not as sturdy as you are, but I suppose if I'm going to be up until all hours tomorrow, I'd better get some sleep tonight."

"I'll wake the two of you up about four-thirty."

Walt handed the box to Loren. "Here you go. See you in the morning."

Once he'd disappeared into the back of the house, Loren tossed the box on the kitchen counter. "I'm not taking one of those. If you're keeping watch, so am I."

He knew better than to smile at her show of defiance, although he felt like it. Neither would he fight her on this. "If you insist," he said. "But I wasn't planning on standing here in the kitchen like a sentry. I thought I'd relax on the living room couch."

"Oh." She hesitated, and he could tell she didn't relish the idea of being alone in the kitchen. "Maybe I'll go into the living room, too, then."

Good. He might still coax her into getting some sleep. "Then you take the couch."

"That's okay. One of the chairs is fine."

What a stubborn woman. "Suit yourself." He flipped off the kitchen light, then the dining room light as they passed through. Then he turned the three-way switch on the living room lamp to its lowest wattage.

She watched him suspiciously. "I hope you're not dimming the lights because you imagine I'll drift off to sleep. I couldn't sleep in a million years."

"I understand you have no intention of sleeping." This was getting almost funny. He sat on the huge, old leather couch, which had been a terrific make-out spot years ago. He imagined it still contained the impression of his body. He'd sat there often enough.

Loren perched on one of two wing-back chairs opposite him, her spine straight, her eyes determinedly open.

He remembered the fabric on the chairs, cream-colored with tiny blue flowers. "Those chairs are in great shape for being as old as they are."

Loren glanced down and smoothed the chair arm. "Mom had them recovered."

"Really? But they look exactly the way I remember them."

"They should." She gazed at him across the room, her eyes misty. "She picked the same pattern. Dad told her he'd always liked the flowers because the color matched her eyes. She special-ordered that fabric from some company that buys up remnants."

That's how it is when you're in love, he thought with sharp regret. "I'll bet you miss her a lot."

"Yeah, I miss her a lot."

"Funny how I keep expecting her to walk down the hall or hear her banging around in the kitchen. Remember how she always seemed to know when we were getting too carried away on the couch? That's when she'd call out, 'How about some milk and cookies, kids?'"

"The old milk-and-cookies ploy," she said, her smile tinged with sadness.

"I'll say this. They were good cookies."

"Josh says I still can't make them as well as she did. So one day I gave *him* the recipe to try, and he made these little things that were as hard as golf balls." She chuckled. "But he wouldn't admit they were bad, and he almost broke his teeth eating . . ." Her laughter faltered and she pressed a hand to her mouth to hold back a sob.

He didn't stop to think, which was probably just as well or he might have hesitated, might not have done the human thing. He went to her, helped her rise from the chair and guided her over to the couch.

"It's going to be a long night," he said gently, sinking onto the couch and settling her into the crook of his arm, his touch devoid of any sexual overtones. "I think we'll need all the strength we can give each other."

She nodded and took the handkerchief he offered to blow her nose. "I . . . I guess you're right," she murmured. "But I don't want to complicate—"

"Hey." He gave her shoulder a soft squeeze. "This isn't about you and me right now. It's about them."

She nodded again.

"We'll get them back safe," he said. "I promise."

"We have to," she whispered. "I couldn't—"

"I know." He urged her head down against his shoulder. "I know."

Gradually, she relaxed as he stroked her hair. She needed to sleep, he thought, as a wave of tenderness spread through him. And he needed to hold her.

Gradually, her breathing settled into a steady, shallow rhythm. She was asleep. He leaned against the couch back and brought her more securely into the cradle of his arms. She moaned softly in her sleep, and he carefully, reverently, kissed the top of her head. "Don't worry," he murmured. "Don't worry, my love."

With a sigh, she cuddled closer to his chest and sank deeper into sleep. His throat grew tight as he absorbed her gift of trust. He had that much at least. But at what cost?

ADAM SLEPT LIGHTLY, in the manner of jungle animals, with a portion of his senses alert. He'd hoped never to have to use the skill again. He awoke before dawn, his muscles cramped from holding Loren all night. Yet, knowing she'd felt secure enough to sleep in his arms made every bit of the discomfort worth it.

"Loren," he whispered close to her ear. "Wake up."

Her eyes snapped open and she scrambled to a sitting position, nearly falling from the couch in her haste. "What time is it?"

"Early yet, but we need to get going."

She pushed her hair back from her face. "Right. I must have fallen asleep. Sorry."

"Don't be." He touched her cheek.

She met his gaze, and pink tinged her cheeks. "Thank you. Did you sleep at all?"

"Some."

"Good." There was a softness in her eyes that made him want to weep. Then she seemed to mentally shake herself, and she was all business again. She stood and glanced down at him. "You go make coffee while I wake Dad. Then we can each shower and change. You can borrow some clean clothes from Dad." She looked at the wall clock behind the couch. "We should make it out of here in half an hour, check you out of Los Arboles and be in the air by five-thirty."

He chuckled. "I thought I was in charge."

She smiled, her arms crossed over her chest. "Oh, really? I don't remember agreeing to that."

As she whisked down the hall, he shook his head and got up to make the coffee. Insubordination had never looked so damned appealing.

LOREN KEPT the schedule she'd outlined, he thought with admiration as he pulled the Geo into the circular entry of Los Arboles a little after five o'clock. Walt followed in Josh's old truck after Adam realized that the three of them plus Daphne's extensive luggage wouldn't fit in the Geo.

Adam drove past the valet and parked by the curb. "This shouldn't take long," he said, reaching for the door handle.

"I'll help." Loren was out of the car in a flash.

Adam didn't object. Her presence comforted him more than a little. He waved to Walt, who had parked the truck behind the Geo and followed Loren into the lobby.

The resort grounds were deserted in the soft, pre-dawn light except for a gardener snipping quietly at a hedge and the pool crew setting up the vacuum hoses. Adam and Loren didn't talk as they covered the distance to his room. He unlocked the door and they walked inside.

The light he'd left on when he'd taken her home was still burning. He remembered standing in this room, looking at Loren holding the envelope possessively against her chest. He would have given anything at that point to know what was wrong. Now that he knew, he wished to hell it could have been something else.

"This shouldn't take very long," he said, walking through the connecting door.

He wasn't even slightly prepared for the emotional effect of seeing Daphne's belongings strewn around, as if she'd be back any minute to change clothes and head out for another adventure. He stood in the doorway, gripping the knob until the metal imprinted itself on his flesh, while he fought the urge to scream and rage at the unfairness of it all.

Loren put a reassuring hand on his shoulder. So this was why she'd offered to help, he realized with a flash of insight. She'd known all along that seeing Daphne's things would sucker-punch him in the gut.

"I'll do Daphne's room, if you'd like," she murmured.

His shoulders slumped in defeat as he realized he'd never get through it without breaking down. "Thanks."

She gave him a quick squeeze of encouragement, slipped around him and began picking up discarded clothes the minute she stepped into the room. Adam turned away. When this nightmare was over, he wouldn't rest until Daphne knew how much he loved her.

Finally, they had everything together. Adam carried the bulk of it while Loren took two smaller bags. He remembered kidding Daphne about how much luggage she'd brought. On the next trip, he'd let her bring twice as much. Just let there be a next trip, he prayed.

They stopped at the checkout desk in the lobby, where a bellman hurried up to take the bags out to the Geo. Adam shoved the keys across the marble registration desk and waited impatiently for the clerk to get the bill off the computer.

"Looks like you had one long-distance phone call," the clerk said, sliding the bill toward Adam. "And of course, the room-service charges. Is everything in order?"

The room-service charges were staggering, but he wasn't surprised. He hadn't made any long-distance calls, so it had to be Daphne. He signed the credit-card slip, folded the bill and put it in his pocket. He couldn't make an issue of one long-distance call. After all, he had brought Daphne here and he had left her alone. He just wished he knew whom she'd called.

CHAPTER SEVENTEEN

"THE PLACE is surrounded with a cat's cradle of power lines." Loren peered through the telephoto lens of her hand-held .35-millimeter camera as her father guided Whiskey Foxtrot over Hoover Dam. She'd suggested using the smaller camera and aiming it out the open passenger window. The prints wouldn't be as detailed as she could get with the Wild RC-10, but they could have them within an hour of landing. Adam crouched behind her and used binoculars with which to study the site.

Loren hadn't noticed all the power lines until Adam suggested that Walt could helicopter her and the kids out of harm's way after the exchange. But now she gazed at canyon walls bristling with transmission towers, each of them sprouting tentacles of high-voltage cable. "It could be a real suicide mission to fly in here, Dad."

"Maybe not," Adam said, his breath warm on her neck. "And the more difficult it looks, the less they'll expect us to try something like that. I think a helicopter could come in over that bluff on the Nevada side of the dam, using the intake tower lights as a guide."

"What's an intake tower?" Loren asked. "All of us aren't engineers around here."

"Those four turrets that look as if they belong on a medieval castle," Adam said. "Two are in the water on the Nevada side of the lake and two are on the Arizona side."

Loren looked below her as Walt banked the plane to the right. The four structures squatted just behind the dam like concrete frogs. "Intake towers. Check."

"Okay, Walt," Adam continued, "when we come around again, look at the bluff right behind the Nevada intake towers. See that break in the power lines?"

"Sure do. I could bring a small chopper in there easy."

"So what?" Loren asked, focusing her camera on the two-lane road bordered by pedestrian walkways crossing the dam. "There's a steady stream of traffic down there where I'm supposed to meet the kidnappers. Where would you land to pick us up?"

"Traffic won't be as heavy at midnight," Walt reminded her.

"It doesn't have to be. One car can louse up the whole plan."

"That's where I come in," Adam said. "I'll rent an eighteen-wheeler in Vegas. At five minutes to midnight, when you're approaching the rendezvous point at the middle of the dam, I'll drive down from the Nevada side. I'll pull alongside you at the midway point, going slow. When you hand over the pictures, I'll stop, blocking traffic in that lane. Walt will land right in front of the truck and take all three of you out of there."

"I see what you have in mind," Walt said. "If they have any sharpshooters stationed on the Nevada side like you think they might, the truck will keep them from getting a clear shot while we load."

Loren's stomach became queasy. Sharpshooters with high-powered rifles hadn't been part of the scenario she'd imagined when she'd agreed to deliver the prints and negatives. But Adam seemed to think they might be there, ready to cut her and the kids down once the pictures were safely in the hands of the crooks. "Won't the noise of the helicopter alert them?" she asked.

"The wind blows up the canyon and will carry some of the noise away," Adam replied. "And the dam itself is noisy. I'll make sure I gun the motor of that big truck a lot, and maybe sound the horn a few times. If it's a small helicopter and it comes over the bluff just before the exchange, I don't think anyone will hear it until it's too late."

"Probably not," Walt agreed.

"Make that pass coming in from the west one more time, Walt," Adam said, "so Loren can get a good shot of it. Then we can head home, get those pictures processed and developed and plan our strategy."

"Will do," Walt said. "The whole thing's crazy as hell, but it just might work."

"Are you confident enough to leave the police out of it?" Adam asked Walt.

Loren held her breath. If her father said no, she and Adam had a problem on their hands. They couldn't pull off the rescue without Walt, so if her father really wanted the police, Adam had agreed to call them. Loren rebelled at the thought of handing her son's fate over to strangers, no matter how highly qualified they might be.

"Hell, I can fly a chopper as well as anybody, I guess," Walt said, and Loren sagged with relief. "If we call in the cops, they won't let me do a thing to rescue my grandson," he continued. "And if they loused it up, I'd never forgive myself."

Loren turned in her seat and caught the slight curve of Adam's mouth. She gave him a subtle thumbs-up.

"This plan of yours has real imagination, Adam," Walt said. "I'll bet you were a damn fine soldier."

Adam glanced at Loren, his expression unreadable behind the aviator sunglasses. "Most of us were," he said quietly. "We had no choice."

THE IRONY of the situation taunted Loren as she drove the lonely stretch of road leading to Hoover Dam that night. Twenty-three years ago she hadn't wanted Adam to know anything about war and its strategies. Now she prayed he'd learned enough in the jungles of Vietnam to see them all safely through the rescue operation.

The night they'd spent together in Laughlin he'd told her he wouldn't have been the same man if he'd stayed, and now she had to agree he was right. Certainly nothing in her civilian experience had prepared her for this sort of confrontation.

She'd been alone since midafternoon, when Adam and Walt had left for Vegas to rent the truck and the helicopter. The hours had seemed endless, with not much to do but think. She'd done a lot of thinking.

She'd begun by trying to blame Adam for dragging her and Josh into the whole mess, but he hadn't intended that, and she couldn't in good conscience make him the scapegoat. The truth was she'd led a sheltered life, and so had Josh. Perhaps too sheltered, she'd realized sometime during the long hours of waiting.

As if repeating her action of twenty-three years ago, she'd fought to keep Josh out of the military, yet his life was in danger, anyway. While pretending to have some control over Josh's safety, she'd had virtually none. Adam was right about that, too. Josh needed to make his own choices and his own mistakes. She'd have to learn to live with the uncertainty and the risks. She'd have to let him go.

At six that evening, she'd left Sedona in Adam's rented Geo, anxiety and adrenaline overcoming exhaustion as she drove to Flagstaff and headed west to Kingman. She'd been treated to a spectacular sunset that had nearly made her cry. By the time she'd turned north toward Hoover Dam, darkness had surrounded her.

Now she pushed the Geo over the speed limit as she crossed a broad valley on Highway 93, passing lighted billboards advertising cut-rate rooms in Vegas. Adam had called from there at five that afternoon and described the truck he'd rented. He'd settled on a white cab as being most visible in the dark. The truck had a long nose and no windfoil. The silver trailer would be unmarked.

He and Walt had bought and tested a communications system that would allow them to coordinate

Adam's arrival with Walt's. She was to park in a lot above the dam on the Arizona side and begin walking toward the midpoint of the dam at exactly five minutes before midnight.

"Are you okay?" Adam had asked her finally, concern in his voice.

"I'm okay," she'd replied, although she felt as if a skateboarder were living in her stomach.

"Remember, three blasts of the air horn means to dive behind the nearest obstacle."

"I'll remember."

"If anything pops near you, run for cover. It means they're shooting."

"Is this what it was like, getting ready to go into the jungle?"

"It was far too much like this. I'd give anything if you didn't have to—"

"Hey," she'd chided. "Up to this point, you've treated me like a member of the team. You wouldn't demote me before I have a chance to show what I can do, would you?"

"Never."

"Okay, then. We can do this."

"Yes, we can. And Lor...thanks for trusting me. It means a lot."

"I do trust you." Trust. Was that the word they'd meant to say, or the word they were using because another one was too dangerous?

There'd been a pause, and the sound of a long, shaky breath. "God, Loren, be careful. I..." Then another silence had hummed along the line.

"What, Adam?" she'd murmured, wishing she could see him, reach out to him.

"Just be careful," he'd said, his voice husky. "See you soon."

"Very soon," she'd whispered, and lowered the receiver into its cradle.

Loren glanced at the Geo's dashboard clock as Adam's last words echoed in her mind. "Very soon," she said into the darkness.

The valley crumpled into hills, and the four-lane road constricted to two as the descent to the dam began. Two sedans preceded her onto the narrowed pavement, and a motor home followed. Loren's heartbeat quickened as the road snaked deeper into the canyon. A flashing yellow light illuminated a sign posting a speed limit of fifteen miles an hour, and red lights popped on in the rear of both sedans. Loren tapped her brake pedal and gripped the wheel tighter as her fingers began to tremble.

One more curve and the dam appeared, glowing in the night. Blue lights winked atop the intake towers and recessed white lights illuminated the rock walls on either side of the road crossing the dam. Fifteen minutes before midnight. Josh and Daphne would be waiting across the canyon for the appointed time. Loren drew comfort from the fact that Adam was over there somewhere waiting, too, and while Josh and Daphne walked toward her, he'd be cruising his truck beside them, ready to act if anything went wrong.

She parked in a deserted lot overlooking the dam, took the envelope containing the prints and negatives from the seat beside her, locked the car and started walking. She held the envelope with both hands, afraid it might slip out of fingers that felt as if they'd been dipped in snow.

Across the canyon on the Nevada side, gray stone buildings housed the administration offices of the dam. Nearby stood a giant flagpole, its stars and stripes spotlighted and billowing in the wind. Loren noticed that the wind blew up the canyon, just as Adam had said.

Vehicles moved slowly across the dam a few at a time, but Loren saw no pedestrians on the sidewalks. Someone would have to appear soon. She'd almost reached level ground, and a glance at her watch showed the time: two minutes before midnight. No white truck appeared on the switchbacks across the canyon. Her blood pounded in her ears.

He'd said he'd be there. He would be there. But what if he'd been discovered somehow? What if the kidnappers driving to the site had become suspicious about an eighteen-wheeler parked in a turnoff and investigated?

Then Loren heard a blast on an air horn. Adam! Her gaze flew to the curving road across from her, where a white semi eased down. He was late. Ahead of him an enormous motor home inched along at no more than five miles an hour. Loren slowed her steps just as she caught a movement near the sidewalk on the opposite side of the dam.

She looked more closely, and her chest constricted so forcefully she could barely breathe. Josh and Daphne were walking slowly across the dam ahead of . . . Barnaby Haskett.

She hadn't expected him to be the deliveryman. He'd said he'd be out of the country by now. Why had the kidnappers wanted a picture of her if they'd intended to send Haskett? Maybe they'd asked him to deliver the picture so he couldn't run away. She glanced up at the cliffs on the far side of the dam and her stomach heaved.

Wanting to put an end to the uncertainty, she walked faster. The fast walk threatened to turn into a run toward the kids. *But Adam wasn't there yet.* It took all her willpower to slow down again. She didn't dare look up at the truck or over at the bluff where Walt would be coming with the helicopter.

She clutched the envelope to her chest like a shield, and walked along the sidewalk on the river side of the dam toward Josh and Daphne. Her heart wrenched at how young they both looked, how vulnerable and afraid. What monsters would threaten such beautiful children?

They'd had a rough time of it. She wanted to believe they looked tattered because they'd been to a boisterous rock concert. But she doubted it. Josh's Cardinals football jersey and the knees of his jeans were stained as if he'd been rolling on the ground. Daphne's silver lamé cat suit was ripped, and her jeweled vest hung crookedly across her shoulders. Her hair, which she'd once tossed with such arrogance, hung in matted clumps. Loren bit her lip to keep from calling out to them.

As she drew nearer, she looked into their faces, rigid with fear. Sweat dampened her armpits and trickled down her spine, and her mouth tasted as if she'd been sucking on pennies, but she forced her lips into a smile. Josh acknowledged her smile with the faintest nod of his head, but Daphne remained stiff, her lips almost white.

Another blast of the air horn sounded, closer this time, but Loren couldn't be sure how close as echoes filled the canyon. Then the engine roared, and Loren knew the helicopter had been summoned. She strained to hear it over the hum of the dam's huge generators, the rush of water below them and the rumbling of the truck. She couldn't.

She judged herself to be about a hundred yards from Josh and Daphne, when her peripheral vision picked up the motor home coming toward her. And behind the motor home was Adam.

The motor home seemed to slow even more as the driver and his portly wife craned their necks to take in the lake to their left and the dam to their right. Loren felt hysteria bubbling in her. Rubbernecking tourists at midnight!

Adam laid on the horn again, and the motor home driver stuck his hand out the window and threw him a rude gesture.

Haskett glanced in the direction of the motor home as it rumbled past, then looked at Loren. He lifted his eyebrows and shrugged, as if sharing a dark joke with her.

The moment was unreal, but then, the whole episode was unreal, a nightmare from which she'd surely awake. Impulse almost had her smiling back at Haskett—until she remembered he was one of the people responsible for kidnapping her child and holding him for ransom. Then ice enshrouded her heart and she stepped resolutely forward as the white semi cruised toward her.

Her timing and Adam's had to be perfect. She moved toward Josh and Daphne, but her concentration was all on the man in the driver's seat of the truck. She had to sense the exact moment to hand the envelope over and grab the kids.

Ten feet away, Haskett moved between Josh and Daphne. Loren looked into his eyes and saw fear. Suddenly, she knew he'd been forced to make the delivery and was terrified something would go wrong. The knowledge did nothing to calm her.

She was within arm's length of him when she sensed that Adam was going to stop the truck. She thrust the envelope forward and felt the tug of an answering grasp a second before the air brakes sighed and a helicopter clattered overhead.

"Now!" she shouted, not sparing even a glance at Haskett as she grabbed Josh by one hand and Daphne by another.

They shot forward, almost knocking her down, but Josh steadied her before they raced for the open door of the helicopter. The wind from the whirling blades ripped at them and drowned out any noise except the frantic battering of the air. Daphne hurtled to a back seat and Josh shoved Loren in behind her. He was only halfway into the copilot's seat, when Walt lifted off.

"Close the door!" Walt yelled at Josh.

Josh obeyed, and Walt arched the helicopter over the dark surface of the lake, under the power lines and up, up to safety.

"Who was in that truck?" screamed Daphne, her fingernails digging into Loren's arm.

"Your father!" Loren yelled back, panting. "He's meeting us down the road at the first lookout point!"

Daphne craned her neck to look back through the helicopter's side window. "He's not!" she cried, and began to sob. "No, he's not!"

Loren's heart slammed against her chest. "Turn this thing so we can see back there!" she shouted to her father.

Walt came around to the right, giving Loren a perfect view of the road across the dam. She clutched her stomach and cried out.

The truck hadn't moved.

CHAPTER EIGHTEEN

ADAM HAD KEPT the last part of his plan to himself, knowing Walt and Loren would never agree to it. But he had learned one immutable truth in the jungle; if you had the enemy in your sights, you never let him escape.

The moment he slammed the truck to a stop, he threw himself across the truck seat and out the passenger door. Haskett had a head start by the time Adam leaped to the sidewalk, but it didn't matter. Adam had been the fastest running back in Flagstaff High's history. Foot races exhilarated him.

He tackled Haskett from behind, knocking the wind from both of them as they hit the sidewalk. From the corner of his eye, Adam saw the envelope shoot across the concrete and stop against the rock wall bordering the dam. His moment of attention to the envelope cost him dearly as Haskett kicked him in the face, dazzling him with pain as his nose crunched and warm blood rushed from his nostrils and into his mouth.

He spat it away and relaunched himself at Haskett as he scrambled for the envelope. A split second before Adam made contact, Haskett grabbed the envelope and crouched against the wall. Adam tried to pin him there, but desperation seemed to give Haskett strength he hadn't displayed before. With one mighty shove he pushed Adam backward.

Adam shook his head and started forward. "Don't be stupid," he gasped. "They'll kill you, anyway. Give yourself up."

"Screw you, Riordan," he sneered. Then he turned and hurled the envelope over the dam.

Adam tackled him low, pinning him against the waist-high wall.

"Now you give up," Haskett said through clenched teeth. "Your evidence is gone, man."

"Then I'll have to make do with you." Grunting with the effort, Adam forced him backward, until Haskett's head hung out over the seven-hundred-foot drop. "Who told you about those pictures?"

Haskett strained against him. "A little...birdie," he panted.

"It's a long way down."

"That's...right!" He jackknifed against Adam, temporarily breaking the hold enough to leap away from the wall. As they circled each other, Adam recognized the stance of a doomed man. Haskett knew he'd gambled with the wrong crowd. He had nothing to lose, which made him the most dangerous kind of opponent.

Haskett closed in, locking his body with Adam's and wrestling him toward the wall. They gasped and writhed, each trying for supremacy.

"One of us...is going over," Haskett said between heaving breaths.

"I vote for you." Adam braced himself against the wall and tried to bend Haskett over it again. The level of fear in Haskett's eyes escalated to panic as he began to slip.

Then the sound of a helicopter beat its way into Adam's consciousness. Oh, God, they were coming back. He looked up, and in that second Haskett flipped him against the wall and began slowly, steadily, easing him over it.

Ocean waves seemed to be crashing against Adam's eardrums. He struggled to maintain his hold on the wall and on the man who wanted to shove him to his death. Haskett pushed his face sideways, so he had to look down the long, shadowed slope of the dam to the concrete below. He wouldn't land in water, though that would probably kill him just as easily. He'd hit a concrete apron at the very base of the dam and be smashed like a bug on a windshield.

He strained to regain his balance while his fevered brain kept asking why the helicopter carrying the people he loved was coming back into the danger zone.

"Since you're gonna die, anyway," Haskett said through clenched teeth, "I'll tell you. It's Anita."

Anita? What was he saying? Then Adam knew. Anita had told Haskett about the pictures. He didn't know how, but she'd gained the information necessary to betray him. And endanger Daphne. The knowledge charged through his body like a lit fuse, igniting an instinct long buried. The mantle of civilization slipped from his shoulders as he forgot the helicopter overhead. Nothing mattered but survival.

With a howl of rage, he heaved upward. For one horrible moment, he thought his momentum would carry them both over as they teetered together on the edge of the wall. Then he threw his weight toward the sidewalk, and they toppled against each other in a writhing mass.

With hell's fury as his companion, subduing his adversary was almost easy. By the time Josh and Walt rushed over to help, Haskett was facedown on the sidewalk, his arms pinned behind his back. A police car roared up, sirens blaring, and two officers loaded him into the back of a squad car almost before the blades of the small helicopter parked on the road stopped whirling.

"Daddy!" Daphne hurled herself into his arms. "You're bleeding!"

He held her tight and looked around for Loren. When he found her standing next to Josh, he recoiled from the look of agony in her eyes. Her lips moved. Although he couldn't hear her one-word question, he knew what it was. *Why?*

Despair gripped him. In the midst of the agony surrounding the kidnapping, hope had flowered. Hope that she understood the kind of man he was and accepted it. Hope that her understanding had fostered more than trust. Hope that they could face their personal problems with the same sense of partnership they'd used to foil the kidnappers. That hope was gone. They were back to the same question that had ripped them apart twenty-three years ago. *Why?*

DAPHNE CLUNG to her father for dear life. She was never letting him go. Never. Then she remembered what had happened with Barnaby.

"Daddy," she said desperately, looking into his ravaged face, "we have to warn Mom right now. If

Barnaby is in with those guys, she could be in danger. We have to warn her."

"I'll have the police contact her, Daphne." Her father smoothed her hair away from her face the way he used to do when she was a little girl.

"But we should call her, too. Maybe from here. We can get the number of the resort in Aspen. Maybe she needs police protection, or something."

"She's in Aspen?" her father said. "Are you sure?"

"Of course I'm sure. I talked to her night before last, and I know she's still there."

Her father had a strange look in his eyes. "You called her the night I was in Laughlin?"

Daphne nodded. "Yeah, I was mad at you, so I called her to whine about it. I'm sorry, Dad. I didn't realize what was going on."

"And I'll bet you told her about Loren and me going to Laughlin to take pictures, didn't you?"

"Yes." Daphne tried to identify the expression on her father's face. He'd looked like that when he'd had to tell her that Great-Grandma Riordan, a woman Daphne had adored, had died in her sleep. Fear closed her throat. "Daddy, she's okay, isn't she? They didn't..."

"I'm sure she's fine, Daphne." He held her more tightly. "But you'll need to give the police the name of that spa in Aspen."

"Well, sure. They probably should protect her. I mean, who knows what—"

"No, Daphne. They'll be arresting her."

Daphne stared at him, not quite ready to accept the meaning of the words he'd just spoken.

"I'm afraid she was in on this, too," her father said gently. "I'm sure she doesn't know you were kidnapped. She would never have wanted you hurt. But she knew Haskett was taking the steel."

Daphne felt as if spiders were crawling over her skin. "No, no, she didn't."

"It's pretty clear she did, Daphne. I'm sorry."

She pushed away from him. "You're not! You're not the least bit sorry. I know who told you this." She spun around, searching for that hated face. "*She* told you my mother was in on it, didn't she?"

"No," her father said. "Loren didn't—"

"She said it just to get my mother out of the way," Daphne continued, advancing on her mother's rival standing there so innocently between her beloved son and her beloved father. "My mother's not even here to defend herself, but I am. I'll—"

"Cool it," Josh said, stepping between his mother and Daphne at the same moment Adam laid a firm hand on Daphne's shoulder.

"Apologize to Loren, Daphne," he said, his voice dangerously low. "She risked her life for you."

"And be quick about it, young lady," Walt added.

She couldn't believe it. They were all ganging up on her. Her careful plans for how her mother and father would get back together were being ruined by this woman. She wouldn't apologize in a million years. Not in a trillion years.

"Daphne." Her father's hand settled more heavily on her shoulder.

"He's right, Daphne," Josh said, moving back to put his arm around his mother in a protective gesture. "You had no right saying that about Mom."

"Never mind, Adam." Loren stepped forward and looked Daphne in the eye. "She's only defending her mother. I don't blame her for that. Anyone would do the same."

Daphne shrank in horror. This was worse. Now Loren was *forgiving* her. "I hate your guts," she said, and walked away, away from all of them.

"Daphne!" her father roared.

She ignored him. Then she heard another voice. Loren's voice. "Don't, Adam," she said. "Leave her alone."

Daphne stood by the wall, tears pouring down her cheeks and spattering the gray surface. She clenched her fists so hard her fingernails stabbed her palms. Her mother hadn't known a thing about Barnaby's dealings. Not a thing. But her father was so in lust, he'd believe whatever Loren said. Daphne had never hated anyone as much as she hated Loren Stanfield.

SOMEHOW LOREN GOT through the maze of police procedure that took up the rest of the night. She was grateful, in a way, that all the flurry of activity kept her from having to face Adam alone. She had no idea what to say. Once again he'd foolishly risked his life. Catching the crooks apparently meant more to him than being with her.

She'd imagined he was beyond taking such chances. She'd even thought that maybe, after this was over, they could reconsider their earlier decision to go their separate ways and try to work things out, instead. She'd imagined they had a chance.

What a joke! And his daredevil behavior was only half the problem. The other half was Daphne. Even if the girl finally accepted the fact that her mother was guilty, her resentment of Loren for being there to witness her humiliation could last forever. If Anita faced prison, Adam's commitment to his daughter would become even more critical. And he couldn't be a devoted father to Daphne with Loren in the picture. Daphne wouldn't allow it.

As dawn approached, it was arranged that the police would give Loren, Josh and Walt a ride to Las Vegas where Whiskey Foxtrot was parked. The police had located Josh's Suburban in Las Vegas and would hold it until someone came to take it home. Adam decided to drive the rental car to Sedona where he and Daphne would pick up the Scorpio plane and return to Phoenix.

Consequently, Loren, Walt and Josh arrived in Sedona before Adam and Daphne. Walt wanted to wait at the airport for Adam, so Loren talked Josh into taking her home in Walt's old truck.

Once there, she fell across her bed, expecting to fall instantly asleep. It didn't happen. Two hours later, when her father tapped on her door and softly called her name, she told him to come in.

"He picked up the plane," Walt said, sitting on the bed beside her. "Took that little bi... that Daphne with him."

She didn't comment.

"And he asked me to give you a message. He said he'd done a lot of thinking on the drive to Sedona. He wanted me to tell you he'd be back."

Loren turned her head and gazed into her father's sympathetic eyes. "Unfortunately, it'll be a wasted trip."

WANTING TO SORT THROUGH his thoughts, Adam had let Daphne sleep on the drive to Sedona and again on the plane ride to Phoenix. She remained silent through the process of putting the plane in the hangar at Sky Harbor and retrieving his Mercedes.

They left the executive terminal in his Mercedes, and the car's air conditioner cooled the interior from one hundred and twenty degrees to a civilized seventy-eight. He thought she might apologize for her behavior at last, but she slumped in her seat and stared out the window. They rode that way as he left the center of town and headed north toward Fountain Hills, with his head pounding, the bandage on his nose driving him crazy and Daphne sulking.

Finally, when he was two miles from the turnoff to his town house, he glanced at her. "Would you like to stay with me temporarily, instead of going back to the house?"

"No. I'll just stay at home and wait for Mom."

"She won't be home until after the hearing tomorrow, and that's only if someone posts bail for her."

"You mean you won't?"

"No."

"Dad!"

He glanced at her stricken face, but was unmoved. "She conspired with Haskett to defraud me, which was bad enough, but she's indirectly responsible for nearly getting you killed. Nearly getting us all killed."

Daphne slumped farther in her seat. "I suppose by *all*, you're including that woman."

"Yes." He held on to his temper with difficulty. "And I suggest you call her by her name. Without her, we might not be having this conversation."

"So, are you going to marry her?"

Adam sighed. "I'm going to see her at least once more, if she'll agree. She may not, and I can guarantee she has no desire to marry me." He glanced over and noticed a smug expression stealing over Daphne's face. "Don't take too much credit for that. Loren and I have problems that have nothing to do with you."

"Like what?"

"Never mind."

She folded her arms and glared at him. "I guess you didn't really mean it when you said you'd start telling me more stuff."

"Don't try laying a guilt trip on me, Daphne." He struggled for patience. "I'm not about to give you information about a woman you've just insulted, a woman I happen to respect."

"I should have figured you'd go back on that promise," she mumbled, obviously not willing to hear what he'd said. "You never did care about me, anyway."

"That's not true."

"It is true. Your business was always more important to you than I was."

"No, Daphne." He sensed this might be a critical point with Daphne and tried to ignore the ache in his head. "I wanted to do things with you. But maybe they were the wrong things. Like on your ninth birthday, I'd planned to take you to an air show, but your mother said you didn't want to go, that you'd rather have a party with your friends."

Daphne frowned. "My ninth birthday? Oh, yeah. That was when she took a bunch of us to lunch and then on a shopping spree at the Borgata. But I don't remember her telling me about an air show. I always wanted to go to one of those." She eyed him suspiciously. "You could be making that up, just to pretend you were interested in doing stuff with me. Because if Mom told me about that air show, I can't believe I wouldn't have picked that over shopping at the Borgata."

"Or," Adam said, voicing a growing suspicion of his own, "maybe your mother didn't give you the choice."

"Why wouldn't she? She was always wishing you'd pay more attention to me, instead of keeping your nose stuck in your steel business."

Adam slowed the Mercedes as they approached a red light. When the car glided to a halt, he gazed at Daphne. "That's interesting. She was always telling me that my ideas for entertaining you were inappropriate for a young girl and I should stick to what I knew, which was the steel business."

Daphne exploded with laughter. "I don't believe that!" Then her laughter died and she flicked him a glance. "Like what?"

He searched his memory. The rejections of his attempts at fatherhood stood out like little sore bumps, and he wasn't eager to touch them again. Daphne would probably agree with Anita's assessment, anyway. "I remember once thinking you'd like a ride in an eighteen-wheeler, but I suppose you wouldn't have wanted—"

"I thought you wouldn't *let* me."

"No, your mother wouldn't let you. Would you have gone?"

"Are you crazy? Any little kid loves those big rigs."

His suspicions grew even more. "Then there was the time when you were doing so well in math, and I wanted to take you down to the office over the weekend and show you the accounting system on the computer. I thought I might even begin assigning you some little jobs, for a small salary."

"Yeah? You wanted me to work for you?"

"Why not? You're very smart."

"Dad."

He glanced away from traffic for a second to look at her.

"Are you sure you're not making this up?"

"That particular one you can check with Donna, our bookkeeper. I remember telling her my idea, and she thought it was great. But your mother said that would be boring for you, and besides, your weekends were too busy with other things."

"Like shopping, I guess she meant."

"Probably. And I knew how much you liked going out to buy new clothes."

"Well, sure, Dad. Most girls like that. But if I'd had a chance to work for you in the office... Why didn't you ask me yourself?"

He shrugged. "I didn't know much about raising girls. I didn't have sisters, so I depended on Anita to clue me in." And in light of what he'd learned in the past twenty-four hours, he'd been far too trusting. "I have a question for you," he said, bringing up the most painful rejection of all. "Why didn't you ask me to teach you to fly?"

"Are you kidding? With all the work you had to do? You'd never have had time to teach me."

"I would have made time," he said quietly.

"Oh, sure. You say that now, but I remember asking Mom if she thought you'd be able to teach me, and she said—" Daphne stopped abruptly.

"She said I was too busy, right?"

"Yeah." Daphne fidgeted with her shoulder harness. "But you *were* busy, Dad. Admit it. You were down at Scorpio Steel six days a week and sometimes on Sunday. I can see why Mom divorced you. She never saw you."

"You're right." He swerved into the circular driveway that led to the elegant home overlooking the golf course, a course he'd never played. "Your mother and I didn't spend much time with each other. Apparently, that made her very angry with me."

"Well, duh! Of course it would."

"But I never thought she was angry enough to take my daughter away."

"Don't be silly. She didn't take me away."

Adam stopped the car in front of the entryway and gazed at her. "Didn't she?"

CHAPTER NINETEEN

IT WAS Georgia's day off, so Adam didn't leave the Fountain Hills house until he made sure there was plenty to eat in the refrigerator. Daphne still didn't believe that her mother had conspired to drive a wedge between father and daughter, but Adam was convinced. He arrived at his town house gritty and exhausted, but he had one call to make before he could shower and sleep.

The receptionist at the law firm of Flannery and O'Donnell said Mr. Flannery was in conference and couldn't be disturbed, but when Adam identified himself, she put him through.

"I was wondering if I'd hear from you," Flannery said. "She's going to need money."

"I know. And I'm willing to provide some. But in exchange, she's going to have to do something for me."

As WALT TAXIED Whiskey Foxtrot toward the Icarus hangar late the next afternoon, Loren saw a red Mercedes parked beside it and her stomach lurched. The luxurious car in that particular color could belong to only one person.

"Looks like you have a visitor," Walt said over his shoulder, a note of satisfaction in his voice. "I didn't expect him so soon, busy as he is."

Loren hadn't, either. She wasn't up to this. Why couldn't he just leave her alone? "We're busy, too," she said, her heart pounding. "I don't have time to fool around with him. You know what our schedule looks like, and with the weather so unpredictable, we—"

Walt chuckled. "It's five-thirty, Loren. Time for dinner. Surely you could spare him an hour while you eat something."

She collected the film canisters. "You still think he's okay, don't you?"

"I guess I do."

"Dad, the guy has a death wish and the daughter from hell. Why would you want me involved with those kinds of problems?"

Her father took off his sunglasses and swiveled in his seat. "Because I don't think you've ever been in love with anybody else."

Heat rose in her cheeks. "That's ridiculous!"

"Is it? People don't always come packaged just like we want, Loren. Life hardly ever turns out the way you expect it to, either. I thought your mother and I would live to a ripe old age together."

Loren's throat constricted. "I wish you had."

"So do I. But even if somebody had told me when I married Fran that I'd lose her to cancer before we reached sixty, I'd still have married her, and been happy for the chance."

Loren put down the film canisters so she could reach over the seat and hug him. Then she drew back and gave him a teary smile. "You're terrific, you know that?"

"Sure." Her father patted her arm. "Give him a chance to say his piece. Then listen to your heart."

Her reply was husky with emotion. "Okay."

He opened the door, then turned to her. "I agree Daphne's a handful." He winked. "But so were you." Then he climbed from the plane.

Digesting that last thought, Loren jumped down onto the steamy tarmac, hauled out the canisters and shut the cabin door.

A plane revved its engine nearby as she walked into the hangar, so Adam, who had his back to the doorway, didn't hear her come in. He was talking to Josh.

Loren pushed her sunglasses to the top of her head and stood listening while she tried to subdue the rush of welcome she felt at the sight of Adam.

"So you're really going in?" Adam asked.

Josh nodded enthusiastically. "I've already contacted a recruiter," Josh said, "and he says to get my degree at MIT, then enlist as an officer." His gaze swerved to his mother.

She gave him an uncertain smile before putting the film canisters on the workbench.

"Mom still doesn't like the idea much, but she's not going to disown me, or anything," Josh said. "So what branch do you recommend? I was thinking marines, but—"

"Josh," Walt said, coming over to put his arm around his grandson, "I think Adam has some business with your mother, and now that she's here, maybe we should let them take care of it."

"Oh, sure. Sure thing."

Adam turned, and Loren gasped. He had two black eyes. That, along with the white bandage on his nose, made him look like a creature from a nightmare.

"Pretty grisly, huh?" He smiled, which looked grotesque combined with the battered upper half of his face. "But you should see the other guy."

Loren shuddered. "I don't even want to think about the other guy."

"No, I don't suppose you do. Look, I'm not the most attractive of dinner partners at the moment, but I would like to talk to you. Are you free?"

Loren nodded, then glanced down at her khaki shorts and blue tank top. "Although I'm not dressed for anything fancy."

"That wasn't what I had in mind, anyway."

"Good." Candlelight and wine would remind her of their last dinner together, when she'd spent the meal trying to think of how to get the prints and negatives away from him. She pulled her sunglasses over her eyes. "Let's go."

Outside the hangar Adam glanced up at the clouds. "I hope it doesn't rain."

"Usually does this time of year." She couldn't believe they were discussing the weather.

"Yeah, I know." He opened the passenger door of his car for her. "If the seat's not comfortable, you can adjust it using those buttons on the door."

The honey-colored leather felt cool against her bare legs. After buckling herself in, she experimentally punched a button, and the front of the seat tilted up an inch or so. She moved it back down. Soon she'd punched all the buttons and tested every position the seat offered. After deciding on a gently reclining mode, it occurred to her that they weren't moving yet. She glanced over at Adam and found him watching her with a smile on his face.

"So I'm easily impressed," she said.

"I sure hope so." After putting the car in gear, he pushed a button on the dash and Roberta Flack began to sing "The First Time Ever I Saw Your Face."

Loren fumbled with her control panel until she brought her seat bolt upright. "How do I shut that off?" she asked, reaching for the dash.

"I thought you liked that song."

"Not anymore." She felt her sense of control slipping away.

"Well, I do. And it's my car."

She resorted to being a smart aleck in order to counter the effect of the heartrending song. "Is that how you're going to be? Pushy?"

Adam's mouth quirked. "Maybe."

She estimated their speed at less than ten miles an hour as they cruised slowly past the hangars to the entrance gate. "Because if you're going to be pushy, I'm getting out."

Adam touched a button on his door and she heard the click of locks.

"Hey!" She pulled up on her door handle and nothing happened. She pushed every available button and the door was still locked. "You can't do this."

He remained serene. "Last time you disapproved of my behavior, you wouldn't listen to my explanation, either. This time I'm determined that you will."

"That's not fair." Her voice was beginning to betray her.

"A lot of things in life aren't fair, Loren. Sometimes even you aren't fair."

"You've locked me in here to insult me?"

"No, to tell you once and for all why you love me."

That rendered her speechless. Finally, she managed a faint comeback. "Who says I do?"

"I say so. The lovee."

She laughed. She didn't want to, but she couldn't help it. Then, as the tender words of Roberta Flack's song filled the car, her throat closed with emotion. She certainly did love him, had loved him from the first time ever she saw his face, just as the song said.

"You love me because I'll fight for what I believe in," Adam said, glancing at her. "And so will you."

She cleared her throat. "Oh, you'll fight, all right. Look at you."

"I may have black eyes, but you could have been shot. I got a call today that confirmed the existence of sharpshooters at the scene last night. I guess Haskett is spilling his guts, hoping the police can keep him alive."

"He almost spilled yours all over the bottom of that dam. When Walt brought the helicopter in close and I saw you hanging over that edge..." She couldn't go on.

"I know." He reached over and squeezed her knee. The casual touch electrified her. "But I had to go after him, just like I had to go to Vietnam. Somebody has to stand up to the bullies in this world, Lor."

"But does it always have to be you?"

He sighed. "Yeah, I'm afraid so."

"It's so hard on me!"

"That's what you get for loving me. You can't have it both ways, which is what I meant when I said you were sometimes unfair." He glanced at her. "You admire me for the kind of person I am, but you don't want to face the consequences of my being that kind of person. I'll take risks to do what's right. It's as simple as that. Deal with it, Loren."

She gasped. "And what if I don't want to?"

He looked at the gas gauge. "I'd estimate about five hours of driving time left. Maybe you'll change your mind."

"You're bluffing. There's no way you'd keep me locked in this car for five hours."

He turned right and started through town. "I don't know if I'm bluffing or not. Until this moment, it never occurred to me you wouldn't immediately see the logic of my argument."

She sat quietly as he maneuvered the car through the press of tourist traffic. He was appealing to her intelligence and sense of fairness. Good techniques, she acknowledged grudgingly. "Are we driving anyplace in particular?"

"That depends."

"Okay, maybe I do see the logic of your argument," she admitted finally. "I don't like it, but I see it. Now what?"

"I guess you have to decide if you can live with me, knowing my habit of sacrificing myself to the cause, or if you'd rather not be around that kind of behavior."

She turned to him, heart pounding. "Did you say live with you?"

"As in husband and wife. We've wasted twenty-three years. I'm not much interested in a long court-ship."

"You must be out of your mind! Even if I thought it over and decided I could accept your tendency to sacrifice yourself to a noble cause, which I'm not saying I've done, what about Daphne?"

"We'll talk about Daphne." He inched past the rows of cars and pedestrians at Slide Rock. "This tourist crush is definitely out of hand. I can't believe there are so many people around."

"Welcome to summer in Sedona."

He grimaced. "I may have to revise my plan."

"Which is?"

He didn't answer, but not far up the road he pulled over, easing the Mercedes between a minivan and a pickup truck. He released the locks and opened his door. "Let's at least see what the situation looks like." He climbed out.

Loren's stomach churned, as she, too, exited the car. This had been their favorite spot, the spot where they'd planned to make love. Except it was July now, not May, and twenty-three years later, when thousands more tourists had discovered Sedona and Oak Creek Canyon.

She met him back by the trunk, knowing he'd have a blanket and picnic basket in there. He did.

He handed her the blanket and hefted the picnic basket with a wry grin. "I guess this isn't more public than any of the restaurants would be."

"That's true." Taking a deep breath, she followed him down the rocky path to the creek. The shouts and squeals of children playing nearly drowned out the music of the water. The scent of grilled hamburger overpowered the fragrance of wildflowers. And yet . . . she responded to the feel of the path beneath her feet with the dizzy excitement she'd had at eighteen.

She'd never returned to this exact spot, so the old associations weren't overlaid with new. Perhaps it was the Roberta Flack song. Perhaps it was sheer exhaustion from the events of the past few days. But it seemed as if she'd been here only yesterday, as if she and Adam had returned to that heady time when life swelled with promise.

They paused at the edge of the creek and looked across. The moss had been worn away from the clearing beside the creek where they used to spread their blanket, rubbed clean by countless others who'd spread blankets there, too. The cottonwood shading their spot was much larger now, its dappled trunk too big to circle with both arms.

A family occupied a picnic table several yards downstream, and to the right a couple of boys were splashing in the water, but Adam and Loren's special place was empty. They could have their picnic, but it wouldn't be secluded.

Adam shrugged. "Oh, well, what the heck. We're here. Let's do it."

A row of boulders created stepping stones across the water. On graduation night, Adam had carried her across those boulders to preserve her white dress. She didn't think he'd try it today. The summer rains had raised the water level, shellacking the boulders with a thin film of moisture, just enough to make them treacherous.

Adam balanced on the first one and crossed to the second, where he turned back and held out his hand. She placed hers within it and felt a current of excitement surge through her at his touch. She balanced on the first rock and stepped to the second while he moved on to the third.

But when she reached the third, she slipped. Grabbing his arm, she pulled them both off balance and they splashed into knee-deep water cold as ice.

"Yeow!" Adam juggled the picnic basket as he staggered in the cold water.

"I'm sorry!" She clutched the picnic blanket. A corner had dipped into the water, but she'd managed to keep the rest of it dry. "I'm a little out of practice for this, I guess."

"You mean you don't come here?" He glanced over his shoulder at her.

"No. Never."

"Why not?"

She waved him forward. "Come on, Adam. Let's get out of the darned water, okay?"

"I'm just starting to get used to it." He steadied the picnic basket on his shoulder and offered her his hand again.

They sloshed to the opposite bank and climbed out. Adam's jeans were soaked to his thighs. Only the hem of Loren's shorts got wet, but her shoes squished with each step.

Adam set the picnic basket in a cradle created by exposed tree roots. "Let's spread the blanket."

She tossed him a corner and they opened the blanket. As they started to lay it on the ground, her gaze met his.

"So why don't you ever come here?" he asked.

"Because."

"Because this is our place?"

"Yes. Are you satisfied now?"

"Not by a long shot. But it's a start." He smoothed a wrinkle from the blanket, stood erect and glanced around. "Just like in the old days, isn't it?"

"Except for your two black eyes and broken nose."

"Actually, I did have a broken nose before, from the time that guy from Holbrook tackled me on the five-yard line and my helmet came off." He pulled off his shoes.

"So you did," she agreed, following suit. "Then nothing's changed, after all."

"Oh, I wouldn't say that. Twenty-three years ago, I wouldn't have had the nerve to do this." He unbuttoned his jeans and peeled them off.

"Adam!" She tried not to stare at his muscled thighs and the glimpse of navy briefs beneath his shirttail.

He grinned at her as he tossed the jeans on a rock. "So what? There's almost no difference between these and bathing trunks, and I'm not going to eat in soggy jeans."

She lowered her voice. "I think that was a deliberate effort to...to..."

He laughed. "Set the mood? It's not a bad idea, but you pulled me into the water, so I can't claim credit. But if it works, so much the better."

"Don't count on it. Not with all these people surrounding us."

"Too bad. Then we might as well eat." He retrieved the basket and opened it. To her surprise, the
basket disguised a small, insulated cooler.

She sat on the blanket while he unpacked a bottle of
wine, glasses and containers of fried chicken, potato
salad and chunks of raw vegetables. "I don't remember anything like this when we were in high school."

He extracted the cork from the wine and poured her
a glass. "I told you some things had changed," he said
as he handed it to her. After pouring wine into the
second glass, he recorked the bottle and raised his
glass in her direction. "To my future wife."

Her stomach clenched. "Adam, there's—"

"Okay." He sipped the wine and placed it beside the
blanket on a flat rock. "We'll eat first and then talk.
How's that?" He dug out plates and began filling one
from the three containers.

"I just think—"

"You're not going to turn down chicken I fried just
for you, are you?"

"*You* fried this?"

"Technically, no." He handed her a plate and a
linen napkin. "But I stood there the whole time it was
being fried at this little take-out place I know, and I
told them to make it extra-crispy because I remembered you like it that way. So I think that counts."

She had to admit everything smelled wonderful.
And if they didn't have all these insurmountable
problems, she might have been able to relax and have
fun. She'd forgotten how easily she and Adam could
do that. But there was a word for not facing reality. It
was denial, and Adam seemed to be deeply into it this
evening.

"We will talk about Daphne, right?" she prompted.

He finished filling his own plate and closed the cooler. "Yes, we will. Now eat."

She did, and everything tasted better than any food she'd had since...their steak dinner in Laughlin. While she ate, she thought about how he'd remembered she liked crispy chicken. He could still pick out the exact spot where they'd almost made love. For nearly twenty years he'd been looking at her picture of Red Rock Crossing. The evidence of his devotion seemed endless. She'd talked to enough women about the men in their lives, and she knew this level of caring didn't come along every day. Some people would call her crazy for turning aside a chance like this. Her father would, for certain.

When she was nearly finished with the meal, he took another linen napkin and walked over to the creek. She watched him, remembering how good those hair-sprinkled thighs felt against her skin.

He returned with the dampened napkin and held it out to her.

She took it and wiped her hands. "Thank you. Thoughtful service around here." She handed the napkin back.

"You missed a spot." He squatted next to her and touched the cool napkin to the corner of her mouth.

She made the mistake of looking into his eyes. And this time she didn't see the bruises around them, or the bandage on his nose. She saw only the fire blazing in the blue depths.

He wiped the other corner of her mouth tenderly, and her lips parted as she gazed up at him. He stroked her lip with his forefinger, and with a quick movement she caught his finger between her teeth.

"Still hungry?" he murmured.

With a soft moan, she released him and looked away.

"So am I. I booked a room. Maybe we should—"

She glanced at him. "No. You said we would talk. Let's talk."

His gaze roamed her face. "Okay." He moved the basket over to the exposed tree roots and sat beside her.

"The subject is Daphne," Loren said.

"Indeed it is." To his credit, he didn't evade the issue.

"She hates me," Loren said. "And considering Anita may go to jail, you're all she's got. You can't desert her to marry me." A raindrop fell with a soft plop on the blanket beside her. Appropriate, she thought. The sky was crying.

Adam took her hand and held it, tracing the lines in her palm. "I wouldn't desert her. She'd have to leave me, leave us, if that was her choice."

"And she might, Adam. You can't take that chance with her right now."

"Oh, yes, I can." He closed her hand into a fist and brought it to his mouth, where he kissed her knuckles. "I'm a risk taker, remember? And so are you. Otherwise you wouldn't have helped me rescue those kids. We're both go-for-broke people and now's not the time to stop. Besides, I have some new insights about Daphne."

Two more raindrops fell. Loren glanced through the trees at the blanket of gray being pulled across the sky. "I think it's going to rain."

"Maybe." He sounded unconcerned. "Do you want to leave?"

She shook her head. "Just thought I'd mention it. I'm getting used to being soaked when I'm around you. Go on."

He nodded, but instead of continuing, he traced the lines in her palm for a long moment. At last he glanced up, and his voice was strained. "It looks as though Anita has spent eighteen years convincing Daphne I have no interest in being a father." He held her open hand against his cheek and rubbed against it. "I guess it was revenge."

"That's terrible!"

"Yeah." His jaw muscle clenched beneath her palm. "I can understand it, but when I think of all those years, gone forever..." He looked away, and his tone grew harsh. "I want her to pay."

The rain was falling faster now, but Adam still didn't seem to care. Loren didn't care, either.

He took a shaky breath and sought her gaze again. "How could I have ever thought I cared for someone as vindictive as that?"

"We all make mistakes," she said gently.

"But some of us don't like admitting them. I didn't see what she was doing, because I couldn't imagine I'd married a woman who could act that way."

"She must have wanted your love desperately."

Contrition replaced the anger in his eyes. "Yes, I guess she did."

"I'm not excusing her behavior, but—"

"I know." He squeezed her hand. "You're a good person, Loren. Eventually, Daphne will see that."

"Have you told her your suspicions about Anita?"

"I've given her some idea of what I think. But I want Anita to tell her the truth. That's the only way Daphne will believe I'm not making everything up."

"But will Anita tell her?"

A cold light came into his eyes. "Yes, I think she will. And I suspect that after she does, Daphne will rethink her position."

"And if she doesn't?"

Adam cupped Loren's face with both hands as large, warm drops pelted them. "I believe she will. I'll do everything I can to convince her to accept this marriage. But if I gave you up to please Daphne, I'd come to resent her so much our relationship would disintegrate. I can't let Daphne keep me from you, Loren. And she won't."

Loren wanted to believe him.

"And one other thing you should know," he said, stroking her cheeks with his thumbs. "I'm selling Scorpio Steel."

"What?" She could see he wasn't joking, but when she thought of the years he'd invested in building the company and how hard he'd fought to preserve it from ruin, she couldn't comprehend his giving it up. "Are you sure you want to do that?"

"I'm sure. It's too time-consuming. Daphne's always resented the place, so the sale is a kind of gift for her, part of my pledge that I'll be more of a dad to her from now on. And besides, the plant's too far from you. Could Icarus use another pilot-slash-mechanic now that Josh won't be around much?"

Her pulse quickened with hope. Selling Scorpio Steel might convince Daphne of Adam's intentions. It just might. "My dad would love to have you work with us, but . . ."

"But you wouldn't?"

"The money's not that good. You're used to bringing in so much more."

The corner of his mouth lifted. "The investment of my profits from Scorpio will keep the wolves from the door, I think. So how about it? Will you hire me?"

She smiled into his rain-dampened face. Maybe they had a chance. Not a perfect setup, but who was given that? Not even her parents. "I suppose you'll want benefits."

"Every damn one I can get." His gaze traveled suggestively downward. "Do you know what? You're wet."

"Drenched." Her taut nipples pushed against the soaked fabric.

"You look good in rain."

"Thank you." She glanced up at him through lashes spiked with moisture.

"You know what else?" He surveyed the area. "Everyone left."

Anticipation tightened the coil of desire within her. "Then we're alone?"

"That's right." He leaned forward and his mouth brushed hers. "Just you and me and some unfinished business in Oak Creek Canyon."

Rain pattered against the leaves over their heads as Adam kissed her . . . and kissed her. She couldn't get enough of his lips, his tongue, his wine-sweet breath, his murmurs of need.

He urged her backward on the damp blanket, his upper body shielding her from the rain. He kissed her wet eyelashes, ran his tongue down the bridge of her nose, licked the drops from her chin. The rain fell harder, bringing forth the pungent fragrance of peat carpeting the forest floor. It was the scent of fertility. With a groan of desire, he entwined his legs with hers and rolled with her to the other side of the blanket in a frenzy of touching.

She straddled his lean hips and peeled her soaked tank top over her head, then shook her dripping hair from her eyes and unfastened her bra. The moment it fell away, his hands were there, fevered and hungry against her rain-cooled skin as he drew her down, down to his ravenous mouth.

Raindrops skittered along her spine as his tongue and mouth slipped over her breasts, smooth as the stones beneath the waters of the creek. Sheets of rain swept through the canyon, curtaining them from the world, anointing them with life-giving moisture.

His mouth still pleasuring her breasts, he lifted her until they lay side by side. Impatiently, he peeled away the rest of her clothes, and she removed his. When they lay unfettered beneath the downpour, they laughed with delight, exploring and sliding their rain-slicked bodies together in liquid friction, as if polishing themselves against each other's skin.

"My water nymph," he murmured, caressing her slippery thighs. "How do I know where the rain leaves off and you begin?"

She wrapped her arm around his wet neck and stretched upward to nibble at his lips. "The rain's cool."

He slipped his hand between her thighs and found her aching center. "And you're warm," he whispered, entering her with questing fingers. "So warm." Her body synchronized to the ripple of his touch, to the ripple of the water in the creek bed.

"Love me," she begged.

He moved over her. "This is for all the years apart and all the years to come. This is forever, Loren."

And as the current surged through the canyon, he came to her, gliding deep, his sure rhythm eroding the anger, the heartache, the loneliness they'd suffered. The flow of his desire eddied against the dam of emotions barricaded within her—promises she'd dared not make, passion she'd dared not feel. She cried out as the dam gave way with a rush, and she was swept into the unending river of his love.

CHAPTER TWENTY

THEY SET the wedding date for two weeks away, at sunrise at Red Rock Crossing. Adam stayed in Sedona for three more days making the arrangements while Loren worked to get ahead in her business so she could afford time off for a honeymoon.

They asked Walt to give away the bride and Josh to be Adam's best man. Crossing her fingers and hoping for a miracle, Loren wrote a note to Daphne, which Adam would deliver when he returned to Phoenix, asking Daphne to be her maid of honor. She didn't expect Daphne to accept. If she even agreed to come to the wedding, they were making progress.

Walt could hardly wait for Adam to come on board at Icarus. Even the question of where Loren and Adam would live was handily answered. Loren hadn't wanted to abandon Walt, yet she craved a degree of privacy with her newfound love. Then, as if planted by woodland fairies, a For Sale sign sprouted in front of the house on the lot adjoining Walt's. The house would need extensive renovating, which Adam looked forward to tackling.

Loren observed his boundless craving for challenge and knew he wouldn't be content with the status quo for long. An empire builder like Adam would eventually advance plans for expanding Icarus. She'd warned her father, who didn't seem to mind in the least. In fact, he'd commented that it was "refreshing" to have a son-in-law who believed in the free-enterprise system.

On the morning Adam had to leave for Phoenix, Loren fought the sinking feeling in her stomach. Everything seemed so perfect—except for one small detail. Adam hadn't told Daphne yet.

"She's no dummy," Adam assured Loren as they stood with their arms wrapped around each other in the driveway of Walt's house. "I think she'll figure out that her resentment is pointless. Especially after she gets the whole story from Anita. I'm hoping that was handled while I've been gone. I left instructions with Anita's lawyer." He took Loren's chin between his thumb and forefinger and wiggled it affectionately. "Don't worry. The prince and princess will live happily ever after."

"You'll call me after you talk to Daphne?"

"Sure will. And after I get home each night, and just before I go to sleep, and as soon as I wake up. If it were any longer than ten days, I'd put in an 800 number."

Loren gazed into his eyes. The bruises were fading. He looked a little more like her Adam than like the creature from the Black Lagoon. "I'm really going to miss you."

He grinned. "That's the idea."

"I suppose you think after you're gone for ten days I'll attack you on our wedding night."

"Yep." He massaged the small of her back. "That's my plan."

His touch reawakened desires that he'd satisfied only hours before in his hotel room. She felt his arousal through the clothes separating them. She nudged her hips against his. "You'd better go while you still can."

"One kiss."

One turned into two, until they were entwined in a breathless embrace that had no end.

At last she struggled from his arms. "Go," she whispered.

With obvious reluctance, he backed toward the car. "I'll bet you still have that effect on me when we're eighty."

"If your intemperate demands don't kill me off at a young age," she said.

He laughed. "In ten days we'll review that statement and see who has the intemperate demands." His laughter faded and he gazed at her, one hand on the car-door handle. "Hold on," he said. "I'll be back."

"I'm counting on it."

As he drove away, she stood with a hand pressed to her mouth. Would she always have this horrible feeling of abandonment whenever he left her, this unreasoning fear that she'd never see him again?

DAPHNE DRESSED for lunch with care. At last she'd have both her mother and father sitting at the same table again. Her mother had been released on bail two days ago, and she'd taken Daphne on a whirlwind shopping spree. Daphne wore one of her new outfits today, a pink silk sundress, whose narrow straps and short skirt managed to show off most of the tan she'd been working on all summer.

During shopping and lunch the day before, Anita had explained that, yes, she'd known a little something about Barnaby's plans to reroute the Scorpio Steel, and she'd considered it a great "joke" on Adam for being so mean to her all these years. Yes, she'd called Barnaby to warn him about the aerial photographs, but she'd never dreamed that would put her darling child, the light of her life, in danger. And now she *hated* Barnaby Haskett. She was also grateful to her ex-husband for posting her bail.

All in all, things sounded good, Daphne thought. Her father had asked for this lunch. What could he want besides to suggest they forget the past and become a family again?

The doorbell chimed, and she raced to the entryway to let her father in.

His black eyes had nearly healed, and he'd removed the bandage from his nose. He smiled affectionately at her. "You look great."

Daphne pirouetted for him on the polished tile of the entryway. "Mom bought me this yesterday."

"Did she?" Something flickered in his eyes, but Daphne wasn't sure what it was.

"Dad, she thinks Barnaby is a real sleaze-bucket."

"That's a fair assessment."

"And she's really happy you posted bail for her."

"Is she? That's good."

Hope blazed in Daphne's chest. This could be the best day of her life. "She's so sorry about all this, Dad."

"So am I." He glanced at his watch. "Where is she?"

"I'm sure she's almost ready. I'll go see." Daphne flew down the hall toward her mother's bedroom. One of her parents' constant arguments had been over Anita's tendency to be late. Daphne didn't want this promising lunch to start out that way.

She found her mother in her underwear, languorously brushing her mane of blond hair. "He's here," she said with a bright smile. "Almost ready?" She could tell that Anita wasn't even close. She hadn't finished putting on her makeup, let alone decided on a dress. That decision alone often took as much as half an hour.

Anita laid down the brush and picked up an eyebrow pencil. "I'm not going to rush just because your father showed up early, Daphne."

Daphne glanced at the crystal clock on the dressing table. "Actually, it's, uh, five minutes after the time he said he'd be here."

"Then he can wait." She peered into the mirror ringed with light bulbs and began drawing a narrow line at the base of her eyelashes.

"Mom, could you hurry a little bit?"

"I'll be ready when I'm ready." She started on the other eyelid.

"Anita."

She jumped, and the line squiggled up toward her eyebrow. "Look what you made me do," she said, not looking at her ex-husband standing in the bedroom doorway. She reached for makeup remover. "Now I'll have to start all—"

"I suggest you get dressed. Now."

Daphne glanced apprehensively at him. His expression was thunderous. "I'll pick your outfit," she chirped, heading for the huge walk-in closet. "I think that jade pantsuit we found yesterday would be just—"

"I'll pick my own outfit," her mother said, "when I'm ready to put it on. Thanks to your father's rude interruption, that will be a while longer."

"No, I think not," Adam said, striding into the room. "I have an important meeting in two hours. I had to cancel lunch with a prospective buyer for Scorpio in order to take care of this. Please be ready in five minutes, Anita."

Her blue eyes snapped. "And if I'm not?"

Daphne braced herself for a wingding of a fight. Or for her father to stomp out of the room.

Instead, he met her mother's gaze calmly in the lighted mirror. "I think you know."

Daphne watched in amazement as the defiance faded from her mother's expression.

"Go wait in the living room," she said. "Both of you. I'll be out in five minutes."

Daphne followed her father down the hall. "How did you do that?" she asked when they reached the living room.

"For the first time in your mother's and my relationship, I'm holding all the cards," he said, his face devoid of expression.

Daphne stared at him, unable to decide if that was good or bad for her plans. Then she remembered something he'd said. "What did you mean about a buyer for Scorpio? You're not selling, are you?"

"Yes." His blue eyes grew warm again as he smiled at her. "I'd meant to tell you with a little more flourish, but yes."

Daphne wasn't sure what to make of it. "Then what will you do?"

"Spend more time fooling around with airplanes. Spend more time with you. You were right, Daphne. I've sunk too much time into that business, and I'm unloading it, freeing myself up."

"Really?" The idea sounded good to her, but she wondered what her mother would say. "Will you... will you be able to make enough money?"

"Maybe not as much as before, but money's not that important, is it?"

Daphne thought this might be a test, and she was jolly well not going to fail it. "No, it isn't," she said. Privately, she thought her mother would have a fit.

As if to underscore her thoughts, Anita appeared, looking rather more thrown-together than usual. Daphne glanced at her watch. Five minutes on the button. "You look nice, Mom," she said.

Her mother waved aside the compliment. "Let's go."

Daphne rode in the back of the Mercedes and fantasized about more such trips with both parents. Except neither of them was saying a word. If they had any hope of getting back together, they'd have to talk to each other. Daphne was glad when they reached the restaurant and the tension-filled ride was over.

Her father had picked a perfect spot for a reconciliation, Daphne decided. It was one of her mother's favorite restaurants, where the tables sported pink linen and heavy silverware, the background music was subtle and romantic, and the generous use of potted plants provided a garden atmosphere. Daphne ordered a full meal, but her parents ordered just soup and salad.

After the waiter left, her father folded his hands on the table. "I called Flannery this morning, Anita."

Daphne smiled to herself. He'd called her mother's lawyer. That could mean only one thing. He wanted to reverse the divorce, or however you did that so you could be married again.

"He told me he'd had no call from you saying you'd discussed that matter with Daphne."

Daphne frowned in confusion. What matter?

"I've been busy." Anita's gaze darted around the room. "Could I have a glass of wine?"

"No."

Daphne's mouth dropped open. He wouldn't let her have a glass of wine with lunch? "Dad, it's not like she's an alcoholic, or anything."

"I didn't say that." His blue eyes were steady and determined. "But I don't want anything to muddy your thinking, Anita. Now, perhaps you'd like to tell Daphne about what you've been up to the past eighteen years?"

Anita took a drink from her water goblet. Her hand shook as she returned the goblet to the table. "Really, Adam, I think you're blowing this all out of proportion. A few chance remarks, a few mistaken impressions..."

"More than a few. I want you to tell Daphne everything you can remember."

"Now? That's why we're having lunch?"

Adam nodded. "Since you haven't seen fit to handle this yourself, I decided to observe and get my money's worth. I figured a public place like this, where you're known, would prevent you from having one of your dramatic tantrums."

Anita pushed away from the table. "I don't have to do this."

"True. I'm sure I can get a refund from the bail bondsman once you're behind bars again."

Daphne grabbed his arm. "What are you talking about? You just got her out of jail!"

"Apparently, she's ready to go back."

"Dad!"

Anita sighed and rested her head in her hands. "All right, Adam." Then slowly she raised her head and gazed at Daphne, who stared at her in fascinated horror. "There have been some occasions in your life when I thought it...more appropriate if you spent time with me, instead of your father." She waved her hand at him. "He wanted you riding in eighteen-wheelers and being an office slave. I didn't."

Daphne glanced at her father in quick surprise. So he hadn't made that up. He'd wanted her with him. The quick burst of joy she felt died when she realized the role her mother had played. But her mother had been thinking of her welfare, hadn't she? "What about the air show?" she asked. "Do you remember Dad wanted me to go on my ninth birthday?"

"Vaguely. As I recall, I couldn't imagine you traipsing around an air show when we could have a nice lunch with your friends and go shopping."

Daphne felt as if someone had squeezed her lungs like a damp sponge. "Mom, I would have loved that air show."

"Then I'm sorry. I thought—"

"But you didn't even *ask* me. You shouldn't have made that decision for me."

"Shall we discuss the flying lessons?" Adam asked.

"Oh, that." Anita waved her hand again. "Any fool could see you were too busy to teach her."

"Except for one thing," Adam said, his voice deepening. "I've been thinking back over our years together. And I remember that afternoon when Daphne got her learner's permit to drive a car. I remember sitting in our kitchen after she'd gone to bed. I'd just bought a new plane for the business, and I was excited about that. Do you remember what I said?"

Daphne listened with rapt attention.

"That was three years ago, Adam. How am I supposed to remember things you said three years ago?"

"Take time to think. I didn't remember it, either, at first. But I do now. It was only days before Daphne started lessons with someone else, too short a time for you to have forgotten that conversation, wouldn't you agree?"

"Well, I—"

"Anita!"

"Okay, okay. Don't make an issue out of it. You said something about wanting to teach Daphne to fly if she ever showed an interest."

"What?" Daphne glanced at her mother, but Anita wouldn't meet her gaze. "But I *asked* you if I should ask Dad, and you said no."

Anita looked everywhere but at her daughter. "I must have forgotten he said that."

"How could you forget something like that?" Daphne's voice rose in pitch. "But you didn't, did you?"

"No, she didn't," her father said. "Her actions were deliberate. Maybe not every time, but enough of the time. I wasn't giving her what she wanted. I'm willing to take the blame for being a bad husband. But what I can't forgive is her calculated campaign to keep us apart, to have you all to herself." His voice grew husky. "She stole eighteen years from us, Daphne."

The truth of it washed over her, making the room spin. One look at her mother confirmed that what her father said was true. Her mother had filled her full of lies just to get revenge. And now her parents weren't going to make up at all. Her father was probably still interested in that woman in Sedona. Daphne had lost them both.

She pushed back her chair and got unsteadily to her feet. Then she retrieved her small shoulder bag from where she'd hooked it over the back of the chair.

Her father shoved his chair away and rose with her. "I'm sorry to spring it on you like this, Daphne, but I was afraid your mother would never tell you if I didn't insist."

"It's okay, Dad." She took a deep breath. "I just need to get away and think. I'll catch a cab to the mall, or something."

Anita's voice was shrill, bordering on hysteria. "Don't let her just go off, Adam."

"Have some confidence in your daughter, Anita. She has a lot more sense than you do."

Daphne gave him a weak smile of gratitude. At least he wasn't treating her like a baby. "Thanks, Dad. I'll call you tonight."

"Do better than that," he said, his gaze intent. "Come over. We'll order a pizza. I have something else to talk to you about."

Daphne had a sick feeling in the pit of her stomach for what that something would be, but she nodded, anyway. Maybe she'd be wrong.

Five hours later, she found out she wasn't.

"Loren's a wonderful woman," her father said, leaning toward her across the kitchen table. "Give her a chance, Daphne."

Daphne picked pepperoni slices from her serving of pizza and squeezed them between her fingers. Dammit to hell. Why did she have to be right?

"She wrote you this note," her father said, sliding an envelope toward her.

She didn't touch it for a while, but finally curiosity got the better of her. Not bothering to wipe the pepperoni grease from her fingers, she opened the envelope and took out the folded piece of paper.

"Dear Daphne," the note read. "Your father and I will be married a week from Saturday in a sunrise ceremony at Red Rock Crossing. Josh will be the best man. I would be so pleased if you'd be my maid of honor. Sincerely, Loren."

Sunrise at Red Rock. She glanced up. "The picture in your office. She took it, right?"

"That's right."

Anger swelled within her. "If you loved her all this time, why did you marry Mom?"

He looked sad, but he held her gaze. "Because I'm human and I make mistakes."

"Was I a mistake, too?"

"God, no." He reached for her hand, pepperoni grease and all. "You're what's made my life worth something."

Daphne fought tears. "But now you have her. You don't need me anymore."

"I need you both."

Sure you do. Daphne stared hard at the note on the table, wondering if she could make it catch fire with her gaze. Finally, she composed her expression carefully before looking up. "Okay," she said. "I'll be there."

He grinned, and she almost felt guilty for what she was thinking. Almost.

"Thanks, Daph." He squeezed her hand.

"Don't mention it." The way she had it figured, she had no choice. Because if she expected to stop the wedding, she'd have to be in Sedona to do it.

CHAPTER TWENTY-ONE

A BRUSHED-PEWTER SKY arced over the russet spires of Sedona as Walt drove Loren and Josh to Red Rock Crossing. Rain the night before had left water dotting the red earth like beads of mercury. Bridal bouquets of wild daisies clustered beside the roadway, lending their delicate scent to the fresh-washed tang of sage and juniper. A soft breeze blew in the open window of the Suburban, ruffling the lace trimming the neckline of Loren's wedding dress.

She and Adam had found the dress in one of Sedona's shops. She'd protested the expense, but he'd insisted, after seeing how the handkerchief-soft material draped her breasts and swirled at her knees. She wore no veil, only a circlet of miniature white roses in her hair. A bouquet of miniature roses and baby's breath rested on the dashboard of the car. When she'd walked into the kitchen that morning at four-thirty, both Walt and Josh had gaped in wonder, then verbally tripped over each other showering her with compliments.

The simplicity of Loren's dress dictated a similar mode for the men. Walt and Josh wore open-necked white tux shirts and gray slacks. Adam's attire would be the same. Daphne's dress would be the only bit of color in the wedding party. Adam had told Loren she'd found an elegant shirtwaist in lavender silk. She would carry the bouquet of violets that rested next to Loren's on the dash.

Red Rock Crossing was in a small state park. Adam and Loren had chosen a relatively level picnic area close to the creek and had hired a furniture-rental company to set up several rows of folding chairs. They'd decided to have no altar and no containers of hothouse flowers. Nature had sprinkled the area with daisies, purple lupine and pink globe mallow, and an altar would be superfluous in the face of the turreted magnificence of Cathedral Rock with the sun rising behind it. A local musician had agreed to play a lilting song on the flute as Walt led Loren down the aisle between the folding chairs, and again when she retraced her steps with Adam. Other than that, the only music would be the bubbling magic of Oak Creek flowing at the base of Cathedral Rock.

Loren glanced around as Walt pulled into the parking lot. The chairs were in place; the flutist stood ready to play, and the minister was just getting out of his car. Everything looked perfect—except for one thing.

Adam's red Mercedes wasn't in the parking lot.

Loren's father leaned over and patted her hand. "He'll be here. You just stay put in the car and I'll make sure the guy with the flute knows when to play and when to be quiet."

"Okay."

"I'll go with you, Gramps." Josh squeezed her shoulder as he climbed out of the back seat. "Don't be nervous, Mom. He'll be here."

The folding chairs filled with guests. After the ceremony, a caterer would arrive with breakfast. Adam had arranged that, too. He was a dynamo of organizational skills. No wonder his business had flourished. He was creative, thorough and...always on time. So where was he?

As the sky lightened to the blue-white translucence of fine milk glass, Loren began to worry in earnest. Five more minutes and they should be starting down the aisle. Ten more minutes and the shimmer of sunlight would halo Cathedral Rock. Twenty more minutes and it would rise. By then they were supposed to be husband and wife.

Walt came to her side of the car. His overly hearty smile told her he was worried, too. Perspiration glistened on his bald spot. "Might as well climb out of there and get ready to walk down the aisle with your old man," he said. "Adam should be here any minute. Probably wants to make a grand entrance."

"Assuming he gets here." She glanced at the gold aura surrounding Cathedral Rock. "He's already ten minutes late. Do you think maybe he's had car trouble? Or an...accident?"

"Not an accident," her father said quickly.

"How can you be sure?"

He touched her shoulder. "We would have heard sirens. But maybe that fancy Mercedes did break down. If you want, Josh and I can cover the route from here to Los Arboles."

"Not yet." Besides, Loren didn't think car trouble would have stopped Adam. He would have commandeered another vehicle, hitchhiked if necessary, to be here. A mere machine wouldn't deter Adam from a goal. But a duty to his daughter might.

And that was what she feared. His sense of duty had taken him away from Loren before. What was to prevent it from happening again?

Only his love for you, whispered a voice. But rays of sunlight streaked the sky behind Cathedral Rock, and Adam wasn't here....

"Here he is!" her father exclaimed. "I told you he'd make it."

Loren whipped around in the direction her father was pointing, and sure enough, the red Mercedes was tearing down the road, far exceeding the park's speed limit. As the car screeched to a stop, Loren's throat tightened. Daphne was not with him. He'd arrived, but had he come to marry her or call off the wedding?

She opened the door of the Suburban and her father helped her down as Adam ran toward her. She braced herself.

He was breathing hard, his hair disheveled. "Let's go," he said, panting. "Sorry I'm late."

At that moment, the sun rose over Cathedral Rock.

Adam glanced up and swore softly. "We missed it," he said gently, turning back to her. "God, I'm sorry, Lor."

She looked at him with brimming eyes as the sun gilded his hair. "We didn't miss anything," she murmured, her voice husky with tears. "You're here."

He took both her hands in his. "Of course I'm here. Did you think I wouldn't be?"

"I...well, Daphne..."

"She thought she could stop the wedding by throwing a tantrum at the last minute. Eventually, I gave up trying to talk her out of her fit and left her there.''

"Do you think she's okay?"

"I bribed a maid to sit outside the door and listen. If she hears anything suspicious or it gets too quiet, she has permission to go into the room and check on her."

Josh walked up, his young face creased in a frown. "Where's Daph?"

Loren noticed his use of the nickname. Coming from Josh, it sounded nice. Familiar and brotherly. "She decided not to come," Loren said.

"Aw, man." His voice rose on the second word as he turned away in frustration.

"It's okay, Josh," Adam said. "We can do this without her."

Josh glanced at them. "Look, I know you wanted this to be a sunrise ceremony and everything, but—" he turned and gestured toward Cathedral Rock "—that program's out the window. How about giving me half an hour? If I can't convince her in that time, I'll drive back and we'll have the wedding without her."

Loren had been thinking as Josh talked. She was basing a lot of hope on his affectionate use of a nickname for Daphne. And the two of them had survived some tough times together. Maybe Josh had more sway than the rest of them. She laid a hand on Adam's arm. "Let him try. Thirty minutes isn't very significant when you consider your whole relationship with her may be at stake."

Walt broke into the conversation. "Caterer's here. She thought she'd timed it so the ceremony would be almost over, but I told her we were running late."

Adam glanced at Loren, and they both seemed to have the idea together. Loren smiled. They were getting pretty good at this mind-reading business. "Why not?" she said. "As Josh said, the plan is out the window, anyway, so let's feed people before the wedding instead of after."

"Excellent!" Josh said. "Can I have the keys, Gramps?"

Adam fished in his pocket. "Take the Mercedes."

Josh's eyes lit up. "Really? Cool!" He trotted off toward the car. "And save some food," he called over his shoulder.

"Save *lots* of food," Walt said, his eyes shining with pride.

Loren watched Josh backing the Mercedes out of the parking space. "Adam, that's a very expensive car. Are you sure you want him driving it?"

"If he can bring Daphne back with him, I'd be willing to give him that car."

She gasped. "But you wouldn't really!"

"No," he said, putting his arm around her shoulders. "I won't mess up the values you've given him. Come on. Let's take a walk and watch the sunrise." Ignoring the curious stares of the guests, he led her down a trail beside the creek.

And as they walked, the chatter of the guests faded and disappeared. Gradually, the magic of her surroundings enveloped Loren. Bird song mingled with the gurgle of clear water and the soft buzz of insects. In the distance a hawk called to its mate as the large birds circled on a current of air high above Cathedral Rock. A cottontail hopped across the path and disappeared in the grass and rushes growing beside the water.

"You know, I think this was the atmosphere we had in mind," Adam said after several minutes.

"Yes. Too bad we can't have a wedding all by ourselves."

He turned and faced her, capturing both her hands and gazing into her eyes. "Have I told you how beautiful you are this morning?"

"Not yet." She smiled, thinking of all the times she'd pictured him as a groom, in tie and tails, with all the formal trimmings. Yet she loved the way he looked now, his shoulders flexing beneath the soft shirt, his throat unconstricted by a tie, the gray slacks hugging his hips with no jacket to obscure her view of his magnificent physique.

"You are beautiful," he said. "You are..." He paused. Finally, he sighed. "I can't find words expressive enough. But all this—" he released her hand and flung his arm out to encompass the spectacular scenery "—all this is nothing when I look at you."

"And I don't care where I am, as long as you're with me."

"So you're not terribly disappointed that we didn't pull it off just as we planned?"

"No. Are you?"

"As long as I have you, I can't imagine ever being disappointed." He gave her hands a squeeze. "Let's start back. No matter what happens, Josh will be there soon, and I'm very impatient to become your husband."

"And I'm impatient to become your wife."

His eyes shone with love as he took her hand again.

They were nearly halfway back when his grip tightened. Two people were walking toward them, their hair golden in the sunlight. Josh and Daphne.

She wore shorts and a rock-concert T-shirt. As she drew closer, Loren could tell she hadn't put on makeup and her eyes were rimmed with red, yet Loren thought she'd never seen a more beautiful maid of honor in her life. Josh grinned, his face alight with success. Her heart swelling, Loren stood with Adam and waited for them.

When they were a few yards away, Josh paused and let Daphne go ahead. Taking her cue from her son, Loren urged Adam forward while she stayed behind.

Daphne looked into her father's face and swallowed. "I'm sorry, Dad. I'd love to be in your wedding."

Loren's heart wrenched as Adam wrapped his arms around Daphne. His head bent over hers and his broad shoulders quivered. They stood in a quiet embrace for several long seconds. Loren caught Josh's eye. He looked a little overwhelmed by emotion himself. Wiping the tears from her eyes, Loren made a circle of her thumb and forefinger and smiled. Josh smiled back.

Finally, Adam released Daphne, reached into his back pocket and offered her his handkerchief. Then he turned back to Loren, love shining in his eyes. "Ready?"

"Just a minute, Dad." Daphne blew her nose and shoved the handkerchief into the pocket of her shorts. "I have something to say to Loren."

Loren held up her hand. "You don't have to—"

"Yes, I do." Her voice quivered, but she came resolutely forward. "You risked your life for me, and you deserve better than I've been dishing out. I...I'm not always such a brat. And I'm hardly ever late."

Tenderness swelled Loren's heart. "I'm sure you're not."

Daphne held out her hand. "I'm sorry, Loren."

Loren's first impulse was to pull her into a hug, but she restrained it. She didn't want to jeopardize this fragile beginning by going overboard. She clasped Daphne's hand and looked into her eyes. "Apology accepted."

Daphne's smile was tentative, but it was definitely there. "Good." She released Loren's hand and glanced down at her outfit. "Josh said I didn't have time to change, so I look like a wreck."

"I couldn't care less what you wear. I think you look wonderful," Loren said. "Now, why don't you walk on back with your dad, and I'll walk with Josh?"

Daphne looked surprised. "Oh, no. I shouldn't."

"I think you should."

Daphne looked as if Loren had just presented her with a precious gift. "Thanks," she said. Her smile was more definite now.

Arms around each other, father and daughter walked together down the path. When they reached Josh, Adam paused. Then he unwrapped his arm from around Daphne's shoulders and offered his hand to Josh. He didn't say a word, but Josh didn't seem to need words. He looked as if he'd been knighted.

"Good going, kid," Loren said when she reached Josh.

"Aw, it was nothing."

"It was definitely something."

He grinned and slung his arm around her waist and urged her down the path. "Come on, let's go get you married so I can eat."

Loren laughed and put her arm around his waist. Then she lowered her voice. "Are you going to tell me how you did it?"

"Well, first I told her that everybody was willing to wait until she got there, and she seemed pretty impressed, but still wouldn't go. Then I started talking about all the fun we could have as a family. See, I've never had a sister, and she's never had a brother. Like at Disneyland, or Magic Mountain, we could go on rides together. Do you know she's never been to either of those places?"

"No."

"I could see she was weakening, so I thought of what else we could all do. I guess the magic word was camping."

"Really? Daphne?"

"The girl is crazy about the idea of camping. I kind of thought so from something she'd said once before. So I, uh, sorta promised her we'd all go pretty soon after you get back from your honeymoon."

"How soon?"

"The next weekend?"

Loren chuckled. "Sure, why not? Anything else you committed us to?"

"Well, yeah. She wants to go skiing this winter, during Christmas break, and maybe rent a cottage on the beach next summer. She's like a little kid, Mom.

She's never done any of the things that families usually do together."

"Then I guess we'll have to do them. I sure do love you, Josh."

"Love you, too, Mom."

THE GUESTS, some of them still holding plates of food or cups of coffee, rearranged themselves on the folding chairs. The flutist raised his instrument to his lips, and sunlight flashed off the shiny flute as he began to play.

Daphne, holding the bouquet of violets kept cool in the caterer's truck, started down the makeshift aisle, her head high, regal as a princess despite her T-shirt and shorts.

With a sigh of relief, Loren knew she'd be able to love this girl, after all. She grasped her bouquet of roses, which had also been saved by the caterer's ice chest, and took her father's arm. Ahead of her stood the minister, his Bible open in his hands, a broad smile on his face. Josh stood to the far right, looking very adult and proud of himself, as well he should be, Loren thought.

And Adam. He awaited her, his face glowing with anticipation, his whole body straining subtly in her direction. She'd fantasized about this moment since she was sixteen. The reality made her dizzy with joy.

When she reached him and took his hand, she was trembling. He steadied her with an arm around her waist. His responses were strong and clear as he gazed into her eyes. She barely remembered hers.

And then, they were husband and wife. He kissed her swiftly, surely, as a victor would claim his prize. The guests broke into applause.

She gazed up at him. "I love you so very much."

"And I love you, Mrs. Riordan."

Her smile trembled. At last. Then instinct took over. Keeping one arm around Adam, she turned toward Daphne and held out her other arm. Adam saw her intention and beckoned to Josh.

Daphne hesitated, but finally she walked over. Josh slid his arm over Adam's shoulder and held out his other to Daphne. Loren's breath caught in her throat. Then, with a little whimper, Daphne stepped into the circle of love.

S HARLEQUIN SUPERROMANCE®

WOMEN WHO DARE
They take chances, make changes
and follow their hearts!

FORBIDDEN
by Ellen James

Having proposed marriage and been turned down flat,
Dana Morgan says to hell with security, her ex-lover and
her old life. Out for adventure, she's prepared for difficulties
and discomfort—and she's eagerly looking forward to the
unpredictable.

What she isn't prepared for is Nick Petrie. Talk about *unpredictable*... And Nick knows it; in fact, he enjoys his reputation.
While Dana tells him to his face that he's a "royal pain," privately she has to admit he's the handsomest, sexiest, most
exciting man she's ever met. Unfortunately, Nick swears
there's no room in his life for love.

Dana's taking the chance that he's wrong.

Watch for *Forbidden* by Ellen James.
Available in April 1995,
wherever Harlequin books are sold.

Harlequin invites you to the most
romantic wedding of the season.

Rope the cowboy of your dreams in
Marry Me, Cowboy!

A collection of 4 brand-new stories,
celebrating weddings, written by:

New York Times bestselling author

JANET DAILEY

and favorite authors

Margaret Way
Anne McAllister
Susan Fox

Be sure not to miss Marry Me, Cowboy!
coming this April

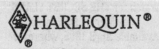 HARLEQUIN®

MMC

THE SECRET YEARS
by
Margot Dalton

Kate Daniels is beginning to regret her impulsive move to the small town of Fox Creek, Alberta. The locals are less than friendly and seem determined to thwart Kate's efforts to revive the old Fox Creek Inn. Only the mysterious—and gorgeous—Nathan Cameron is prepared to help. Then Kate finds a treasure hidden in the walls of her hotel—a diary kept by another young woman who had come alone to Fox Creek ninety years ago. From the diary, Kate learns answers to questions that have plagued her since her arrival. Answers that cause her to view Nathan Cameron in an entirely new light...

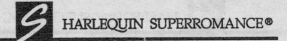

HARLEQUIN SUPERROMANCE®

FAMILY MAN

**He's sexy, he's single...and he's a father!
Can any woman resist?**

First Love, Second Chance
By Amanda Clark

Julia Marshall is leaving New York City and going back to the Pennsylvania town where she grew up—even if there's not much to go back for. She'd been raised by cold, unloving foster parents. And she'd been betrayed by *Tommy Black*, the love of her teenage years. He'd promised to wait for her, to marry her, to love her forever. And he hadn't....

Now, ten years later, Tommy's a family man—with a family of two, consisting of him and his five-year-old daughter, Charlotte, better known as Chipper. When Julia comes back to town, Tommy discovers that he'd like nothing better than to make that a family of three....

Watch for *First Love, Second Chance* in April.
Available wherever Harlequin books are sold.

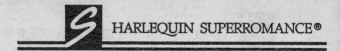

HARLEQUIN SUPERROMANCE®

Introduces

Laura Abbot

This talented author's first Superromance, *Mating for Life*,
appears in April 1995. You'll meet Josie Calhoun and
Mackenzie Scott—and their story will involve you,
move you and warm your heart!

Watch for it next month, wherever Harlequin books are sold.